WHO WALK IN DARKNESS

Who Walk in Darkness

☾

Chandler Brossard

With a New Foreword by Steven Moore

HERODIAS

NEW YORK LONDON

Introduction © 2000 Steven Moore

Published by HERODIAS, INC. 346 First Avenue, New York, NY 10009
HERODIAS, LTD. 24 Lacy Road, London, SW15 1NL

www.herodias.com

Manufactured in Canada
Design by Charles B. Hames

Cover and frontispiece photo by Louis Stettner
"Steam from Manhole," Times Square, 1952
from *Wisdom Cries Out in the Streets* (Flammarion Publishers)

LIBRARY OF CONGRESS CATALOGING-IN-PUBLICATION DATA
Brossard, Chandler, 1922–1993
Who walk in darkness / Chandler Brossard.—1st Herodias Classics ed.
p. cm.
ISBN 1–928746–12–8 (alk. paper)
1. Authors, American—Fiction. 2. Beat Generation—Fiction.
3. New York (N.Y.)—Fiction. 4. Young men—Fiction. I. Title.
PS3552.R67 W48 2000
813'.54—dc21
00-024248

BRITISH LIBRARY CATALOGUING IN PUBLICATION DATA

A catalogue record of this book is available from the British Library

ISBN 1–928746–12–8

1 3 5 7 9 8 6 4 2

FIRST HERODIAS CLASSICS EDITION 2000

Life in the United States in the years following World War II, according to the official *Life* magazine version, was just swell. America had won the war and emerged as the leader of the free world, the economy was booming, and college classrooms had begun filling with veterans taking advantage of the GI Bill. But our sharpest writers, as usual, were having none of it. The best literary works to appear in the decade after VJ-Day painted a different picture of America, one characterized by a sense of loss and disappointment, even disgust. Salinger's Holden Caulfield complained about the phoniness of people, while William Gaddis extended that complaint to expose postwar America as a counterfeit culture in his massive novel *The Recognitions*. Among the Beats, Jack Kerouac mourned the disappearance of redbrick small town America, Allen Ginsberg howled "I saw the best minds of my generation destroyed by madness," and William S. Burroughs attacked conformity and repression in the hallucinatory routines that would eventually be served up as *Naked Lunch*. And of course James Baldwin, Ralph Ellison, and Richard Wright pointed out with varying degrees of rage that the American dream still had a sign warning No Coloreds Allowed.

Who Walk in Darkness brought a French existentialist sensibility to this American malaise. While all of the above works are exuberant, dramatic works that display a kind of grim hilarity at times, for his take on postwar America Chandler Brossard stripped language of all its unnecessary literary trappings and reduced it to the flat, unemotional voice of a black-and-white documentary movie. The lean, chaste language reminded many reviewers of Hemingway, specifically of *The Sun Also Rises,* with which it has a superficial similarity, but a more illuminating parallel would be *The Stranger* by Albert Camus. Susan Sontag notes in her essay "On Style," "Sartre has shown, in his excellent review of *The Stranger,* how the celebrated 'white style' of Camus's novel—impersonal, expository, lucid, flat—is itself the vehicle of Mersault's image of the world (as made up of absurd, fortuitous moments)." This image of the world is shared by Brossard's narrator Blake Williams (a stunted William Blake?), the passive recorder of a month in the lives of his Greenwich Village circle at the beginning of 1948. The Camus parallel is significant for other reasons: *Who Walk in Darkness* may or may not be (as it is sometimes called) the first Beat novel—George Mandel's *Flee the Angry Strangers* and John Clellon Holmes's *Go* were published the same year (1952), though I believe Brossard wrote his earliest—but it certainly appears to be American literature's first existential novel.

Narrator Blake Williams's first spoken word is "Nothing," a word carrying the full weight of both Sartre's *Being and Nothingness* and Camus's *Myth of Sisyphus.* Like Mersault, Williams describes rather than explains, and like *The Stranger, Who Walk in Darkness* is a demonstration of (rather than an argument for) the existential absurdity of life. Wanting only to perform "clean work" someplace where "you did not have to tell lies," the narrator documents his movement toward love and authenticity by contrasting it with his nemesis Henry Porter's flagrant inauthenticity. Williams displays none of the "self-righteousness" poet Delmore Schwartz ascribed to him in his review of the novel; Williams's observations are as objective as a scientist's, taking special care to avoid subjective judgments of any sort. Only after he experiences tenderness with Porter's girlfriend Grace—her name carries as much religious symbolism as godless existentialism allows—does he venture a few speculations and metaphors, eventually working up to such remarks as his sardonic response to a recording of Khatchaturian's

"Saber Dance" sung by the Andrews Sisters: "It sounded like the swan song of my decade. After that there could be nothing."

Who Walk in Darkness can be said to take place in what Jewish mystics call the Abyss of Nothingness, which Brossard knew (if from nowhere else) from Milton Klonsky's 1948 essay "Greenwich Village: Decline and Fall," which Brossard reprinted in his excellent sociological anthology *The Scene Before You* (1955). Klonsky took as his epigraph this quotation from Gershom Scholem: "Rabbi Joseph ben Shalom of Barcelona maintains that in every change of form, in every transformation of reality, or every time the status of a thing is altered, the Abyss of Nothingness is crossed. . . . Nothing can change without coming into contact with this region of pure absolute Being which the mystics call Nothing. . . . It is the abyss which becomes visible in the gaps of existence."

Everyone in the novel is in this state of transformation (as was Greenwich Village at the time, as Klonsky shows), and the flat narrative tone and general meaninglessness of the characters' actions are meant to evoke this abyss of nothingness. Nothing in the novel is sensationalized or melodramatically exploited, even though both the narrative and setting offered numerous temptations that would have overpowered a less ascetic writer. Burroughs faced and overcame the same temptation in *Junky*, another even-toned "documentary."

Brossard's superb control of tone also throws into high relief any dialogue contaminated by the slightest dishonesty, ambiguity, or pretension. Only Grace's dialogue approaches the purity of the narrator's, and she consequently emerges as the only other person of "good faith" (to return to Sartre) in the novel. Henry Porter, Max Glazer, and (to a lesser extent) Harry Lees all illustrate Sartre's inauthentic men of "bad faith," and Brossard accomplishes this as much by the inauthenticity of their language as by their actions.

This philosophical demarcation is dramatized by the Coster-Phelps boxing match that lies at the heart of the novel. Blake and Grace favor the former: "Coster was a skillful, clean-fighting boy who knew his way around in the ring. He never bragged. He played by the rules." Porter favors Phelps, a brutal, dirty fighter; Max is too busy putting the make on a girl to participate, and fastidious Harry doesn't know if he's attracted to or repulsed by the fight. A boxing match may seem an inadequate, overtly masculine objective correlative for an existential crisis, but clearly Brossard incorporated it because the boxing ring is one place where inauthenticity of any sort is quickly exposed. Coster's defeat at the hands of the vicious Phelps, however, seems to suggest that those who fight clean and play by the rules are endangered most by those who have no rules, like the ubiquitous hoods in the novel (who mug Harry and leave him for dead) or "underground" men like Max and Porter. It is for this reason that the novel ends on a fearful, apocalyptic note as Blake and Grace realize that "escape" is their only protection against the violently absurd world in which they are condemned to live.

❰

Brossard had difficulty finding a publisher for *Who Walk in Darkness,* and even more difficulty after he did. It was rejected by all the major New York houses, but fortunately, Brossard met the eminent French novelist and publisher Raymond Queneau during a visit to the States and let him read the manuscript. Queneau liked it and not only offered to publish it in France with the prestigious Gallimard publishing house, but recommended it to his American editor, James Laughlin of New Directions, who also liked it and offered to publish it. Brossard was delighted.

Then Delmore Schwartz stepped in. Laughlin's literary adviser at the time, he was miffed to learn than an American novel had been accepted without his approval. Laughlin let him read the galley proof as compensation, and Schwartz quickly realized that a few of Brossard's characters were apparently based on mutual acquaintances: Henry Porter resembled writer Anatole Broyard, and Max Glazer seemed to be based on Milton Klonsky. (Brossard always insisted that his characters were just that: characters, not portrayals of real people.) Schwartz informed these two of the situation, and they threatened to sue New Directions unless changes were made. On the other hand, novelist William Gaddis saw something of himself in the character Harry Lees, the Harvard dandy who drinks too much, but he didn't object to the portrayal. Cap Fields was based on the noted Village character Stanley Gould.

Brossard reluctantly made the required changes, the most difficult beginning with the novel's opening line: instead of "People said Henry Porter was a 'passed' Negro," he had to change it to "People said Henry Porter was an illegitimate." This change was not only factually wrong—Broyard was indeed a light-skinned Negro who passed for white—but lexically wrong: a black man can't choose to be illegitimate, but he can choose to be inauthentic, and making such choices is what the novel is all about. One further change was Laughlin's: the original title of the novel was *Night Sky,* but he wanted something different, so Brossard took *Who Walk in Darkness* from part five of T. S. Eliot's "Ash Wednesday," who had taken it from Psalm Eighty-eight, the epigraph to the novel. (Incidentally, when the novel was published in France in 1954, it not only retained Brossard's original title, translated as *Ciel de Nuit,* but used Brossard's original, uncensored text.)

Who Walk in Darkness was published by New Directions in 1952, in England later that year, and in paperback by New American Library in 1953; it went through several more paperback editions in the 1960s. It wasn't until 1972 that Brossard was able to publish the original version of his novel with Harrow, an imprint of Harper & Row. That unrepentant, unexpurgated version is the one used for this new edition of Brossard's underground classic.

Steven Moore

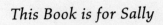
This Book is for Sally

Lord, why castest thou off my soul?
Why hidest thou thy face from me?
I am afflicted and ready to die from my youth up;
while I suffer thy terrors I am distracted.
Thy fierce wrath goest over me: thy terrors have cut me off.
They came round about me daily like water: they
compass me about together.
Lover and friend have thou put far from me,
and mine acquaintance into darkness.

PSALMS

People said Henry Porter was a "passed" Negro. But nobody knew for sure. I think the rumor was started by someone who had grown up with Porter in San Francisco. He did not look part Negro to me. Latin, yes. Anyway, the rumor followed him around. I suspect it was supposed to explain the difference between the way he behaved and the way the rest of us behaved. Porter did not show that he knew people were talking about him this way. I must give him credit for maintaining a front of indifference that was really remarkable.

Someone both Porter and I knew quite well once told me the next time he saw Porter he was going to ask him if he did or did not have Negro blood. He said it was the only way to clear the air. Maybe so. But I said I would not think of doing it. I have always been quite willing to let people keep their secrets to themselves. I have never had the desire to uncover them. I felt that if Porter was part Negro and ever wanted that publicly settled, he would one day do so. I was willing to wait.

The story went that his father had been a seaman turned jack-of-all-trades and his mother a hostess in a restaurant. They lived together for a few weeks and then one day the old man just pulled out. Porter was given to some of his mother's relatives to raise and she went back to what she had been doing before this interruption.

Porter had been living downtown, in New York City, in the section of the Sporting Club Bar for about three years when I knew him. He had come there right from San Francisco. Until he became literary-minded, Porter liked living in San Francisco. He was rather popular at school, he was a tennis champion, he was an accomplished dancer, and because he was good-looking and bold he had early successes with women. He had his first affair when he was sixteen. The woman was a professional singer, a Mexican. She had two abortions before they finally broke up. She paid for the abortions herself. They cost a hundred dollars each at that time.

Porter went to college—Berkeley—for three years, quit, and was drafted into the army. When he was mustered out he returned to San Francisco and married a local girl who was Spanish. Her father paid for a lively neighborhood-type wedding and many of her relatives gave them small presents of money.

Porter's best man was a boyhood friend, a Spanish boy. Five years later when this best man was in a hospital bleeding to death of knife wounds received in a street fight, Porter could not find the time to visit him.

The Porters had a child, a boy, but something was wrong with it and it died at three months. Porter and his wife went to the movies quite often and she spent a good deal of time in her kitchen preparing fine meals for him. He had a job in a publicity office. Soon after his child died Porter became very literary-minded. He decided that his wife was a burden to him and that the life he was leading in California was nowhere. So he left. He left his job and his wife and came to New York to begin his literary career.

I was told that his wife forgave him for leaving her. She knew that he was really very fond of her but that he was ashamed of her origin and thought she would interfere with his new career. I understand they wrote friendly letters to each other until the day she remarried.

It was odd, but Porter was occasionally quite talkative about his wife. Mostly he bitched her, but not vehemently. He laughed about her fondness for housekeeping, her ignorance of cultural matters, her confusion at the contradictory feelings he had about marriage. You would think that he would have kept all this to himself, too, because of the questions it might raise. But there you are.

Downtown Porter lived for a while on veterans' unemployment checks. He read a great deal and looked in nearly every book shop he passed and he met as many people as he could. He worked hard to get rid of his Western accent. He did this by trying to "model" his accent. But the Western part was not so easily cut off, and the result of his labor on his speech was that it sounded slightly odd. Also, Porter began to dress like a Harvard man.

With what he had left of his share of his and his wife's savings, Porter bought a couple of Brooks Brothers suits. Those suits are the Harvard man's identification. Henry Porter wanted to be taken for a Harvard type. This was one of the contradictions in his character. Porter hated Harvard men. Whenever he got the chance he put them down. He always said they were exotic and over-mannered and inclined to be faggy. He always secretly envied and publicly put down Harry Lees.

Unfortunately, he did not have the style for dressing this way. You have to have a certain style to go with Brooks clothes, and Porter did not have it, that was all. And despite his hard understudying Porter missed a point here and there. He got the wrong kind of ties. His ties were nice-looking but they were the wrong kind. And he tied the knots too big. His shirts were never exactly right, either. So nobody took him for a Harvard man. He was looking hard for a style.

Along with the Brooks suits, Porter began to go after the kind of girls Harvard men usually go after.

One night at a big party Porter had got himself invited to he met a Bennington girl who was distantly related to Harry Lees. She was with a date and other men were following her around, but Porter, slightly tight, made use of his boldness and his expert dancing, and took her away from all of them. Later he took her home. He stayed with her for three months in her apartment. She was tired of over-mannered Harvard types and Porter seemed to be what she was looking for. She went for him in a big way. She wanted to marry him. But first she thought he could use a little psychoanalysis. She had four or five thousand dollars in the bank that she said she did not need and she told him he should use it for an analysis.

After some persuasion Porter finally went to an analyst, for five weeks, for kicks. He stopped going and at the same time left this girl. She never knew just why. She was quite a nice girl. Being with her had convinced Porter that he could make the grade with her type. It gave him confidence to know this. It made him feel he was beginning to acquire style.

When his money ran out Porter got a job writing promotion copy for a publishing company. On the side he pursued his literary career by writing fiction and book reviews. His fiction was not bad. It did not knock me out, but it was not bad. Three or four of his stories were accepted by small literary magazines. This gave him some literary status. His reputation with women gave him more status though. I had to hand it to him. He could pick up almost any woman he saw.

Almost all of the people we knew well went to the Sporting Club Bar. We went there nearly every night. There were other bars around like it, but we did not go to them. I do not know why we all selected the Sporting Club instead of another place, but we did. None of the other bars felt the same to us afterward. We did not like the people who went to them. We did not think they were very hip.

I was not working at that time. I had recently been fired from a job because I had not been able to hide my feelings that the place was no good. I should have been smarter about it, I guess, but I was not interested in being smart that way.

It was early summer. I had finished working at home and decided to go to the Sporting Club to see who was around. It was about six o'clock. I left my third-floor apartment on Dover Street and went outside. Standing on the sidewalk in front of my building were several Italians. They belonged to the Sorrento Social Club downstairs next door. They shot pool there and played cards and made bets on the horses and watched the television screen. Some of them wore large-brimmed hats with the brim turned up all around. This made them look tough and like underworld characters. They wore splashy ties. They were arguing about the Dodgers.

I walked by them. They looked at me as they always did and I looked back. We did not speak although I had seen them every day for several months. I walked on up the street to the corner of Spring Street. It was warm out. Across the street in the candy store the juke box was playing loud. The owner was standing outside the store watching the street. You could hear the juke box all the way down the block. On the corner of Spring Street in front of the bar were the three bookies and their friends. They were in front of the bar all day long taking bets. One of them was holding a baby and talking to a woman with a baby carriage. They were all Italians.

I crossed Spring Street and walked to Prince. I passed the kids playing stoop ball against the side of a red brick warehouse and ducked when one kid threw the ball to home plate as I was passing through them.

Women were leaning out of the tenement buildings and talking from building to building. I walked by the vegetable pushcarts parked in the gutter facing the sidewalk, smelling the fresh, clean, fragrant smell of the fruit and the freshly watered lettuce and radishes and spring onions and dandelion greens in big boxes. Then by the fish market downstairs with the blackshelled mussels clinging in bunches and the spiraled scungili shells in bushel baskets and the big basin inside the window full of the small black live eels wriggling through the clear running water. The fish smell was strong and sharp.

I stopped to look downstairs into the store at all the different kinds of fish piled neatly in layers on the slanted shelves with chopped ice thrown over them. The store was crowded with fat women talking loud in Italian and broken English.

I crossed Prince and walked up Sullivan Street past the Jesuit school playground, past the Mills Hotel with the drunks leaning unsteadily, beaten-faced, against the walls, and the smell of piss and cheap wine hanging in the air, and on to the park.

The park was leafy green and full of children playing and their mothers sitting on the benches watching them and talking among themselves in groups. Walking by the benches I looked at all the young mothers. They were pretty and lightly dressed and looked cool and happy and desirable and I liked them very much. I wished I knew a couple of young mothers. I looked toward the big circle in the middle of the park. There had been a large fountain in the circle at one time but its flowing had been cut off and the circle was used now for sitting in. I did not see anyone I wanted to visit. A few easy-sitting hipsters and their girls were sitting on the periphery of the dry circle. I had seen them around but I did not really know them. One of them saw me and jerked his head back in a motion of hello. I did the same thing, and went on walking. Then I saw Cap Fields. He was sitting with a girl. I thought of going over to sit with them, but then decided not to.

I walked south through the park, looking at the people on the benches and enjoying it every time I passed one of the young models who were always walking in the park in their absolutely stylized way, walking haughtily but obviously liking very much being looked at. I came to the south side of the park. I crossed Elkin Street and walked up the block, turned the corner, and went into the Sporting Club Bar.

No one I knew was standing at the bar. I looked around the booths. Max Glazer and Henry Porter were sitting in a booth in the corner. They were with a girl I had never seen before.

"Hey, Blake!" Porter shouted, seeing me. "Come on over, old sport."

The girl looked at me, and away. I walked to the booth and sat down next to Glazer. Neither he nor I spoke to each other immediately. He always waited before greeting anybody he knew.

"What's new, man?" Porter asked me.

"Nothing," I said. The girl was quite nice-looking. Her hair was cut short like a boy's. She faced away.

"Everything is pretty dragged right now," Porter said.

"Hello, there, Blake," Max said, playing with his beer glass.

"Hello, Max."

I motioned with my head to one of the two waiters standing around. He came to the booth and I ordered a glass of beer. He did not say anything. I liked him less than any waiter I had ever seen. He looked deadpan at us, and went to the bar for my beer. The Italians who worked in the restaurants down there disliked all non-Italians. Some of them disguised it better than others.

Porter and Glazer kept looking around the place. A few more people had come in now. "This is Betty Graham, Blake," Porter said suddenly. "This is Blake Williams."

We said hello. She was slightly tight-faced but rather nice-looking. Max winked at her without smiling and sipped his beer and went on glancing around. The waiter brought my beer. I took a long drink of it. It stung my nose. The waiter stood there at the booth waiting to be paid for the beer. I gave him a dime and he left. I wondered who the girl was with, Porter or Glazer.

"What are you going to do for a vacation, Blake?" Porter asked me.

"I'm not sure. Maybe I'll go to Harry Lees's father's place up on the Cape. Maybe we could all of us go there. He has a whole beach house to himself."

"That so?"

"Yes. His old man went to Europe and left him the house for a couple of months."

"He'll miss his old man," said Porter.

"You're too hard on the guy," I said. "Why don't you lay off him?"

"I don't mean anything."

"I'll ask him what the chances are of our going up there."

"Sounds great. Work on it, man."

Just then Cap Fields came in. Max watched him with sudden interest. Cap nodded to us and took a chair from a near-by table and sat down with us.

"Did you get it?" Max asked him.

Cap nodded his head. "Listen, man," he said. "This is really great charge. The best. I know. But it will cost you."

"How much?" Max asked.

"An ace for two sticks."

Cap talked thick and strange. He was really high. He moved his head in a jerky way when he was lit up and talking.

"That's steep, man," Max said. "Are you getting anything out of this?"

"No, man. Not a thing. There's nothing in this for me. You can buy it or not. I'm doing you a favor. But you should really dig this charge. It's the best."

Max looked across the booth at Porter, squinting. I used to think this was an affectation, an irritating one to most people, until I found out that he was nearsighted. He looked at Porter for a couple of seconds before speaking.

"Can you lend me some gold?" he asked Porter.

"I'm low. How much do you need?"

"Can you lend me an ace?"

Porter took the money from his watch pocket. "I want this back," he said.

"You'll get it. You'll get it."

The girl watched Porter give the money to Max. Max now looked around the place. Cap did, too. Then Cap took a pack of Luckies from his shirt pocket. He offered the pack to Max. Max took the two thin sticks of marijuana from the Luckies and put them in his pocket. He slipped the dollar to Cap.

"You won't regret it," Cap said, his voice thick and funny-sounding. "It's the best in the city. You won't need more than half a stick each. I know. I've been on it for three days."

He laughed.

"You really like it, huh?" Max said, turning his head to look around the place again.

"That's what I've been saying," Cap said. He laughed again. He was really on.

Max sipped his beer, finishing it. "Want to blow this place now?" he said to the girl.

"I'm ready," she said, tight-faced.

"That was a fine pun, man," Cap said, laughing. " 'Want to blow this place.'"

I stood up so that Max could get out of the booth. The girl got up quickly. She was about nineteen.

"We'll see you around," Max said to Porter.

"Okay. Call me. Take it slow."

He looked at me, smiling slightly. "So long, Blake."

"So long."

"Thanks," he said to Cap. "I'll remember this."

"Do that," Cap said.

Max and the girl left, the girl not saying good-by to any of us. The surly waiter came up to the booth. "You want anything more?" he asked, picking up the glasses.

"I want another beer," I said. "What about you?" I said to Porter.

"None for me. I don't like the stuff."

"Cap?"

"Sure. I'll drink anything. Beer. Wine. Whisky. I love it all, Jack." He smiled and jerked his head around. "I feel so good," he said, and laughed.

Porter smiled and shook his head. The waiter left.

"Who was the chick?" Cap asked Porter.

"A girl I used to know."

"Now Glazer knows her?"

"Yes. I got her for him."

"That's very lovely, man. You really look out for your buddies. Wish somebody would look out for me." He laughed. The waiter brought our beers. I paid him and gave him a tip. He picked up the money and left.

"He's cute," said Cap. "Don't you love these surly wops? You know something? I saw this guy beat up a man one night who had only one arm. And the man was drunk, too. What do you think of that?"

"They are the worst," I said.

"They're so far underground they don't need eyes any more," Porter said.

Porter waved at someone in another booth. I looked up to see who it was. It was the editor of a literary magazine Porter had done some reviewing for. I did not know him well enough to wave at him. At least that is the way I felt about it. Porter left us and went over to his booth to talk to him. Slapping the editor on the back and talking loud and laughing. Promoting something. A drunk radio writer sat down in the next booth with a girl. He began talking loud about his IQ.

Porter came back and I asked him if he wanted to eat dinner. I was getting hungry.

"Sure. Anytime you say, sport."

"You don't want to eat here, do you?"

"Suppose we leave then. What about Enrico's?"

"Not that dump. It depresses me. Too many cornballs go there. Besides, the floor is always so dirty."

"Where do you want to go then?" I did not want to argue about a place to eat.

"What about the Eagle?"

"All right. Let's go there." I looked at Cap. "What about you, Cap? Are you hungry?"

"I'm always hungry," he said. "But I think I will stick around here for a while. Maybe something beautiful will happen to me if I stick around long enough." He laughed. He was certainly on. He probably could not even see the ground, he was so high.

Porter and I started out. Porter told Cap Fields to take it slow. I motioned so long to him with my hand. Halfway down the block we ran into Grace. She was walking toward the Sporting Club.

"Hello, Slim," Porter said, grabbing her around the waist. "Where are you headed?"

"Looking for you," Grace said. "As if you didn't know."

She was smartly dressed. She was the best-looking Italian girl I had ever seen. She did not look Italian. She had more of a Jewish beauty. Most people at first thought she was Jewish.

"See, you found me," Porter said, laughing. It was a dry ha-ha laugh. "Want to eat with us?"

"What do you think?"

"Come on then."

We walked on. I could smell Grace's perfume. She bad good taste in perfume and clothes. I liked her. I felt sorry for her that she had ever connected with Porter. There were lots of people she could have gone with. You could tell in a minute that she was in some way in love with him. I was sorry for her.

"I thought you were going to call me," she said to Porter.

"I got involved," he said.

"Involved. You're really an involved person, aren't you?"

"Okay, okay. I'm sorry."

"All right. But I expected you to call me."

She linked her arm with mine as we walked. "Let's ignore this involved person, Blake," she said. "Tell me what you have been doing with yourself. Have you involved a job yet?"

"Not yet."

"Do you think he is crazy?" said Porter.

"Listen, involved. We're ignoring you. Are you worried about a job, Blake?"

"No. I don't need one for a little while yet."

"It's horrible to be worried about a job," she said.

We passed the cafe espresso place with the iron wrestlers in the window, and by the Coco Bar which the uptown tourists always crowded, and waited on the corner before crossing as a low red foreign car drove by us. Porter watched the car drive by. Grace held both our arms now.

"You're the Italian expert, Blake," he said. "Wasn't that a wop car?"

"Yes. It was a Lancia."

"They are sharp-looking but they probably don't last long."

"Are you the Italian expert?" Grace asked me. "I thought he was."

"He says I am."

"I decided it was time somebody else was the Italian expert," Porter said. "I'll rest on my laurels."

Grace looked at him, and at me, and made a mock puzzled expression and then shrugged.

"Let's go dancing tonight," she said. "You're still the dancing expert aren't you?"

"I am," said Porter. "The only one around."

"Want to go along, Blake?" she asked me.

"Fine. I'll get Joan."

Now we walked along the south side of the park. It would soon be dark. It was still warm out. Several New York University students came by. We walked through their straggling crowd and turned the corner and went toward Sixth Avenue and the Eagle. I was trying to remember Joan's telephone number. It had slipped my mind.

Grace looked up at the sky. It was clouding up.

"I hope it doesn't rain tonight," she said.

"So do I," I said.

Porter looked up at the clouds, too, but he did not say anything.

CHAPTER II

After dinner we walked from the Eagle Restaurant to Sheridan Square. I bought a *Post* from the newsstand operated by the blind man at the entrance to the Seventh Avenue subway. I handed him a quarter and watched his lid-covered eyes and then his hands as he gave me change from the metal change holder clipped to his belt. He put the right change in my hand and in my watching I dropped a dime.

"I'm sorry," he said, smiling, eyes covered.

"No. That was my fault."

I quickly picked up the dime fallen on the stacked papers. It had been my fault. I should not have watched him like that.

Porter and Grace were standing several feet away from the newsstand, talking. They had not seen me drop the dime. I went over to them and opened the paper. They looked at it over my shoulder. The Russian barricade was still in effect in Berlin and the Allied planes were flying over it with their cargoes of food for the Germans in the American zone. I turned to the back of the paper. There was nothing about the big fight.

"What can you do about the Russians?" Grace asked disinterestedly.

"Go over their heads," Porter said.

Grace and I both laughed.

We looked around the square. Over the entire square was the exhausted underground smell emptying out of the subway entrances. The neon horses over Jack Delaney's Bar chased the bright red fox. On the other side of the square the gang of Italian hoods stood outside the entrance to the bowling alley. Max called them the Goths. They stood around with their hands in their pockets, leaned against the wall, talking and watching. The ground beneath us trembled as the subway trains rolled in and out of the Sheridan Square station. The exhausted smell of the underground was all around us. The southbound traffic on Seventh Avenue was going very fast. I watched the cars driving by us through the brightness of the square and followed them as they sped into the darkness of the avenue below the square.

"I want to clean up and do a couple of things be fore we go dancing," Porter said.

"I do, too." I said.

We walked down Fourth Street. Grace's arm was linked with Porter's. The smell of the underground was still in my nose and mouth. I inhaled and exhaled deeply to get rid of it. Now Grace put her arm around Porter's waist, and he put his on her shoulder. They walked this way for a while. But just before we came to the night club called the Nineteenth Hole Porter took his arm from the shoulder and her arm from around his waist and held her hand instead.

"Why did you do that?" Grace asked.

"The other way was too exhibitionistic," he said.

"Oh nuts. Don't be silly."

"I'm not. Certain things embarrass me in public." Grace shook her head and looked at me. I indicated that it beat me, too. Outside the Nineteenth Hole was a life-sized cardboard picture of a red-haired strip-tease artist, her arms crossed in front of her naked breasts. Billy White, the sign said. She looked pretty good. The uniformed doorman sat on a stool at the entrance drinking coffee from a paper container. Two couples who looked like tourists stopped in front of the place. The doorman told them the show was going on in half an hour. He did not say anything about the three-fifty minimum per person.

We walked down Fourth Street past the book shops with the tables of second-hand books and back issues of literary magazines out in front. Several people, tourists, too, were standing in front of a jewelry store window watching the jeweler work. The entire front of the shop was a window so that people could watch him work. Nobody I knew ever bought anything there.

We walked by Mack's Bookshop and both Porter and I waved to Mack inside sitting at his desk. He waved back.

We crossed Sixth Avenue, still going east, and passed the Pepper Pot and the Chinese restaurant downstairs and the Rider Bar where there were never any customers to speak of. At the next corner we stopped. From this point on Porter and I went in different directions.

"Suppose I meet you in the circle in two hours?" I said.

"That will be plenty of time," Porter said.

"Maybe I will call Harry Lees and tell him to get a date and come with us."

"If you want to."

"Yes, call him, Blake," said Grace. "He would be nice to have along."

I smiled at her, then asked Porter if he wanted the newspaper. I was through with it.

"No thanks," he said. "I almost never read them."

"Do you sleep in your pajama tops?"

"No. Why?"

"Nothing. Well, I'll see you in a couple of hours."

They went down the west side of the park and I went down Sullivan Street to my place.

CHAPTER III

I did not have to call Harry Lees. A few minutes after I had showered, while I was rubbing myself dry, he came up.

"Here I am," he said when I answered the door with the towel around me.

"It's a good thing, too. Sit down, Harry."

"I will, thanks." He turned around and looked at the door. "Come along. Don't just stand there," he said, looking at the door.

"What's that?"

He sat on the edge of the day bed. "It's the other half of my split personality," he said. "He's always hanging back. He's uncertain and shy. Thinks nobody likes him. I don't have a bit of respect for him."

I started dressing. "I think you ought to come off that kick, Harry."

"I wish I could." He watched me get a clean shirt. "Listen. Am I interrupting something?"

"No. I was going to call you. Porter and Grace and Joan and I are going to go out dancing uptown. Why don't you get a girl and come with us."

"You aren't inviting me just because I happened to show up, are you, Blake?"

"You know better than that."

"All right. I believe you." He leaned back on the day bed, resting on his elbow. "You know, you're the only person around who I don't think would kid me. The only one."

There was something about the way he said it that made me feel funny. "Want a beer?" I asked him. "I don't have any whisky."

"Oh. I forgot." He reached into his inside jacket pocket and brought out a pint of Courvoisier brandy. "I brought this."

The bottle had not been opened yet. "Here," he said. "You open it."

I took the bottle and with my door key I cut through the lead foil around the cap. I put the bottle on a lamp table and got two glasses from the cabinet. I was not surprised that Harry had brought the brandy. He wanted very much to have people like him. He thought he had to bring a gift to make his presence more desirable. Maybe he knew that this was not really necessary, but maybe he could not help himself. I poured the drinks, pouring more for Harry than for myself.

"Here it goes," he said, and drank down the brandy.

I drank all of mine and put my glass down and went to the closet for my jacket. Harry poured us another drink. This time he poured more for me than for himself. He sat far back on the day bed.

"Why don't you call somebody, Harry?" I said. I was completely dressed. In another half-hour I was supposed to pick Joan up.

"Who? I don't know many women. Who can you suggest?"

"What about Millie?"

"Millie? No, not Millie. She makes me sad and guilty."

"You could get Louise Parsons. Anything wrong with her?"

"Yes. She is always talking about jobs. She is too ambitious."

Harry finished his drink and put his glass on the floor. "Would it be all right if I just went along the way I am? Do I have to get a date?"

"It doesn't matter to me," I said. "Go any way you like, Harry."

"Swell."

The telephone rang and I answered it. I said hello twice and then someone asked for Burke. It was a wrong number. I told them my number and hung up. I sat down again. Harry had poured himself another drink. I did not want another one yet. I could tell that Harry wanted to get tight. I did not.

"Wrong number," I said. "Unless you told somebody to call you here under the name Burke."

"That is not as far-fetched as you think," he said. "Are you interested in fantasies, Blake?"

"Why? Have you got some?"

"A great one. Listen. In the fantasy I have I am myself but I am somebody else, too. Say I am in court for some reason. I get up to plead my case. Well, I am the guy pleading my case but I look like somebody else. Somebody I know. It is as though he is fronting for me. Say I get into a fight. Some other guy is there doing all the fighting, and I am hiding inside him and nobody knows it but me. What do you think of that?"

"It's very strange. Does it bother you?"

"That's it. I don't know whether it bothers me or not. I have this fantasy all the time."

I looked at the clock on the mantle. "It's getting late," I said. "We'd better be going."

"Right."

He got up from the couch and went to the little table and put the Courvoisier bottle back inside his jacket. "Let me know if you want to hear about some dreams sometime, Blake. I've got some real beauts."

"You think too much about them."

"You would, too, if you had my dreams."

Harry went out first. I turned out the lights and followed him. Outside we passed the social-club gang. They looked Harry up and down. He was just the sort of person who would get them. He obviously had the style of the people who the social-club boys thought ran the game in America and who thought of the Italians as wops or guineas. Harry did not have to do a thing. He had just to look the way he did. That was enough.

We walked west to Sixth Avenue and caught a cab. I could not afford a cab but I did not feel like walking over to Joan's house. I was late. We could walk from her place to the park. I gave the driver Joan's address and settled back against the seat. It was dark and roomy in the cab. It smelled coldly of imitation leather and rubber. The smell of the Twentieth Century. The driver drove north for two blocks, took a left turn, and headed for the river. I tried to read his identification card in the back but it was too dark.

"Blake, why is Porter such a preposterous bastard?"

"You tell me."

"It's funny. I think he is a preposterous bastard, yet I sort of like him. There is something likable about the guy."

"Yes. But what is it?"

I was not looking at Harry as we talked. I was looking up at the night sky through the glass window in the top of the cab.

"Somebody ought to set the guy straight," Harry said. "Do you think he is aware of the way he acts?"

"Most of the time. Sometimes I think he wants to be the way he is. I mean, a bastard."

"Too bad."

Now through the open windows of the cab I smelled the strong river smell. Oily and damp. I liked it as much as any smell I knew of. A fog horn sounded twice. We drove down to West Street right on the river where the warehouses and docks were and then the driver made a left turn and came up Joan's street. I paid for the cab, and Harry and I got out and went inside the vestibule of Joan's apartment. I did not want to go up three flights of steps to get her, so I rang her bell on the mail box, and we stayed downstairs and waited for her.

We leaned with our backs against the wall. Then I heard her door close. I followed the click of her high heels through the halls and down the three flights of stairs, the clicking getting louder and harder as she came nearer us waiting there for her. She came down the last flight.

We said hello. Harry bowed to her and took off his hat. We went out.

"You're getting lazier, Blake," Joan said.

"You mean the stairs?"

"Yes."

"You really didn't want us to come up, did you?"

I had known her for a long time and we had got by the point where we meant anything special to each other. We could be relaxed if not very excited together. We knew each other too well.

"I guess not. Surprise me sometime, will you?"

"Would you like me to surprise you sometime?" Harry asked her. We were walking up Tenth Street now.

"I'd love to have you surprise me, Harry," she said, laughing.

"How would you like to be surprised with a drink of brandy?"

"Oh fine."

Harry stopped and took the bottle of Courvoisier from his inside jacket pocket. He took the cap off and handed the bottle to Joan. The warehouse night watchman across the street was staring at us.

"Here's looking at you," Joan said, taking a drink. Harry offered the bottle to me, but I did not feel like a drink just then, so I shook my head. He took a drink and put the bottle back inside his jacket. The night watchman across the street looked at us as we walked up the street. Maybe it was the first time he had ever seen a woman take a drink on the street with two men.

"Makes me feel wild, like the Twenties," said Joan. "That must have been a great time," said Harry. "I wish I had been around then."

"Why don't you stick in your own time?" I said. "What's wrong with now?"

"Something," he said. "But I don't know exactly what it is. I'll tell you when I've put my finger on it. It will be a big exposé."

"Good old Harry," said Joan, putting her arm around him. "You will show them, won't you?"

I looked at him when she put her arm around him. For just a moment he looked pained, then his expression changed, relaxed, and he looked all right.

We passed the paper box factories that were now dark and closed and quiet and crossed Hudson Street against the light and headed for Bleecker Street.

"Do you think these people will mind our being in their dance hall?" Joan asked me.

"How do you mean?"

"Well, won't we look out of place, being the only white people there?"

"They don't care. Besides, they are not all Negroes. Many of them are Puerto Ricans and Cubans."

"That's the same thing, isn't it?"

"Not quite."

"Well, as long as we don't have any trouble with them."

"We won't."

I looked at the sky. It did not look like rain.

Henry Porter and Grace were already at the circle in the park when we got there. Some people were sitting on the ledge inside the circle, but it was too dark for me to make out anybody. Grace and Joan said hello and Harry Lees smiled and raised his hat to Grace.

"Who is that well-mannered chap with you, Blake?" Porter said.

"Oh, hello, Porter," Harry said.

"What do you know, old sport?"

"I know you."

"I guess that's enough."

Porter jumped up from the rim of the circle and slapped Lees on the shoulder. "Well, let's get going, everybody," he said. "We want to get a table before the place gets too crowded."

I was low, so I suggested we take a bus uptown. It was lousy being broke. Three Fifth Avenue buses were waiting at the south side of the park. This where we were now was the end of the line. Two of the buses were new single-deckers. The other one was a double-decker. Joan and Lees and I started walking to one of the single-deckers.

"Not that," said Porter. "The double-decker. They are better to ride on." Grace was holding on to his arm.

"Okay," I said. It did not matter much to me.

We got on the double-decker. I put two dimes in the coin box for Joan and myself and we all went upstairs. We were the only ones on the top deck. We went all the way to the back to sit down. I let Joan sit on the inside next to the window.

"I can lend you some money," Joan said.

"I don't want it."

"Sure?"

"Uh-huh."

She shrugged her shoulders and looked out of the window. "All right then."

Lees sat by himself in the seat in front of us. Porter and Grace sat in the seat directly across from us. Grace was on the outside. She was looking out of the window past Porter's face. He was looking straight ahead and drumming with his hands on the edge of the seat as though he were playing finger drums. Now other people were coming to the top deck of the bus. I had hoped we would have it all to ourselves for a while. A beautifully dressed blonde, heavily made-up, came by us followed by a thin young man. Porter turned his head to look at her.

"Okay. Okay?" Grace said. "Don't break your neck?"

"I thought she looked familiar," said Porter.

"I wouldn't be surprised," Grace said. "But just remember that you are with me tonight."

"All right, Slim. All right."

Harry turned around to look at the girl, too.

The bus jolted starting up. It turned around through the park and drove jerkily up Fifth Avenue. The evening breeze came in through the open windows. I smelled the brandy on Harry's breath carried back by the breeze.

"Say Harry, old man," Porter said from across the aisle. "Where's your woman?"

"Probably out with her father."

"Don't take it so hard."

"I couldn't care less."

"Maybe there will be something up there," Porter said.

"Maybe there will be."

The bus stopped to pick up people at Eleventh Street. We passed Longchamps' sidewalk café, the people walking on the sidewalk looking over the boxed hedges at the people drinking at the tables, the whole place in a reddish haze from the red tiles and red-painted lights shining from inside the open doors.

As we drove on I noticed for the first time that the street lights along this part of Fifth Avenue were amber. All the other street lights in the city were white, but these down here were amber. The amber light gave the street a soft rich tone. I settled back in the bus seat for the long ride uptown, feeling Joan's body soft against mine, but feeling it with no particular body pleasure.

CHAPTER IV

We got off the bus at Central Park. The dance hall—the Montana—was diagonally across the street from the bus stop. The intersection traffic was heavy. We waited on the corner until the light was in our favor and then we made the crossing. The traffic was dangerous, and we had to be careful crossing.

The front of the Montana was brilliantly lit with hundreds of light bulbs. It looked like the front of a big theater, with a marquee. There were two places, the Montana and the Skylight, with different entrances, but both in the same building. One upstairs, one downstairs.

Glassed-in sections of the entrances were filled with photographs of the entertainers and orchestras that had appeared at both places. We looked at the photographs before going in. All of the entertainers and the members of the orchestras were Puerto Ricans or Negroes. The women in the photographs were plump and looked middle-aged. They seemed to be enjoying themselves immensely. Harry walked around the entrance looking at all of the photographs. He looked at every one carefully, and came smiling back to us.

Standing outside the entrance were several Puerto Rican sharpies. Even in their sharpiness you could see something elegant. They seemed very sure of themselves. A couple of them were quite handsome. Several couples passed us going in, the women in evening dress.

"Are we going in?" Grace said, pulling on Porter's arm.

"I feel like an outsider," said Joan.

Porter and Grace went in first. Two Negro policemen stood at the ticket office. They were there in case of trouble. When these people fought, knives were brought out and somebody always ended up in the hospital, or dead. Next to one of the policemen stood a powerful-looking Negro. He held his arms folded on his chest and he looked at everyone that came in.

Porter went to the ticket window. "One and one," he said.

"Why does he say one and one?" Joan asked me.

"Maybe that is the style here."

"That's the way he learned to count," Harry said.

We bought our tickets and walked through the lobby where several sharply dressed Negro couples were talking and laughing politely, and into the ballroom. A large band was playing on the stage at the far end. The ballroom was huge. It must have been the size of a square block. The tables were lined up along the sides. A balcony with tables looked out over the floor. The band leader was singing-talking into the microphone. He was smiling big and he kept shaking two small gourds as he sang and talked into the microphone. The band was playing very loud and fast.

"The place is beginning to jump already," Porter said.

"It looks wonderful," said Grace. "It's exciting just being here."

We kept to the side of the dance floor out of the way of the dancers and walked to an empty table down near the bandstand. Most of the tables were already occupied. On the way to the empty table I caught a strong smell of tea. It was a charged sweet odor that penetrated all the other smells of cigarette tobacco and beer and whisky and perfume and body. Porter smelled it too. He looked at a crowded table, four light Negro women there where the smell was coming from and looked away. We sat down.

A fat woman with a white apron came to our table and we ordered a pitcher of beer. The orchestra was right at our back. The drums were going steady and loud. The man playing them sat to one side of the band. He held the little drums wedged between his thighs and hit them hard with his fingers. His torso kept moving while he played and he smiled big. He watched the dancers as he played and smiled.

"That's Beaujean," Porter said. "He's really great. A real wild man. He is the best drum man in the city."

Porter was playing the drums on the table.

"Love these dark ladies," Harry said. "What do they do when they aren't dancing?"

"Don't you want to dance, Blake?" Joan asked me.

"Let's wait until the beer comes."

"Oh, let's dance first. Drink the beer afterward."

"All right."

"Come on, Grace," Porter said, pulling Grace up from the chair. "We'll show these squares. Remember, Blake, this is no fox trot."

"I'll stay right here until you come back," said Harry.

Porter and Grace danced off in the direction of the orchestra and Joan and I moved out into the crowd in the middle of the floor. I did not know how to dance well to this music and I wanted to be inconspicuous as I danced the best I could. I hated to feel foolish in public. I saw several couples in the middle of the floor just moving back and forth, in a simple pattern, a kind of rumba. I thought I could do that, at least. I might even be able to fake better dancing to this music. I liked the music. I was angry with myself that I could not dance expertly to it—as well as Porter. This was a feeling I did not like to have for long. It made you feel so good to do these things well. I wanted to be an expert at it.

"We'll build on a rumba base," I said to Joan. "Okay?"

"Sure. If you want to invent something as you go along, go ahead. I'll try to follow."

"You're game, anyway."

"I have nothing to lose."

The floor was now very crowded. We bumped into a slow-dancing couple.

"Excuse me," I said.

They danced on and did not say anything. Then someone bumped into us. They did not say anything nor did we. It was easier that way. I felt we were dancing all right. The Negro and Puerto Rican couples danced smoothly and without seeming to notice they were dancing. No one seemed to be paying any attention to us. I thought they would, but they were not. The men were quietly absorbed in their dancing with their women. I had not seen anything like it before on a dance floor. There was nothing cute, nothing grinningly exploited in their dancing as it was with most ballroom dancing you see.

"What is happening over there?" Joan asked.

I looked around. Several couples had stopped dancing and had formed a circle around someone. We danced over to the circle and then stopped to look in.

Two young Puerto Ricans were dancing. The boy looked very sharp, drape-suited and wore smoked glasses. The girl fine-faced and tall. They danced apart holding their arms at their sides, shoulders moving rhythmically, making short repeated dance patterns, each complementing the other dancer's, arms still at their sides, then they came together, the boy in a rush taking the girl and together making wider steps and patterns and bending and spinning around the circle formed by the couples who had stopped dancing to watch, now dancing held close together, stomachs rubbing, now breaking, the girl twisting away from the boy, he holding her hand lightly, she now turning completely around, hand held so lightly, by the boy, and now he pulling her to him in a rush, swiftly swept in, and now the close Staccato steps again, and the watching dancers clapping and whistling.

"Isn't that amazing," Joan whispered to me.

More dancers were stopping their own dancing to watch this girl and this boy. They were dancing farther apart now, circling each other clockwise, and the steps being danced by the boy were slightly different, looser in their design, and he was changing them slightly all the time as he circled the girl who was dancing without changing the steps she was taking. He was pursuing her. Then he came in swiftly to her and caught her and spun her and then bent slightly backward, pulling her in to him, one leg slanting back off the floor, her leg with it, both bent together, and the music ended.

Everybody clapped and whistled. The boy and the girl were laughing and the boy was daubing his face with a large white handkerchief. The girl then left the boy and went through the crowd alone to a table and the boy stayed on the floor with his friends.

We walked through the dancers who were still standing on the floor and back to our table.

"Why, that wasn't even her date, was it?" Joan said.

"Probably not. They dance with whoever looks good and afterward go back to where they were before. They like to dance."

"No complications afterward."

"No complications."

"You seem to like it that way."

"Apparently so."

Porter and Grace were back at the table with Harry. I was hot and sweating. Harry had taken off his jacket. He seemed drunk. He must have finished the Courvoisier. We sat down and I poured beer for myself and Joan. Then I took off my jacket, too.

"Listen, man," Porter said, leaning over and taking Harry by the arm. I want to see you dance this next one."

"I want to see myself dance it," said Harry with controlled drunkenness in his voice. "But I don't have the nerve to try it."

"Oh, sure you do. Anybody can do it. I'll let you dance with Grace."

"It would be too embarrassing for you, Grace," Harry said.

"Don't be silly. I'd like to dance with you, Harry."

"Everybody is being so nice about it," Harry said. "But I really don't have the nerve."

"If I can do it, God knows you can," I said. Harry smiled and drank the rest of the beer in his glass. He poured himself another, and said, "We'll see. We'll see."

Just then the young drummer came by our table, going in the direction of the bar. Porter jumped up. "Beaujean! Amigo!"

"Hey, amigo!" Beaujean shouted, turning around and taking Porter's hand. Porter put his arm around Beaujean's shoulder and walked with him in the direction of the bar, talking loud and fast in Spanish.

"Do you think Porter wants me to dance just to see me make a fool of myself?" Harry asked me.

"I doubt it."

"Do you really believe he would, Harry?" Joan asked him.

"I wouldn't put it past him. I think he likes me but I also think he would like to see me look foolish. Would do him some kind of ego-good."

Harry looked across the table at Grace. "I'm sorry, Grace. Do you mind my saying this about him?"

She shook her head. "I know him pretty well."

Porter came back with Beaujean, his arm around Beaujean's shoulder. He introduced him to us. Harry stood up to shake Beaujean's hand when they were introduced. Porter spoke in Spanish to Beaujean, motioning for him to sit with us. Beaujean told him something.

"He says he would like to sit with us but he has to get back to the band," Porter explained.

"Tell him I am sorry I don't speak Spanish," said Harry. "I would enjoy talking with him."

Porter told Beaujean this. Beaujean smiled and leaned across the table and shook Harry's hand. Then he slapped Porter on the shoulder and nodded to us, saying good-by in Spanish, and went back to the bandstand.

"He is really terrific," Porter said, sitting down. "When he starts to play again, listen to how he carries on a conversation with the big drums. It will knock you out."

Now the music started again. The leader began singing-talking into the microphone and shaking his small gourds. A fat woman in a green satin dress came out from the side of the stand and began singing, too.

"What are they singing about?" Grace asked Porter.

"About their love. She is telling him what she will do to him if she catches him playing around with another woman."

"What will she do?"

"She says she will cut off his *cojones*."

"She has the right idea," Grace said.

Porter turned to Joan. "Come on, Slim. Let's dance. Blake won't mind, will you, Blake?"

"Go ahead."

Grace got up now. "This one is ours, Harry," she said.

"I haven't got the nerve," said Harry.

"Yes you have." Grace took him by the arm and he stood up. "We'll go over to the other side," she said.

"You can't back out now," said Porter. Then he and Joan began to dance.

"Okay," said Harry. "But I warned you."

Harry and Grace danced slowly and awkwardly out into the middle of the floor. I lost sight of them. The last I saw of them it looked as though Grace were leading him. I drank my beer and caught the eye of the fat waitress. In a couple of minutes she brought another pitcher of beer to the table. I paid her and she left. Now I drank the beer and listened to the band and watched the dancers. And I began to hear the conversation Beaujean was having with his drums and the big cylindrical-shaped drums farther up in the band.

Beaujean was smiling wide all the time. His end of the conversation was faster and more varied than the other drums. When the conversation was over, the band still playing, Beaujean lit a small gas burner standing near his chair and held his drums over the flame. He took the drums away for a second, then held them back over the flame. Then he turned the burner off, sat there with his drums on his lap, doing nothing, watching the dancers, then he began to play again, but this time with the entire band, not only in conversation with the other drums.

The big Negro who had been at the door walked by our table. He looked over the dance floor and at the people sitting at the tables. One of the men at a crowded table jumped up and held out a pint of whisky to him. He shook his head but the man persisted. He took the bottle and drank from it and gave it back to the man. The man laughed, spoke to him in Spanish, slapped him on the back, and sat down. The big Negro moved on.

The music stopped. Harry and Grace came back to the table.

"I've disgraced myself permanently," said Harry.

"You did not," Grace said. "You did very well. He really did," she said to me.

Harry looked at me and shook his head.

Porter and Joan came back. Grace looked at him and at Joan. Porter and Joan were both smiling. Grace was not. I guess she suspected anybody Porter did anything with.

"Henry is going to play those drums," Joan said.

"It's about time you entertained us, Porter," Harry said. He leaned far back in his chair. "Can you really play those things?"

"Sure I can. I think Beaujean will let me sit in once."

Porter walked to the bandstand and spoke to Beaujean. Beaujean nodded and Porter jumped up onto the stand. Beaujean spoke to the other musicians and they smiled and nodded, smiling, at Porter. Beaujean gave Porter his chair and the drums and sat down on the floor next to him. The music started. Porter began to play away on the drums. He was not laughing the way Beaujean had laughed. His face was very serious.

"He looks good up there," I said.

"Yes. He certainly does," Grace said.

"Seriously. I wasn't being salty."

The band leader was singing-talking into the microphone.

"Where did he learn to play?" Harry asked.

"He used to hang around musicians a lot when he was a kid," I said. "Isn't that right, Grace?"

"I believe so."

"Why didn't he do something with it?" Harry went on. "Why didn't he turn professional?"

"He became interested in other things."

"Drums are pretty interesting," Joan said.

The big Negro walked into the center of the dance floor, twisting carefully through the dancers despite his bigness. A plump Jewish woman in her thirties was dancing with a young Puerto Rican boy with a small face and long lashes. The Jewish woman was drunk and she was dancing in a very, very affectionate way with the boy. The big Negro twisted carefully through the dancers. He grabbed the boy by the shoulder and yanked him away from the Jewish woman.

They began arguing. The Jewish woman looked very surprised. The big Negro was now steering them off the dance floor to their table along the side of the floor. He was talking angrily and rapidly.

"No good. Not here. Not here," he said. He spoke to the boy in Spanish, looking angry. The Jewish woman looked as though she might cry.

"Okay. Okay," the boy said. He was looking away from the big Negro.

"Got to keep the place clean," Harry said.

Porter's drum playing sounded good. It was not as sure nor as interesting as Beaujean's, but you were still convinced by it. He still looked serious. The fat waitress brought us another pitcher of beer. The place was completely crowded. Many people were standing along the sides of the floor because there were no places left to sit down. All of the women were in evening dress. They talked very little among themselves as they stood watching the dancers.

The music stopped.

Porter stayed on the bandstand talking to the musicians for a couple of minutes, then he came down to the table. "Well," he said, "how did you like it?"

"It was impressive," I said.

"I used to be a lot better. But I'm out of practice."

"You do damn well for somebody who is out of practice," said Harry.

Porter laughed. I was not sure he got what Harry meant.

"Anybody like a little beer practice?" Joan asked, holding up the pitcher of beer.

"I would, please," Grace said.

Joan poured Grace a glass, then poured some in Porter's glass.

"No, none for me," he said. "I'm getting bloated. Listen," he said, to Grace. "I've been invited to a jam session later. You don't mind if I go, do you?"

"Can't I go with you?" she asked, frowning.

"No women are going to be there."

"Is this something you just cooked up?"

"I swear it isn't. Ask Beaujean, if you want to."

"I still don't believe it."

"Oh, Christ. Come off it. I'm telling you straight." She looked at him without speaking. I wished I did not have to watch this. Harry and Joan were looking over the dance floor, trying not to notice anything. I drank my beer and looked away, too.

"You mean you can't even take me home?" Grace asked him.

"You can go home with the others. What's wrong with that?"

Harry turned back to the table now. "I'll see you home, Grace," he said.

"See? Here's a real gentleman. Thanks, man."

"When is all this going to happen?" Grace asked.

"After the next piece. This band leaves then and another one takes over. Why don't all of you stay on, though?"

"I think we've had about enough," I said. "Another dance and I'll be ready to go. Won't you, Joan?"

"I suppose so. It is getting late."

"Don't get mad," Porter said to Grace. "This is a sociological experiment for me. You know that."

"Oh, nuts. You and your sociological experiments." She turned her head. "Oh, well, let's drop it. Nothing is going to change you."

The music started.

"Let's make this one," Porter said.

"I don't feel like dancing," Grace said.

"Come on. It will do you good."

Grace got up. They went out on the floor. Joan and I went out on the floor, too. I was slightly drunk and hot and did not want much to dance. But I did not want to sit and watch, either.

"Why doesn't she drop him?" Joan asked me.

"She likes him too much."

"She's a sweet kid. She ought to let Porter alone. He's not in her league."

"I think she knows that. But she can't do anything about it. Right now, anyway."

It was difficult to dance because there were so many people on the floor. Most of the couples were almost standing still, just moving their feet back and forth a few inches, staying in the same position, dancing close together. I was tired and tight. I was sorry I had drunk that much beer. Beer always made me tired. Joan's hair was rubbing against my cheek.

"So what's with you?" she asked me.

"The same old story."

"Aren't you trying to change it any?"

"A little."

"And?"

"And I still don't feel that I can make it with anybody."

"Why, Blake?"

"I'm not quite sure. I just feel empty most of the time. That is the closest I can come to describing it."

"I'm very sorry."

"I wish that helped."

"So do I. I wish I could do something."

Though I was tired I felt the music with more pleasure now. I was digging it better. I listened closely to the drums.

The music stopped.

The band leader was making an announcement in Spanish as we walked back to our table.

"You could get awfully lonely in this place after a bit," Harry said.

"Just about now," I said.

Porter and Grace returned. Harry got up from the table and we were all standing.

"Well, I'll leave you all here," Porter said. "The band is going out the other way."

"Always a back door," said Grace. "You seem to be in quite a hurry to go."

"The band is. I'm not. Listen, Harry, I really appreciate this."

"You should," Harry said.

Porter smiled and said, "Call me, will you, Blake?"

"Somebody will one of these days," Grace said.

"That was a mean one. Call me."

"All right So long."

"So long."

Porter squeezed Grace's shoulder. Then he went the other way. Going out the back way with the band. We walked out the front way, passing the still watchful police.

Outside it had begun to drizzle. Harry whistled down a cab and it drove up in front and we all got in. We drove down Fifth Avenue along Central Park. I was listening to the slick, wet whining the tires made against the wet street. Then I heard Grace crying.

CHAPTER V

A couple of days later I had to go downtown to sign for my weekly unemployment compensation check. It was an embarrassing business, bad on the morale, but if I did not go down I would not get the twenty-six dollars a week I was supposed to be living on. It is even worse on the morale not to eat. The same morning I got a letter in reply to an ad I had answered three weeks ago about a job. The letter was from a large automobile company. Would I please come in to see a Mr. Baxter at three-thirty that afternoon? The job was doing publicity. I did not want it, but I decided to go anyway. More out of curiosity and for laughs, I guess, than anything else.

The unemployment office was not far from my apartment, so I walked to it. The day was warm and bright. On the way I stopped in a lunch counter and had coffee and rolls. The coffee was sour and chicory-tasting. But it was hot. The rolls were fresh and smelled of the bakery. I finished up quickly and left.

I crossed Spring Street, dodging a long-distance truck going through a red light, and walked up to Greene Street and then down Greene Street toward Canal. Greene Street was jammed with trucks loading and unloading at warehouse platforms. I had to walk in the street half the time because the trucks barred the sidewalk. I reached Canal Street and walked east. Out in front of all the cut-rate stores were the shallow boxes full of marked-down goods, hardware, stationery, clothing, Army surplus. Crowds of men and boys were bending over the boxes examining the stuff.

At the unemployment office at 277 Canal Street I got in my regular line and waited my turn to report. There were ten lines of people waiting to report. The people waiting there were mostly unemployed waiters and waitresses, cooks, laborers, truck drivers, and clerks. In my line a drunk holding his jacket in his arms weaved drunkenly in and out of his place talking to himself. In the line on my right a large young woman was eating potato chips and laughing at the drunk. Several lines away an old man was talking loud in Yiddish to one of the reporting clerks.

"I can't help it," the clerk was saying. "There isn't anything I can do about it. I can't help it."

Someone touched me on the shoulder. It was the man in back of me. "Is this the five-five-one-five line?" he asked me.

I told him it was not. That line was two lines away.

"I'm in the wrong line?" he said, looking surprised, and walked to the other line.

My turn finally came. I took out the duplicate of my last unemployment check and my reporting card and put them on the counter in front of the girl clerk. She asked me if I had worked any days of the last week. I said no. She asked me if I had refused any work in that period. I said no again. She gave me a pencil and told me to sign my duplicate check. She marked something on my reporting card and handed it back to me.

"Next Wednesday at the same time," she said.

I walked toward the door marked "Exit." An old lady with red blotches on her face was standing in front of the writing ledges on the wall.

"They've got no damn pencils here," she was saying. "Somebody has stolen all the pencils."

I had a small pencil in my lapel pocket. I gave it to her.

"You're a gentleman," she said. "Now I can fill my card out."

Downstairs I felt better. I had felt tense and bothered in the unemployment office. I bought a *Times* and started home. As I came near the Post Office on Canal Street I remembered some letters I had put off answering. I stopped in and bought half a dozen three-cent stamps. The walls of the Post Office were decorated with those corny Midwestern-type murals that were already beginning to resemble the calendar propaganda art of the Russians. What a laugh.

Outside on the corner of Canal and Thompson a pitch man was demonstrating a radio gadget on a big floor-model radio. A crowd of young men watched him. I went closer. The pitch man had the voice of an announcer at a boxing match. I stopped on the edge of the crowd. The radio screeched with static. The pitch man plugged in his device, a static eliminator. The static stopped. The radio sounded great. He took the static eliminator out. The static screeched in again. It was the oldest pitch in the business. Inside the radio was a device that created the static. It was disconnected when the other device was plugged in. People began buying the device. I walked away.

In front of my apartment building I walked through the crowd of loafing Italians who used the same obscene words over and over again in telling anything, and stopped in the lobby to see if I had any mail. A letter from the family and a bill from the gas company. I went upstairs. The telephone was ringing as I got to the door. I got to it on what must have been the last ring.

It was Henry Porter. Was I doing anything tonight? Nothing special. He had a date with a model, but she was with a girl friend, another model, and did not want to leave her. I had to come along for the other girl. His girl was the best piece in New York, he said. I told him I did not have any money for a date.

"That's all right, man," he said. "I've got enough for both of us."

I said I would meet him at seven in the Sporting Club Bar. I undressed and took a shower.

I often tried to analyze just what it was about Porter that I disliked and what I liked. This was easy to do with some people, but not with Porter. For instance, I disliked one person I can think of because he never bought anybody a drink. Porter often bought people drinks. The best analysis I could come up with was that Porter gave you the feeling that he was trying to get the jump on you. And because he set up this feeling, you found yourself trying to get the jump on him. Or at least feeling you should. This gave relations with him an unwanted competitive aspect. Unwanted because it was never clear just what you were competing for.

Perhaps he was a "passed" Negro. And perhaps this made him feel he had to operate in any way he could. He had learned a few things from Max Glazer, who then had a part-time job in a publishing house. Porter had been a protégé of Max's for a long time. Max was his literary adviser and I think his model, too. Porter wanted to be able to do anything. He did not want to be held back in life by any rules that held back other people. Max had been around a great deal and knew a lot of the angles, and Porter wanted to learn them from him. Max was his closest friend. He had been psychoanalyzed and had got quite a few angles in the process, and he passed them on to Porter.

I finished showering and went into the next room and dressed. Then I read the *Times*. I bought the *Times* because it had the best classified ads of any paper. Otherwise it was almost unreadable. There were jobs listed for compositors, counselors, engineers, and young men between eighteen and twenty-five with high-school educations who wanted to start a career in the stock room of some business. But no jobs for me. I turned to the sports section and looked for news of the fight between Jimmy Coster and Joe Phelps. It was going to be the best fight since Cerdan stopped Tony Zale in the eleventh round to win the middleweight championship of the world.

Grace knew Jimmy Coster. They had grown up together out on Long Island. Coster was not his real name.

Finally I found an item about Coster and Phelps. It was a couple of paragraphs about where they were training. Phelps at Stillman's Gym and Coster at a place in New Jersey. That was all. Some write-up.

I turned to the book-review page. The book reviewed that day was a book of literary criticism written by a man I had met at a couple of uptown cocktail parties. His book was an eight-hundred-page attack on literary critics. I read that one whole chapter was devoted to proving that one well-known critic and poet was really a plagiarist and a psychotic. The only critic enthusiastically praised was a man I knew was responsible for getting this writer a cushy teaching job in a girls' school.

It was time for me to be going for the interview with the automobile man.

I went outside and walked up to Sixth Avenue and caught a subway train to Rockefeller Plaza. Uptown walking under the skyscrapers through the plaza toward Park Avenue I stopped to watch the ice skaters on the sunken rink. The smooth cold sound of their skate runners gliding over the ice came up to me from the rink. I watched the skaters waltz around the rink twice and then went on.

The man at the automobile company kept me waiting for half an hour in the coldly air-conditioned waiting room before having me sent into his office. This soured me on the whole situation. I just wanted to get it over with quickly. In his office now he asked me about the jobs I had had and why I had left them and some things about my personal life.

"Which branch of the service were you in?" he asked me.

"None. A back injury kept me out."

"I see. Well, what fraternity were you a member of in college?"

"I wasn't a member of any fraternity."

"Oh? What about clubs? Didn't you belong to any clubs?"

"No. I went in for other things."

"I see."

He leaned back in his big desk chair and told me about the job. He kept twisting a school ring on his left hand as he talked. I asked him a couple of questions the answers to which I could easily have guessed at. The job was mostly writing news releases, handouts, to be sent to newspapers. And taking visiting businessmen around the local plants.

"The job would also involve some traveling. How would you feel about leaving New York?"

"It would depend on where I had to go."

"Detroit, California, Texas."

"I really wouldn't be able to tell, I guess, until I had tried it."

He smiled. "I guess you are right about that."

He stood up. "Well, I've enjoyed talking to you, Mr. Williams. We want to interview a few more people before we make our decision. Thank you for coming in."

"Not at all," I said.

The corridor outside his office was empty. The sound of my footsteps was very loud as I walked out. I knew I would not be hearing from him. That was settled. And I had not had any laughs, either. What a waste.

CHAPTER VI

I got to the Sporting Club Bar early. Porter was not there yet. I saw Max and Harry Lees sitting together in a booth. I sat down with them. Harry was tight. I asked if they had seen Porter.

"He'll come around," said Max. "What's up?"

"We have a double date."

"Who with? Anybody I know?"

"I don't know. A couple of models."

"Oh. He didn't say anything to me about it."

"Would you like to know something about Max, Blake?" Harry asked me.

"I'll listen."

"Well, Max is the New Man. I'm the Renaissance Man and he is the New Man."

"How do you figure that?"

"I've made a study of it. Max can do things I could never dream of doing. He can do anything and not be bothered by it. For instance, he can call you up and invite you for dinner and when it's over he can feel insulted if you don't pay his check."

Max laughed. "What are you telling the man?"

"It's true," Harry said. "That is what happens all the time."

The surly Italian waiter came to the booth and I ordered beer.

"Most people have preconceived ideas of how to behave," Harry went on. "Like myself. Renaissance ideas. Not Max. He acts any way he feels like acting. Nothing is either good or bad, dignified or undignified. There's no experience he is not capable of having. He is completely mobile. For example. If when we sat down at this booth there were two half-full glasses of beer left by the previous occupants Max could finish them. He really could. It would not bother him a bit. He would feel like having some beer, and there some was, and he would drink it. That is the real Modern Man, Blake."

I laughed. "Maybe he is the only one who will succeed in this world," I said. I was thinking I was probably a Renaissance man, too.

"Do you know he has used my name three times to get invited to parties without my knowing it?" Harry said.

"Why does everybody pick on me?" Max said, smiling.

"We Renaissance men envy you, Max," I said.

"To be or not to be Max Glazer. That is the modern dilemma," Harry said. "The Hamlet of the Underground."

The surly waiter brought my beer.

"Giulio," Max said to him. "Can you lend me a buck? Until tomorrow?"

"Lend you a buck? Christ, I haven't even made fifty cents today in tips. Maybe you could lend me a buck."

"Blake, could you buy me a beer, man?" Max asked me.

"I won't buy him any more," said Harry.

"All right," I said.

"What did I tell you?" Harry said.

I looked around the place. In the center of the bar a group of young men were clustered around a big blonde girl who was talking a great deal and laughing in shrieks. You could spot the boys a mile away. No good place in town was safe from them any more. They eventually hunted down every good place and then ruined it. Those always-happy young faces—even the middle-aged ones looked nineteen. They were always having such a gay time. They brought the uptown tourists and then eventually the hustlers and the hoods came, too, for their share of the gravy. You could not do anything about them, either. They knew it and they acted very superior about it.

A small one with a crew haircut was doing the talking now.

"Can you imagine it? The whole island was a circus. I mean a circus. And what should happen? The police arrested some man and his wife for bathing in the nude at night. Isn't that a scream?"

Everybody giggled. The blonde shrieked. The bartender was watching them from the end of the bar. He looked at someone sitting in a booth and shook his head.

Another one looked the place over and said to one of his friends, "I wonder if there is anyone here I should know."

"Why don't you cruise around and find out?"

"Delicious, aren't they?" said Harry.

"They certainly are," I said.

"They always seem to wear their trousers high," said Max.

Then Porter came in with our dates. Both were redheads. They were perfect looking models. I had seen photographs of both of them in magazines and newspapers.

"You're early," Porter said to me.

We all said hello and Porter introduced the girls. Gloria and Margaret. Harry and I stood up when we were introduced. Max remained seated. I could not tell which girl I was supposed to be the date of. It did not make much difference.

"We will have to cut out shortly, Blake," Porter said. "Margaret has to get back early."

"Whenever you say," I said.

Max was almost staring at Gloria.

The waiter came by and we ordered more drinks. He gave the girls a quick once-over before leaving our table. I started talking to Margaret when a bummy-looking guy who was always around the bar came to our table. He looked at the girls and then looked at Porter, smiling.

"Hello there," he said to Porter.

Porter looked him over and then looked away.

"What's the matter?" the bum said. "Don't you speak to people any more?"

"I don't know you," Porter said.

"Sure you do. I met you one night with Jimmy Butler. Sure you know me."

"Okay. So I know you. Hello."

"That's better. You can at least speak to people."

He stayed at our table looking at us and at the girls and sipping his beer.

"All right. I said hello," Porter said. "Now what is keeping you, Jack?"

Margaret and Gloria seemed amused.

"I thought I might look at these gorgeous women," he said, smiling at them.

"You've looked. Now why don't you beat it."

"Aw, don't get excited. Don't get excited." But he left and went back to the bar.

"They ought to keep guys like that out of this place," Porter said.

"But who was he?" Margaret asked.

"Just some jerk looking for somebody to mooch on."

"He is a lonely hanger-on that nobody seems to like," I said.

"Doesn't he have any friends?" Gloria asked.

"Not that I know of."

"That's awful. That's simply awful."

"Nobody loves a hanger-on," Harry recited.

"This is no way to entertain women," Max said. He reached across the table and put his hand on Margaret's. "Do you like the movies?"

She laughed.

"I'm serious," Max said. "Don't you like the movies?"

Porter looked at Harry Lees. "Hey, man. Where's your tie? You haven't got a tie on today."

"I thought I would look casual today."

"What would they say in Cambridge?"

"I couldn't care less."

"But you look almost like one of the people, Harry," Porter said.

"Oh come off it, will you?"

"Okay, old chap."

"Why don't you rib him, Harry?" I asked him.

"Yes. Rib him," Gloria said.

"What's the use?" Harry said. "I don't enjoy it."

Porter laughed. I began to feel uncomfortable. Max was telling Margaret about some experiences from his childhood. I had an uneasy feeling that Grace might walk in. I don't know why I worried so much about this, but I did. I did not want her to see Porter with another woman, and be there myself.

"How about it?" I said to Porter.

"Right."

"We're leaving," Porter said to Margaret and Gloria.

"Oh. We are?"

Max patted Margaret's hand as she got up. "How's Grace?" he then asked Porter.

Porter shrugged his shoulders. "She's all right, I guess."

It did not even bother him. Harry stood up, waiting for us to leave.

"Always a gentleman," Porter said. "Take care of Max, Harry. Don't let him get into any trouble."

"Solid, old fellow. Solid."

"So long."

"So long."

"Take it slow."

"What a strange person." Margaret said as we were walking outside.

"Who?" I said.

"Max. He gave me the feeling I was supposed to make *him*."

"I love this section of town," Gloria, the taller of the two, said. "Everything is so nice and quaint."

"You said it."

Porter slapped me on the back. I guess he was thinking of a pun.

We turned left at the corner of Volta Place and headed toward Sixth Avenue. Gloria looked in the Tavern. "That is an interesting-looking place," she said. "Is it?"

"No," I said. "It is nowhere."

"Oh. Nowhere? Why?"

"It's full of squares. Retired detective-story writers and women real-estate agents."

"What do you do, Blake?"

"Nothing."

"Nothing? You mean you don't write or paint or anything like that?"

"No. I don't do anything."

"You're just fooling me."

"He wishes he were," Porter said, ahead of us.

"I'm the son of a rich man," I said. "My father is the tuna-fish-salad king."

"You're funny. I like you."

"Thanks."

I saw Cap Fields coming toward us. He was walking light-footedly.

"You haven't seen Max, have you?" he asked us.

"He's back at the Sporting Club," Porter told him.

"You mean he's at home," said Cappy. He laughed dreamily. He was on all right. I guess he was on most of the time. "I've got a little something for him." He laughed again. Then he walked up the street, waving good-by to us.

We walked down Volta. It was a dark and narrow street and the sidewalks were narrow and slanted down toward the gutter. You felt the houses on either side were slanting in, too. The street got almost no sun. Along the sides of the sidewalks next to the buildings were three or four basement stairways. They went down eight or nine feet below the side-walk level, dropping away sheerly. There were no rails guarding the entrances. You had to walk by them carefully. They were very dangerous at night. Finally we reached Sixth Avenue. I was glad to be off the street. We caught a cab. Uptown.

CHAPTER VII

The dinner uptown was not too bad, but it was not much fun, either. The food was good. Gloria, who was my date, and I got tight on martinis. Porter was sober. We had a shrimp cocktail and sweetbreads and artichokes. Porter did most of the talking as usual. He kept using the expression, "anthropologically speaking." And he made a point of telling us how interested he was in "cultural configurations."

He was telling Margaret all about primitive dancing. He talked too loud. I was slightly uncomfortable because of this. So was Gloria. I knew because she looked at me and smiled while he was talking. This made me feel less comfortable.

"The dance symbolizes the man-woman relationship," Porter said. "The woman dances regular time to the music, being very obedient. But the man makes riffs. That is, he improvises steps on the offbeat. This expresses his independence. It shows he is master of the situation and can do anything he wants to do."

"Is it true that they have a dance about lovemaking that ends up with the dancers making love?" Margaret asked Porter.

"Yes. But it isn't a very subtle dance."

"Have you ever seen it?"

"No. It doesn't particularly interest me."

"It sounds fascinating," Gloria said. "Where do they have these love dances? Do they have them in public?"

"No. More or less privately."

"What do you mean you aren't interested in love dances?" I asked Porter. "Do you mean you aren't interested in love-making? Is that it, Henry?"

"Of course not," he said. "You aren't baiting me by any chance, are you, Blake?"

"Of course not."

He looked seriously at me. Then he said, "All right. I thought you might be."

"I think white people should have dances like that love dance, don't you, Blake?" Gloria said.

"They must have had them at one time," I said.

"White people make lousy dancers," Porter said. "We are all afraid to express anything in our dancing."

"You're an exception then," Gloria said. "Blake told me you were an expert dancer."

"There are exceptions," Porter said.

I wanted the conversation to reach something. I had had just enough to drink to want some kind of trouble. But then the waiter came and asked if we wanted anything else. He wanted us to finish up and leave the table. We were keeping him from serving more people and getting more tips. He stood over our table breathing heavily while we decided about some thing else to have. We ordered coffee. Two small coffees and two large coffees.

"Two small, two large," the waiter said, and shuffled away, a tired old man whose feet hurt him. He came back in a minute with four large coffees. He set them down on the table very noisily.

"We said two large and two small," Porter said.

"It doesn't matter," I said quickly.

We drank the coffee and Porter paid the check. He left a much bigger tip than he should have left. He always did this. Outside Porter suggested that we take a walk up Fifth Avenue and look in the windows. This last for Gloria and Margaret.

"I can't," Margaret said. "I've got to get back. I really must. Peter will be coming in any minute now."

"Oh," Porter said, making a gesture of displeasure. "I know," Margaret said. "But he's still my husband. I've got to get back to my place."

Porter was standing apart now. He was standing with his back against the wall of the restaurant building. He looked at

Margaret who was standing apart from him, and then he looked at Gloria and me. I did not want to say anything. I waited for him to say it.

"All right," he said.

He grabbed me playfully by the arm. "Come on, Blake. You and Gloria ride up with me to Margaret's house. Then we can all ride back downtown together."

"It's too much out of the way, Porter," I said. "Perhaps we will see you later?"

"Oh, you're abandoning me, man. You're abandoning me. You can't do that."

"Nobody is abandoning you," I said.

Two taxis were in front of the restaurant. I opened the door of one. Porter looked hurt. He shook his head at me. I was almost beginning to feel sorry for him.

"Perhaps we will see you later at the Sporting Club," I said again.

"That is really white of you," he said.

"It isn't a question of color. Don't get sore, Henry."

Then Gloria and I said so long to them and got in the cab. I asked Gloria where she lived, and gave the address to the driver. I felt good after it all.

"That was fast," Gloria said.

"He is even faster," I said.

"Is that why you did it?"

"Part of the reason. He would have made quite a play for you on the way back. With three of us it might have turned into a free-or-all." I said the last as though it were a joke I was making.

We were at Times Square. The smell of it was like the used smell of the subway. Only this was not underground. Or maybe it was. Maybe it was at that. The sidewalks and the streets were crowded with thousands of people. They were walking slowly up and down. They overflowed the sidewalks. The huge neon signs lit up the sky and the square. It was all colors.

We had to wait for the light and the crowds. The Pepsi-Cola sign took up the north sky. In front of us a mammoth Ingrid Bergman in a suit of armor was charging on a horse. On my left a Union Pacific train was racing through the Rocky Mountains. In the eastern sky a giant mouth was blowing Camel-cigarette smoke rings over the square, over the crowds of people below.

The thousands of lights were so bright they seemed to make a noise in the sky. But that was it. They were not. I felt something was missing in the scene before us. Then I realized what it was. There was no noise. It was all quiet.

CHAPTER VIII

We were outside Gloria's apartment building. The cab ride had cost me nearly all I had. We were standing alone on the sidewalk.

"You can come up if you want to," she said.

"I can?"

"Yes."

"Swell."

"Is it?"

"Yes."

She smiled at me. It was a quick smile. Then her face was stiff again She looked again like a model. She looked younger when she smiled. I did not know how old she was. That was not important. That or whether she smiled or not. Though I did like the smile when she made it.

We went inside her building. It was a remodeled brownstone walk-up. She lived on the second floor. She went first. The steps were covered with thick carpet. You could not hear yourself walking. Her dress in front of me made a nice swish-swish sound as she walked. An empty trash can was outside her door.

"Would you bring that in, please?" she said.

"All right. I don't mind being a porter."

"I thought we abandoned him?"

I laughed. "So we did."

Inside her apartment she walked to a small pantry.

"Put it in here," she said.

I did. Then I sat down in the big easy chair next to the phonograph and record stand. Most of the records were symphonies, but there were a few albums of jazz and bebop. I put on some records by Danny Blue and Dizzy Gillespie and Coleman Hawkins. The machine had an automatic changer. It was a good machine. It did not make any mechanical noises as the records played. On the wall directly across from me was the usual Rouault. I looked away from the Rouault and listened to Danny Blue. He was blowing all by himself now, without the orchestra, blowing on and on and up and up, blowing one variation after another variation on what he had been blowing, getting hotter and faster, more alone in what he was doing, until I thought he was going to come right off the record. A real junkie. He was loaded with heroin on this record. He flipped his wig when it was finished and they took him to a sanitarium.

Now Gloria came back. She had changed into slacks and a sweater. She had a drink in her hand. "Here," she said, and handed me the drink. She sat on the floor near the phonograph and began looking through the records. She put some more on.

"Aren't you having one?" I said about the drink.

"No. I can still feel the martinis."

So could I but I drank the highball anyway. Even though I did not need it. It took away the dry heavy after-drink taste in my mouth but it did not make anything happen. I felt the same as before. I had gone as far as I could go. The exhilaration was over.

"Not a bad setup," I said. "You alone?"

"Yes," she said, sitting facing me with her legs crossed. "Isn't everybody?" She took a cigarette from a copper case on the coffee table behind her and turned the music down low.

"Pretty much so. I guess." I drank some highball. "How long have you been at it?"

"At what? Being alone?"

"No. Modeling."

"Oh, that. Two years."

"You must be pretty good."

"Sometimes I think I am. I guess I must be. I make a lot of money. So I must be."

"That's a good enough measuring stick."

"One measuring stick is as good as another." She smiled. "What's the matter? Do I smell envy?"

"No. Not really."

Dizzy was playing now.

"Don't blame me if people pay a lot of money for something I happen to have. It's not my fault."

"I'm not blaming you for anything. I'd like to make half what you do."

She looked at me without saying anything, smiling and looking at me but not saying anything. Then, "Why don't you make me instead?"

Then, kissing her there, standing up, her hands moving along my buttocks, the lipstick taste and the whisky taste mixing in my mouth strongly, my own hands moving, hers still so, she touching me, I her, she moved a little and turned the lamp off because the window was open and across the way people could see in and then moved again against me to move toward the bedroom.

Afterward lying on my back in the bed, I felt her breathing there against me, and coming up now out of the small aftersleep I turned my head and my nose just brushed her hair, head turned the other way toward the window, from me. I was now awake and the same again. I lay on my back feeling her smoothness on my skin and listened to her steady breathing. She was asleep. I did not move. I did not want to wake her up. I lay there listening and feeling her breathing against me and looked around the room and smelled the mixed smells of love. In my mouth now was the whisky and lipstick taste. The night breeze was coming in through the Venetian blind that was down. It felt clean over my body.

Lying there listening and feeling but unmoving in the darkness of that room I heard the repeated noise, faintly. I did not know what it was, then I did. It was the record. It was the same record. It had been playing all this time, over and over again. I listened to it. Now it stopped, she breathing next to me, then the click of the automatic arm, and it started playing again. I felt lonely and sad and empty. *La muerte chiquita.* The little death, the Spanish called it. I had died the little death and now I was alive again. I could still smell and feel the little death in the room. Was I alive again? Was I?

I knew I must go. I had to get out of this bed and go away. Twisting around carefully, muscles tensed, I got out of the bed, hoping I would not wake her up who was sleeping with her head the other way, away from me. I wanted to go while she was sleeping. My feet felt our clothes on the floor of the room. I lifted up something with my foot. It was not mine. I put it on the chair. Finally I found everything and dressed. I started walking out of the bedroom.

"Where you are going?" she asked.

I stopped. But I did not turn around. "I have to go," I said. "I'm sorry I woke you up."

I heard the record playing, playing.

"You didn't, really. Can't you stay?"

"No. I've got to go."

All this in the darkness of the two rooms, the record still playing softly over and over again.

"You really have to go?" from the bedroom.

"Yes."

"Oh. All right. If you say so."

I remained there for a moment.

"You can turn a light on if you like," she said.

"That's all right. I don't need it."

"Would you turn off the record before you go?"

So she had heard it, too.

"Sure." I reached out and turned off the record that had been playing all this time and walked to the door.

"Thanks. Maybe soon again?" she asked.

"I don't know. Maybe." My back still to her and standing there with my hand on the door knob.

"All right. Maybe then. So long."

"Good night," I said.

I was not far from where I lived. I walked. My head felt clear in the cool night air. On the dark south side of the park I watched a man coming toward me. He came toward me slowly, weaving a little. We were the only people on the entire dark block. I knew what was going to happen. He was a drunk bum. Now he stood in my path waiting for me. His face was dirty and drunken and beaten-up-looking. Then he asked me.

"But I don't have anything," I replied.

He asked me again, pleading, standing with his hands in his pockets, weaving slightly.

"I'm not kidding you," I said. "I don't have a thing. I'm cleaned out."

He shrugged his shoulders and said okay and something else I did not catch, said mostly to himself. But he kept standing there. I walked around him and went on. Walking on, I looked across into the park. It was deserted. It was pretty late. I saw a cop walking slowly by the empty benches swinging his night stick.

Then further on I passed the Sporting Club. Some people were hanging around outside, talking. Without stopping I looked in through the big windows but the crowd inside seemed sort of dead. I did not see Porter, but he may have been there. The owner of the place came out in his undershirt and he said hello to me very politely, too politely for it to have any effect on me. I said hello back and kept on going toward home.

CHAPTER IX

Grace came by to see me the next afternoon. It was Thursday. I had just finished writing the letters I had been putting off. I had put them off as long as I could. One was to my sister, asking her for a loan. That was the one that I had put off the longest. And I was pretty sure it would put her off, too.

"This place is in a mess," I said to Grace. "Forgive it."

"Forgive it. Forget it. I'm a mess, too, Blake."

"You look pretty good to me."

"Keep saying that, will you? I love it."

"All right. You look terrific. You do, you know."

"Lovely, lovely."

She looked very fresh and young, younger than she actually was. She was wearing a blue summer dress.

"I wish I had something to offer you," I said, thinking of a drink.

"You have. A lot. More than anybody I know, I think."

"You kill me."

"Why? You look pained."

"I'm always embarrassed when people say things like that. It's easier when people insult you."

"Is that so?"

"Yes. You can always say something sharp then. I'm thrown off by compliments."

"Is that actually the way you feel, Blake?"

"Most of the time."

She shook her head.

"Let's walk in the park. Do you feel like doing that?"

I said I did. I put my jacket on and put the letters in the inside pocket. They just fitted. Then I asked her to remind me to buy some more stamps. I needed some for the future. I did not really need a reminder, but I thought it would make her feel good if I asked her to do this for me. She said she would. We went out, and downstairs the Italians really gave her the once-over. Almost rudely. They stopped talking as we went by. She did not even look at them. I could feel them turning around to watch us as we went by them. I knew they saw her for an Italian. They were wondering why she wasn't with another Italian. Well, let them wonder. I think she felt what was going on, too. But she did not show it if she did.

We were walking along Thompson Street. "How did it go the other night?" she asked me.

"How did what-go what other night?"

"Weren't you out with Porter last night?"

"Yes."

"And the models?"

"Oh. Did you know about that?"

"Uh-huh. I knew."

"Did he tell you?"

"No. I just knew. How did it go?"

"It went We didn't do much. Just dinner."

"And then?"

"You're putting me on the spot, Grace."

"I'm sorry, Blake."

"And then I don't know. Porter took this girl home—just dropped her—and that was the last I saw of him."

"Were they pretty? Was she?"

"All models are pretty, in their way. You know that."

"Style?"

"Mostly style."

We stopped talking and walked. The sidewalks were cluttered with empty boxes and carts and kids and trucks and we had continually to skirt them to keep going. Some young truck helpers were standing on the sidewalk in front of an Italian delicatessen eating those sandwiches of salami and cheese and ham in a loaf of Italian bread cut lengthwise and they were washing it down with Pepsi-Cola. Ahead of us was the park.

"Were they very bright?" Grace asked me without turning her head.

"You shouldn't do this, Grace. You're only making it worse for yourself."

"I can't help it. Were they?"

"Not extremely."

"I'm glad of that."

I took her arm and we crossed West Third Street where the Fifth Avenue buses end their run. They were lined up empty. The drivers were standing together on the sidewalk, smoking. They were holding their steel change carriers in their hands. The young mothers were all there with their baby carriages. The little boys were wrestling on the grass.

"Want to sit in the circle?" I asked her.

"Let's sit on a bench. Do you mind, Blake? I always feel I'm sitting in an arena when I'm in that circle."

"Let's sit on a bench then. It will be more comfortable."

I saw some people we both knew sitting in the circle. I thought Grace might have seen them and for that reason, because she did not want to see many people she knew, she did not want to sit in the circle. We found an empty bench. Across the park sitting with a girl and a dog was Cap. He was making wide gestures with his arms. And moving his head. Now Grace lit a cigarette. She tucked the used match into the match folder.

"Did Harry get in touch with you about going to his father's house?" I asked.

"Yes. Henry said something about it, too."

"Sounds fine, doesn't it?"

"Very nice." She took a deep inhale.

"I've got a secret, Blake."

"Oh? Go on."

"Do you know of an abortionist?"

"Do I know of an abortionist?"

"That's right."

"Who wants to know?"

"I do."

"You mean for yourself?"

"Nobody else."

"I wish it were for somebody else."

"So do I. God, so do I."

I felt scared for her. I knew she had been raised a Catholic, an Italian Catholic, and I knew that she had never slept with anyone until she slept with Porter, and no one since, and I knew that this had been a great thing with her because she wanted to keep herself for the man who married her, absolutely, that her family knew nothing of this, that they would probably excommunicate her if they did, and I knew how it had been with her to keep all this to herself and watching Porter at the same time, still unmarried, and I knew that she regarded abortions as murder. She was sitting next to me, smoking a cigarette and waiting for me to go on with the conversation.

"Are you sure?" I asked her. "You know, it isn't unusual for anxiety to keep it back once or twice. It could be a number of things. You could even have a cold."

"I know. I told myself all those things a month ago. But now I know for sure."

"How long has it been?"

"Two months."

"Jesus Christ."

"Don't, Blake. You'll scare me."

"I'm sorry. Don't be scared. Why are you asking me this, Grace? Did Porter tell you he didn't know of any doctors?"

"He doesn't know about it."

"You mean you haven't told the guy?"

"That's right."

"But why? It's his isn't it?"

She turned around and looked at me. "You know it's his. I don't have to tell you that, Blake. I didn't tell him because, well, it would only confuse things. I don't want him to know about it."

"But you should tell him. He's responsible."

"He'd say it was my fault. It can be done without his knowing about it, can't it?"

In front of us the double-decker buses were turning past the circle and coming to a stop with their air brakes hissing, and then the automatic doors banged open and the people emptied out in two big packs. Waiting empty now, then to be full and turn around and go back uptown, and the people who emptied out disappeared in the park.

"I guess it could be done without his knowing it," I said.

"How long would it take?"

"You'd have to take it very easy for a day or so after."

She asked me then if it could be arranged for next week. Porter would be out of town then for three days. He had to go to Philadelphia for an account he was working on. I told her about the doctor. He was a refugee living in Brooklyn. I knew of three cases he had handled and they had all been quick and simple and clean. Nobody had had any relapses. Of course I did not tell her there is always the first time, and before you know it you have bled to death. But I thought that happened only when it was three months or more. I explained to her how it was done. It would cost two hundred dollars. She said she had some money in the bank. All right. I could call and arrange it for next week. I told her I would go along with her.

"That will be very fine of you, Blake," she said.

"It isn't anything. While we're at it, you may as well stay at my place those two days you are recuperating. Unless you would rather not."

"Could I really do that, Blake?"

"That's what I just said."

"I'll never forget it. I never will."

"I think you should. You ought to forget the whole thing. As soon as possible."

I leaned back on the bench and looked up at the green-leafed trees. A little bell was ringing. It was the Good Humor man with his bicycle truck. The kids were around him.

"Like an ice cream?"

"I'd rather have a drink," Grace said.

"Fine. Let's go to the Brevoort. We can sit outside and the martinis are cheap."

Now we walked toward the big imitation Arch of Triumph. A group of young Stalinists from N.Y.U. gathered around one part of the circle were singing Stalinized American ballads to a guitar. People were sitting all along the edge of the circle. Inside the circle the people were sitting on the stone tiers looking around at each other and talking. Then I saw Johnnie Place strolling around, alone. He was a bop musician. He was wearing dark glasses. He saw us and waved and came over.

I introduced him to Grace. "How do you like the music?" I asked, nodding my head in the direction of the young Stalinists.

"They're groovy, aren't they? They've already sung 'Go Down Moses' three times."

Grace laughed.

"They can't seem to make him go," Johnnie went on, seeing Grace laugh.

I asked him where he was playing.

"Well, we were blowing a couple nights a week at a place on Second Avenue. But all of a sudden they started charging us for our drinks. We weren't getting paid but we were getting our drinks free. But now, I don't know. We're looking for another place."

I knew he wanted to come along with us. Ordinarily it would have been fine. But this time no. I told him we had to cut out. I said I had to take Grace home. I hoped he believed me. I think he did. I did not want to hurt his feelings. People like Johnnie have very delicate feelings.

"Listen," he said, just as we were parting. "There's going to be a kind of jam and party at Mary Fenner's place the night after tomorrow. I'm supposed to be telling people. Bring somebody with you. Bring a bottle, too, if you can."

I said we would make it.

"Okay, Blake. See you."

"See you."

"Glad to have met you, Johnnie."

"Same here."

"So long."

Crossing Fifth we cut behind a bus and the hot exhaust of it came up in our faces. We walked to the Brevoort. We took a table next to the boxed hedges. It seemed we were miles away now from where we had just been. A white-jacketed old waiter with a German accent took our order for the martinis. I felt we were really uptown. Everybody else at the tables had an uptown look. Maybe we did, too. Though I hoped not. But there was something about the uptown look that every now and then was pleasant. For a little while. The uptown look was a safe look. In a place like the Brevoort you felt safe from whatever you thought was after you. From what I did not know for myself. Grace and I, finished looking at the other people, now looked at each other. I winked at her. The waiter brought the martinis.

"Don't they look beautiful, Blake?" Grace said, picking her glass up. "They are the loveliest-looking drink."

Tiny pieces of ice were floating on the top of my drink. I picked up my glass. "To Modern Man?"

"Modern Man? Who is he?"

"Some jerk or other."

"All right. To Modern Man, then."

Almost as soon as the first swallow went down I felt it mounting to my eyes and to the back of my head, covering my face and head with its soothing prickliness. I took another swallow. Everything seemed even safer now. Already the noises of the street seemed cushioned. I wanted to sit there all night feeling safe.

"Why are you doing all this, Blake?"

"It would take too long to tell you."

CHAPTER X

That night, Thursday night, Grace went out to Long Island to see her family. She regularly went to visit her family. They thought something was wrong if she did not make a regular visit. I called Joan. I had borrowed two books from her that she wanted returned soon. She was going to be home for a while, so I told her I would drop by and leave the books.

The books were *The Sky Is Red* by an Italian named Berto and an anthology of pieces printed by a little magazine in Chicago. Some of the things in the anthology were fairly good. Most of them were very sad. I had not been able to get the books in the branch library and I had borrowed them from Joan because of that. I walked to her place.

"I'm sorry you can't stay very long," she said when she let me in. "But somebody else is coming up. You know."

"Sure."

I sat down in her antiqued-oak porch chair after putting the books on a table.

"Want a quick one?"

"I don't think so. Thanks."

"Do you mind if I finish fixing my hair while you are here?"

"Not at all."

She went into the bedroom. I walked to the bookshelves and looked over them. I picked up a book that looked familiar. It was. I had given it to Joan some time ago. On the fly leaf I had written something sentimental. I put it back. There were very many books on psychoanalysis. She was gone on the subject. She was humming in the bedroom as she fixed her hair. She called in and asked me how everything was. I said it was all right. She said something I did not quite get. I did not bother to ask her to repeat it. I sat back down in the oak chair. She came back in.

"I got a letter yesterday from Harper Baily and his wife in Italy," she said. "He says Florence is so chic that even the whores look like ladies of quality."

I had never especially liked Baily or his wife. But I asked about him anyway. "Is he getting any work done?"

"He seems to be. They're going to live in Perugia until he gets his thesis done. Then they are going to Sicily."

"That's good. I wish I were going." I looked out of the window. Then I got up. "I'm going along, Joan."

"All right. I'm sorry you couldn't stay longer, Blake. You seem very restless. You should have come up earlier."

"I have to go anyway," I said.

"Say hello to the others."

"I will."

She saw me to the door.

When I got outside the apartment building I started up Tenth Street. Then I decided that I would rather walk along West Street. I turned around and walked to West Street. Between the warehouses I could see the river. The river smell was in the air, clean and of tar and oil, and then there was a smell of fresh vegetables being blown down from the vegetable warehouses up near Horatio Street. I walked south on West Street all the way to Christopher. The street was empty and dark. A police squad car cruised by. I passed two old stevedores standing in front of a garage, talking low. There was the noise of a derrick working somewhere. There was no other noise in the street and that made the derrick noise very loud. I turned up Christopher Street and headed for Sixth Avenue.

On Sixth Avenue near Fourth Street I saw Porter coming out of a book shop. He was carrying a large Manila envelope. He did not see me. I hesitated for a moment whether I should go on or wait for him. Then he saw me.

"Hey, Blake," he shouted. "Wait a minute."

I turned around.

"I was just in Larry's." He talked so loud people turned around. You could hear him all over the place.

"Did you steal any good books?"

"They have some great stuff in there," he said. We were walking down Sixth Avenue.

Have they got any good abortionists in there? I said to myself.

"What's in the envelope?" I asked him.

He opened the Manila envelope and took out a small book. "It's a novel by Raymond Queneau. I just bought it for my model, Margaret."

"Why are you keeping it in that?"

"To keep it clean."

There was nothing I could say to that. There was nothing wrong I guess with wanting to keep a book clean. I had never thought of carrying a book in a Manila envelope. I don't know who else it would have occurred to but Porter.

"What happened to you the other night?" he asked. "I waited for you later in the Sporting Club."

"I went home early after that. I did not feel so hot."

"Is that a pun?"

He was quick in getting them sometimes. "No," I said. "It was the truth."

"Didn't you do yourself any good?"

"Uh, yes."

"Well, I had a couple of beers waiting for you, then turned in. I had some writing to finish up. What did you think of Margaret?"

"Nice."

"Nice? Man she's terrific. She kills me."

"She does? What about her husband? Does he kill you, too?"

"A jerk. She stays with him because he is a father substitute. She really doesn't like him. He is much older than she is. She wants to leave him and live with me."

"That should be cozy."

"She has been down to my place a couple of times already. She calls me the sex trap of New York."

In the middle of the block was a clam cart where you could get six clams on the half-shell for twenty-five cents. As Porter talked about Margaret I wondered if it was really true that oysters and clams were good for what they said. If it was just another myth.

"How about some clams for an appetizer?" Porter asked me. "Have you had dinner yet?"

I told him I had not.

"Let's have some clams then. Have some on me.

You could probably use some."

"Speak for yourself."

"I was just kidding."

At the clam cart Porter ordered half a dozen clams for each of us. The man there shelled the clams quickly and put them all on one plate for us. I liked them best with just lemon juice, but before I could do anything Porter was shaking ketchup on all of the clams. I squeezed lemon over my half-dozen. We ate the clams out of the shell without using a fork, sucking up all the juice left in the shell.

"There's Max," Porter said, looking across the street.

Max was crossing the street. Watching the traffic nearsightedly. He was crossing against the light. The cars came very close to him. He bent his red head toward them.

"Max," Porter shouted.

Max looked in our direction. He made no recognizing gesture. You could not tell whether he had seen or heard Porter.

"My favorite food," Max said, coming over to us and looking at the clams and not at Porter or me.

"We used to eat these all the time when we were kids."

"They are great appetizers," Porter said.

"They are great anytime," said Max. "Why don't you stand me some? I'm starving."

"But you owe me a fin already. What am I? Your keeper?"

"You'll get your money," Max said. "I just got an extra job."

I wiped the clam juice from my fingers with my handkerchief. Hellos were often not used with Max. They were not necessary.

"All right," Porter said. "I'll stand you some clams then." He told the man half a dozen more. "What is this extra job?"

Max watched the man open his clams. He began eating them before answering Porter. "I'm going to teach a rich woman how to write poetry," he said. "They say she's worth about ten million." He laughed.

"You're kidding."

"No, I'm not. It's the truth." He laughed again. "This broad wants to be a poet. I give her two lessons a week and she pays me thirty dollars."

"What exactly are you supposed to do?" Porter asked him.

"Twice a week I go out to her house and read what she has written. I tell her what is good and what is bad about it. Then I teach her a trick or two. And I tell her what books to read.

"Is that all?"

"That's all." He finished the clams. "Got a handkerchief?" he asked Porter. Porter gave him his and he wiped his fingers on it. "She lives out in a big place on Long Island. She has a sister that's trying to be an actress. Not bad, either."

"Are you going to teach her anything?" I asked him.

"Maybe she can teach me something."

"I doubt that."

He shook his head. "What a salty character."

"I think it was a compliment," I said. I really think it was, too.

"What sort of a woman is she?"

"All right. She's eager."

"That must make it even simpler," I said.

"Well, what if she writes lousy poetry?"

"What do I care? I don't care how she spends her money."

"Think of that. Thirty bucks a week just to be some cornball's literary adviser. Jesus."

Max was now nearsightedly examining the people walking past us. Porter paid the man for the clams. I walked to a newsstand a few yards away and bought a *Journal-American*. A Senate committee was still investigating war-contract profiteering among government officials. One of the highest men in the Army had already been convicted of profiteering and sentenced to five years in the penitentiary. I turned to the sports page, walking back to where Porter and Max were standing. I read that middleweight contender Tony Giuliano was being suspended in New York for failing to report an offer made by gangsters to throw a fight. One hundred thousand dollars was the offer.

Porter and Max stopped talking. Max asked me what was in the paper. I told him about Giuliano.

"What do those jerks expect?" Max said. "Do they expect him to act like a boy from the YMCA? How dumb can you get? The guy was brought up in the streets and his friends are gangsters and hoods and he's expected to report a bribe probably offered him by one of his friends. Jesus. What a laugh."

"He's a bum, Giuliano," Porter said. "He has all the marks of an hysteric."

"Think he ought to be analyzed?" I said.

The Coster-Phelps fight was going to be held in a few days. Coster was training at Pompton Lakes, New Jersey. I wanted to see him train. "Let's go over to see Coster train," I said to Porter. "Grace can introduce us to him."

"I guess she could," he said. "I don't know whether I want to see him train, though. He doesn't send me. And besides, I would have to take a day off from work."

"It would be worth it," I said. "I'd like to meet him. Ask Grace if she won't go over with you. Maybe we can all go over."

"Maybe. But I'm not too excited about it. I'll speak to Grace and let you know."

"What about you, Max?"

"It is too far to go."

"All right, then."

I wanted to see Coster win this fight. Phelps had a reputation for being quite a rat. He was a neighbor-hood bully who liked to get into street fights. He had once given two black eyes to the sixty-year-old sheriff in his home town. And he was always bragging. I wanted to see Coster knock his head off. If he did he would get a chance at the title. But Phelps had a long string of knockouts to his credit. He could hit as hard with a right cross as most middleweights could, maybe harder. Coster was a clean boy who lived at home with his parents. He was a better boxer than he was a puncher.

Porter suggested we have dinner. We tried to decide on a place to have it.

"Any place but an Italian place," Porter said. "I'm sick of Italian food."

It did not make any difference to me. I would just as soon eat Italian food as any other food. I mentioned a place on Christopher Street where we could get Austrian food. It was cheap and fairly good. Max wanted to go to a kind of luncheonette where you ate at the counter. We decided against that and for the Austrian place. Porter told him they might have cheese blintzes there. He was just making this up. If Porter wanted to persuade Max that way, all right.

We strolled down Sixth Avenue to Bleecker Street and then turned west and walked up Bleecker toward Seventh Avenue. The stores and carts were just finishing up their day's selling and out in the street the street cleaners were sweeping the broken wood crates and bad vegetables into big piles and then shoveling these piles into the back of the white garbage truck that was following them. The truck made a constant churning noise as the garbage was cut up by the machinery inside the truck. The cart owners and the store people stood on the sidewalk, talking loudly in Italian. They were short and built thick and ugly.

Walking toward us was a Negro boy with a white girl. They were holding hands. The Italians they passed on the sidewalk stopped talking and stared after them. The couple looked straight ahead. The girl was quite good-looking. They passed us, avoiding looking at us.

"These spade intellectuals really think they've made it when they get a white girl," Porter said.

"The guy is crazy to do that down here," Max said. "The Goths beat up three of these dark boys last week for doing the same thing."

"What about the cops?" I said.

"The cops? What a laugh," Max said. "The cops don't care if these guys are beaten up. Most of them approve of it."

We passed the meat market. Whole calves split up the middle, their hides still on, were hanging head down from hooks in the window. The hides were splotched with blood. Then we passed the delicatessen with the big provolone cheeses hanging in the window with the cans of imported delicacies and coming strongly through the open door of the delicatessen was the mixed smell of olive oil and garlic and salami and cheese and spices.

At the corner of Seventh Avenue and Bleecker Street we had to wait for the light. Waiting there we turned and looked into Ray's bar. It was already crowded with sailors and local Italian girls. There were four sailors to every girl at the bar. The sailors were most of them drunk. The juke-box music was playing loud.

"Some nice delinquent stuff in there," Max said, squinting into the bar.

"It's too dark," Porter said, "and too short."

"You're crazy, man. Too dark and too short for what?"

"For me."

"Okay. For you, then."

Max kept squinting into the bar. A girl came out alone. She looked about eighteen. She was crying. She stood outside away from the door.

"Look at that," Max said.

"You better stay away from her," I said.

"But she's having a bad time."

"You'll have one, too, if you mess around her. Four sailors would jump you just for the fun of it."

"Come on. Let's go," Porter said.

The girl looked through the window of the bar. She dried her eyes with a handkerchief and walked back into the bar.

"Well, well," Max said, as we turned away and walked across the street, "back for more. They are all masochists, I guess."

The food was good in the Austrian place. We had pot roast and potato pancakes, and, after that, strudel and coffee. An ex-movie critic with nothing more to say came in with a girl who was a notoriously easy make. I wondered whether he and Max would speak. Max had circulated some pretty nasty stories about him and his bed abilities and the stories must have got back to him. But Max was the first to speak to him.

"How have you been, Roy?" he said, waving his hand. "Haven't seen you around lately."

"I've been around," the ex-critic said.

"Sure you have. Nobody doubts that. But where? Where?"

The ex-critic smiled broadly and shook his head and made a slow throwing-down gesture with his arm. Porter and I had nodded to the girl he was with. Porter had been with her. So had Max. She and Max apparently were not speaking.

"He used to be pretty sharp," Porter said about the ex-critic. "But he's going to pieces."

"How do you know?" I asked him.

"I can tell just by reading his stuff. The guy is very fragmentary. And look who he's with, man. Couldn't you tell just from that?"

I shrugged. I had nothing against the girl.

"She's not a bad piece," Max said.

Then he told us about one of the times he had been with her. They had got high on tea and Max had spent the night in the apartment she shared with a widowed cousin. He had set the alarm for an early hour so that he could leave before the cousin's two children got up and saw him there. But they slept through the alarm. Later he woke up, and standing next to the bed looking at them were the two kids.

"Man, I could see the neurosis rising up from their toes," Max said. "Then one of the kids picked up a ball and threw it on the bed. 'Come on,' he said, 'Let's play ball.'"

"Did you?" Porter asked.

"What else could I do?"

"What did she do?" I asked.

"She told them to be quiet. That it was too early for games."

The picture of it was clear in my mind. I looked around the restaurant, hoping the picture would go away but it stayed in my mind. Then slowly it went away and other pictures came in its place.

"What's the matter, Blake?" Max asked. "You look as though you didn't like that story."

"It doesn't make any difference whether I like it or not."

"Why should there always be this sentimental crap in a relationship?" Porter said. "A piece is a piece."

"Okay," I said. "A piece is a piece."

We got the check and examined it and got up from the table.

"Good-by," the girl said suddenly from the other table. "Good-by, Max."

"So long."

Porter and I said good-by to her. I gave Porter my share of the check and he paid it. Outside he counted the change in his hand. "Just to make sure," he said, seeing me watching him.

CHAPTER XI

We stopped in at the Sporting Club Bar to see what was going on there. Harry Lees was standing at the bar with a girl named Julia and a man I had never seen before. The man was expensively dressed in sport clothes and he had a crew haircut. The place was jumping. It was jammed. You could barely move, it was so crowded.

"Come on over here," Lees shouted across the bar.

"I'm going to case the place first," Max said. "I'll be over later."

He walked through the crowd, examining everybody.

Porter and I went over to the bar. We said hello to Harry and Julia. Porter called her Slim.

"I want you to meet Russell Goodwin," Julia said. "He is an account executive and he makes four hundred dollars a week."

"That's quite an introduction," Goodwin said, smiling. "I'm very glad to meet you. Won't you have a drink with us?"

We said all right. I said it was nice of him to do this.

"Don't mention it," he said. "It gives me a great deal of pleasure."

"It does, too," Julia said.

"Four hundred dollars a week," said Harry.

Goodwin laughed. "Don't keep saying that. You'll make me feel self-conscious."

"Not a bad way to be self-conscious," I said.

The bartender put our drinks on the bar and Goodwin paid for them from a long pigskin wallet he kept inside his jacket, and handed the drinks to us.

"Here's mud," he said. We drank. "Harry," he said, "I think you and Julia need yours freshened up a bit."

He called for two more Scotch-and-sodas. He looked at the crowd around us. "I'm crazy about this place," he said. "I just stumbled on it tonight."

Porter and I looked at each other, and Porter made a questioning gesture with his eyebrows. Then he slapped Harry on the shoulder. "Hey, old sport. What have you been up to?"

Goodwin was watching and listening and smiling. I could not help noticing again how well-dressed and set up he was.

"That is an ambiguous question, old sport," Harry said to Porter.

I felt Harry was doing this just for fun, not for any other reason. Goodwin had handed Harry his new drink and was watching him and Porter.

"I don't know exactly how to answer you," said Harry. "When you say what am I up to do you mean what am I capable of doing? Or do you mean to what point have I risen? The assumption being I am low and going up. You see, old sport, it's very ambiguous."

Goodwin laughed. "That's very clever, Harry. I had never thought of it that way."

"Take it anyway you like," Porter said.

"All right. To be honest, Porter, I haven't been up to anything. I've been pretty low."

"Won't you have another drink?" Goodwin asked me, looking at Porter, too.

"No, thanks," Porter said.

"Are you sure? Come on. Have another."

"Don't be dull," Julia said. "Have another drink, Porter."

"I'm not a drinking man," Porter said. "It makes me dizzy and confused."

"Are you afraid somebody is going to put something over on you when you are tight?" Harry asked him.

"No. I just don't like feeling confused."

"I'm not afraid of feeling confused," said Harry.

"But you will have one, won't you, Blake," Goodwin said to me.

"Sure. Blake will have one. He's not afraid of getting dizzy."

"Thanks," I said.

"That's the boy, Blake. Stay with us," Julia said. "Don't let us down."

"Or bring us down."

"Oh. I get it," Goodwin said. "I get that one. It's a jive expression. Right?"

"You're in," Porter said.

"He's a very solid citizen," Harry said. "He makes four hundred a week."

"What do you do?" Goodwin asked Porter.

"I write fiction."

"Really? I used to write fiction, when I was in college."

"And?"

"It was pretty good. I gave up writing because nobody bought my stories. But it was good. Now I wish I had kept at it."

"You're doing all right," Julia said.

"Oh yes. I do all right. Harry, when do you expect to finish your book?"

"Are you writing a book, Harry?" I asked.

Goodwin answered me. "Didn't he tell you? He told me he's doing a book on the end of the Renaissance. Aren't you, Harry?"

"I'm not only doing it, I'm living it. Which reminds me. What happened to that underground man you came in with?"

"He's casing the joint," Porter said. "He'll be back."

"What do you mean by the underground man?" Goodwin asked.

"The man who will do anything. He's a spiritual desperado."

"He means Max Glazer," Porter said. "He's a very smart guy. Really very hip."

"I didn't say he wasn't. He is a desperado, though. Do you know what his ideal is? His ideal is to look like a street-corner hoodlum and be the finest lyric poet in America at the same time."

"He sounds remarkable," Goodwin said. "I would enjoy meeting him."

"Don't say it that way," Julia said. "You'll meet him."

"There's a booth. Let's get it."

We pushed through the crowd on our left and got to the empty booth just ahead of some other people. "Very sorry," Goodwin said to them, smiling nicely. They did not say anything and went away.

"Tell me some more about the underground man, Harry," Goodwin said.

"I'm writing a book about him, too."

"It seems that you are writing these books with your mouth, Harry," said Porter.

"It is a new literary form," Harry said. "Anyway, about the underground man. Max. His favorite reading is Andrew Marvell and the Daily Mirror comics. You might say he is the Neanderthal man of the new world."

"Here he is," Julia said.

Goodwin stood up. We all looked at him as he did this. He held out his hand to Max. "You're Max Glazer, aren't you? My name is Goodwin, Russell Goodwin. We've been talking about you."

Max did not return Goodwin's greeting, though he did shake his hand gently. He made a surprised expression and smiled at us.

"Sit down, Max," Goodwin said, and gave Max his seat in the booth.

"I'll get a chair from the dining room." He shouldered through the crowd and went back to the dining room.

"I don't dig this guy," Max said. "What's his story? Is he a fruit or something?"

"He's not a fruit," said Julia. "He's just lonely."

"Julia and I met him at the bar," Harry explained.

"He was alone and he asked us if he could buy us a drink. Just like that. He makes four hundred dollars a week."

"He is an uptown operator, Max," Porter said. "But he might be good for laughs."

"You're a cool son of a bitch, Porter," Julia said.

"Are you so hot?"

"Oh, nuts to you."

"Even though the guy is uptown, he's an interesting sociological study," Porter said to Max.

"You don't say?"

"What are you drinking?" Max asked me.

"Scotch. He's been standing everybody liquor. You can't stop him."

"Who would want to? Give me a drink, will you?"

I let Max take a drink from my glass. Goodwin came back with a chair. He sat down on the outside. "You will have a drink, won't you, Max?" he asked.

Max said he would. Goodwin ordered from a waiter passing us with his hands full of empty beer glasses. He was one of the good waiters.

"*Subito, subito,*" he said. He liked to speak Italian every now and then. He thought it was amusing. He spoke it with a sharp northern accent. Everyone liked him. He was never sullen. The place was very noisy now. The bartenders were shouting for the dining room waiters to pick up their drinks. People were standing in both doorways, talking and drinking and looking all around. You could not tell whether they were on their way in or on their way out.

A headache was beginning to work up the back of my neck and head and I was feeling the drinks. I was thinking about Grace's abortion and about the big fight and about going away for a few days to Harry Lees's father's place up on the Cape.

And about a job. Goodwin's being there made me think about the job. An uptown job. There were no other jobs. They were all uptown. And you had to go uptown to keep them, too. I did not want to do that.

"You'll have another drink, won't you, Blake?" Goodwin asked me.

"No thanks, Goodwin. I'll nurse this one."

"You're sure?"

"Yes. Thanks anyway."

Max smiled at me. "Why do you play tag this way with corruption, Blake?"

"I'm not playing tag. I just don't want another drink."

He kept on smiling. The others were watching him. "That isn't what I'm talking about. You know that."

"What are you talking about, Max?" Goodwin asked.

"I'm talking about your buying Blake a drink. Blake feels it's corrupt to let people buy for him. And he feels nervous because you're buying it the way you are."

He was right. And he was not stopping there. "How am I buying it, Max?" Goodwin asked him.

Max laughed softly. "You're buying in," he said.

"Oh, nuts, Max," Julia said. "Why do you have to get so salty when people want to have fun?"

Goodwin's smile had gone now. He was looking into his drink. Harry was looking at me. We were both thinking the same thing. I guess Goodwin had it coming to him. Here or someplace else.

"You're right, Max," Goodwin said, looking up. "You're quite right. That's what I've been doing."

"I didn't say there was anything wrong with it," Max said. "I just said that's what you're doing and that's what Blake was feeling bad about. Blake thinks things like that are bad."

"How long have you known everything?" I said.

"Let's forget it," Lees said. "I'll tell a dirty joke."

"Why should you feel bad about this?" Max asked Goodwin. "You get in however you can. In this case you buy in. One way is as good as another."

"You really think you have everybody taped, don't you, Max?" I said.

He smiled and shook his head and patted my arm. "Slow down, man. Slow down. Don't take everything so personally."

"Do you dislike me for doing this?" Goodwin asked, looking at Porter now.

Porter shrugged. "I don't know you well enough to either like you or dislike you, old man."

"Come on. Let's drop it," Julia said. "Tell the dirty joke, Harry. Or whistle 'Dixie.' Do something."

Harry told the dirty joke. It was not so dirty. But it was funny. It involved a Jewish man catching something from a hustler in Atlantic City. Porter laughed very loud when it was over, laughing that ha-ha-ha, loud laugh. Goodwin laughed too. The joke seemed to have relaxed him.

"How do you make this four hundred a week?" Max asked Goodwin.

"I am an account executive at an advertising agency."

"You must live pretty well."

"Well, I guess I do."

"Let me guess. You live up on the upper East side and you probably have a charge account at Abererombie & Fitch."

"You're doing very well."

"And you read the *New Yorker* regularly and think it is really terrific. And you often tell your friends you heard something funny the other day which you think you will send to the *New Yorker*."

"Go on."

"Your idea of a vacation is to go to Fire Island and you probably listen to WQXR very often. You see all the shows at the Museum of Modern Art."

"You are batting a thousand. Go on."

"You see all the French movies and you think they are much better than the American movies."

"You're doing great."

"You still think you would like to live in Paris for a year. Because that is where things happen."

"I do, too."

"What are you doing down here?"

"Oh, looking around."

"Pretty expensive looking, isn't it? One way or another."

"That is what the four hundred is for, Max."

Max smiled and finished his drink. "You're okay, Goodwin, you're okay."

"Thanks, Max."

"Underground Max," I said. "Working overtime."

"You're underground, too, Blake, old boy. You're the Arrow Collar man of the underground."

"Would anyone like to hear another joke?" Harry asked. "This is getting too serious for me."

"By all means, another joke, Harry," Julia said.

"Jokes drag me," Porter said. "One joke was enough. Tell something else, but not a joke."

"That is your trouble, Porter," said Harry. "You are a one-joke man. Spread out. Be a two-joke man."

"Don't let it worry you, old sport," Porter said, laughing and slapping him on the back. "I leave the clowning to the clowns."

"I'll tell you about the time I got drunk in Boston and a couple of jokers put me in the dumb-waiter. I fell asleep. The next morning a lady tenant in the building pulled the dumb-waiter down to put her garbage on. She saw me and screamed and fainted. She thought I was a dead body."

"Wonderful, wonderful," Julia said, shrieking.

"What was it like? Back in the womb?" Porter asked.

"Yes, and I liked it."

"It is amazing," Goodwin said. "Did it really happen, Harry?"

"No. I made it up."

"Well I'll be damned."

"Are you disappointed?" Porter asked him. "Do you want everything to be true?"

"Perhaps I'm naive."

Goodwin signaled to the waiter as he passed and asked for another round. "Just this last one," he said, smiling at us.

"Don't apologize," Julia said.

"Let's make it quick, though," Porter said, "because I have to be leaving. I have to finish some work."

"All right, man, all right," Max said. "Take it easy."

The waiter brought the drinks. None for me or Porter. I wanted to go home. They drank up. Porter was looking nervously around the bar. Afraid he would miss something or somebody. Max was looking at Julia. Examining her nearsightedly. Goodwin and Harry were talking about clubs. I was the first to get up.

"You may not believe me," Goodwin said, getting up with the others, "but I've really enjoyed this. I want to get together with you again. How about coming up to my place next week for dinner? Will you?"

"We would love to, Goodwin," Max said.

Goodwin wrote his name and address down on the back of a card he took from his wallet. "Next Tuesday, say at eight," he said. Then he left a big tip for the waiter. I knew none of us would go to Goodwin's house.

"They'll think you're crazy," Julia said about the tip.

"I don't care," Goodwin said, smiling. "I'm driving uptown. Can I give anybody a lift?"

We all said we were walking. All except Julia. She said he could give her a lift. Harry looked at her, surprised.

"But I thought I was going to walk you home," he said.

"Forgive me, darling," she said. "But I'm tired, really beat. Honestly."

Lees cocked his head and looked that way at Julia. "Okay," he said.

"Some other time, Harry," she said.

We left. Outside Goodwin and Julia got into his Buick convertible.

"Next Tuesday then," Goodwin said. "Don't forget."

We said we wouldn't. Julia waved good-by and they drove off. Lees just watched them, not waving.

"She can drop dead," he said.

"Don't take it so hard," Porter said. "She's just a tramp."

Max said he was going to a movie, a double feature on Forty-Second Street. There was nothing else to do. Porter said that must be the fourth movie he had gone to in the last week. Max said so what. He liked movies.

Porter and Max were going in the same direction. We said so long and they walked off.

"I'll walk home with you, okay?" Harry said to me. "I have a lot of time to kill."

"Sure. Come on."

I did not feel like passing by the Mills Hotel and the bruise-faced drinks there so instead of going up Bleecker as I usually did we went south toward Houston Street. We walked for a while without talking.

Harry said, finally, "I don't blame her. She played it smart and went with the better man.

"Don't say that. You'll begin to believe those things about yourself after a while."

"I do already, Blake. That's the crumby part of it."

"No you don't, Harry. You're talking yourself into it. Don't do that. You've got to keep up some sort of a front, even for yourself."

"Do you believe that?"

"That's the only way you can make it. That's the truth."

"I wish I could do it."

"If I were Porter I would call it a 'personal myth.' But whatever you call it, you have to have it."

Now the street darkened. I felt the darkness suddenly. I had not remembered this street being so dark. As Harry talked I kept feeling the darkness of the street. Then I saw why. The two street lamps were out. I thought somebody had stoned them out. But this was not so. The glass was not broken. The lamps had just gone out. I could see a bunch of the local hoods standing together way down at the corner we were approaching.

"Maybe I should get analyzed," Harry said. "I've often thought of that."

"It's tough. A lot of strange things happen to you."

"I know it's tough. You know something? I'm afraid of it."

"So are a lot of people."

"I'm afraid it will make me just like everybody else. That it will take some special juice out of me. Then I'll be a mediocrity. Maybe I am one already and don't know it."

"That would sound like a symptom."

"I guess it does, Blake. And then I'm afraid of a lot of things it might bring up."

I knew that even before he told me. He had always given me that feeling, as long as I had known him. He was keeping the lid on. Sometimes I thought it was better he did keep it on. It was safer for him that way.

"That's what makes it tough," I said. "But you are supposed to feel better after you bring it up."

"Like puking."

"Something like that."

"Blake, do you have bad dreams?"

"Doesn't everybody?"

"I mean really bad ones."

"Sometimes. Why?"

"I wondered if you had them like mine. Do you mind if I tell you about a dream?"

"Go ahead."

"Well, I have this one a lot of times. Someone is after me. I think I know who it is, then I am not sure. He is close behind me. I am scared. Scared stupid. So scared I want to scream. Then I run into a building. A building just going up. This person is getting closer. He is dressed in black. Now I run up a flight of stairs. I hear him jumping up the stairs. I think I might get away up the stairs. Suddenly the stairs end in a blank wall. I could scream. I hear him after me. He is almost on me. Then I find myself running in another part of the building. He's still after me. I run up another flight of stairs. Just then the stairs end in a blank wall again. And he's almost on me."

"Jesus Christ. Then what happens?"

"I keep running up these dead-end stairways. Then I wake up."

I wanted to say something enlightening about the dream that would make Harry feel better. But I could not think of anything that would not sound dumb. So I just said the dream sounded horrible. We were getting closer to the group of hoods.

"I wish I knew what the goddamn thing meant," he said. "Do you have any idea?"

"Nothing that would help."

Harry had been talking with his head turned toward me or looking down at the ground and apparently he had not seen the hoods at the corner. But now he saw them. I could feel him tighten as he looked at them. They were standing all over the sidewalk. Blocking the way. They were looking our way now. Harry was staring at them. There were eight of them.

I could feel the way Harry was holding himself tight as we came toward the hoods standing there on the sidewalk blocking it. Harry was staring straight ahead at them. I heard them talking now. I could feel Harry's fear.

They were standing in our way unmoving. Then we walked through them. Brushing against them. They moved slightly. We passed through them and on. We did not say anything.

We crossed Houston Street and walked east on it toward Greene Street. There were no cars in the big cobbled street.

"Those sons of bitches give me the creeps," Harry said.

I could feel his fear relaxing now.

"There are too many of them for us to start anything," I said. There were many stories around about the hoods ganging up on people.

"It makes you sick to be so outnumbered," he said.

"I know it. But what can you do?"

"Nothing, I guess. They don't have any rules to keep them back. You can't do anything with people who don't have any rules."

"To hell with them, Harry. Forget it."

"I guess so. I'll have to."

I slapped him on the back. "Old Renaissance Man."

No people were in the streets but us. Harry was walking with his hands in his pockets and his head down looking at the sidewalk. I watched the street lights blinking red and green in the deserted street, no cars to obey them. They were blinking for blocks down the street. We turned into Greene Street and walked south on it.

"Speaking of Renaissance men, Blake," Harry said, "what was this Max said about you being the Arrow Collar underground man?"

"That's what I am," I said, laughing a little. "Partly underground."

"Do you think you will ever go all the way?"

"I wish I could tell."

"It is like a joke become serious," Harry said. "I don't know when to take this underground business as a laugh or when to take it as a real thing."

"Neither do I."

We came to my building. "Want to come up?" I asked him. I really wanted to go to sleep.

"Thanks, Blake, but I had better be going along. I might start in on some more dreams."

"Don't let them get you, Harry."

"I have one of the best collections in the country. Like a jewel collection. Maybe I could sell it to the American Association of Head Doctors."

"You might try."

"Are the buses still running down here? I don't want to walk back."

"Yes."

"Good. Adios, kid."

"So long."

I went upstairs. When I got into bed I did not feel so sleepy any more. I lay awake, thinking.

CHAPTER XII

Porter called me the next day, Friday, about going to New Jersey to see Coster train. He had talked to Grace and she would go with us. We could borrow a car from a painter friend of Porter's. Porter said we could go that afternoon. He had nothing better to do, he said. There was nothing doing in his office. Grace could take sick leave from her office. She had a lot coming to her. Porter said he would pick up Grace first and then they would come by for me before lunch. We could have lunch somewhere on the way over. In return for the favor of the car we were to leave the painter a tank of gas.

I went to the small desk where I kept my cash to see how much I had. There was very little. I was almost broke again. I thought of calling Harry and asking for a loan. Then I decided not to. He would do it too willingly. That would make it bad. Make it bad for me, not for him. Well, there were still the books.

I looked over the shelves to select three or four books I could sell. It seemed funny to me. I had never thought of their paying off in just this way. What a laugh. I was glad now that I had put all that money in books when I had it. It was a new way of looking at literature. Not how good is the book going to be. How much can you get for it when you have read it. That is the point. You had to think of these things. I picked out four that I was quite sure Mack would buy and put them on the desk. Then I took a shower.

Before leaving I poured myself a glass of grapefruit juice. I went outside and up to Sixth Avenue to a small diner to have coffee and Danish pastry. The pastry was fresh and the syrup on it still sticky. I had to keep wiping the syrup off my fingers as I ate. As I left the place I noticed a window card announcing the Coster-Phelps fight. Coster with that baby face. He was smiling. What the hell was there to smile about? Phelps looked like just what he was. A real killer. A little crazy. It was a very convincing look. His eyes were slanted down with scar tissue. This made him look old. Coster looked like a kid. A nice, easy-going kid.

Mack's Bookshop was not yet open. I had come too soon. I bought a *Times* in the cigar store next door and went into the coffee shop on the corner and sat at the counter and ordered coffee. The waitress who served me was a good-looking Negress. She served me and went back to the end of the counter where she had been talking to a sporty-looking Negro boy. They were getting quite a kick out of whatever they were talking about. They laughed as much as they talked. I tried to guess what they could be talking about. Then I dropped it.

I read the *Times* and watched the clock on the wall to see how much time I was killing. One of the columnists in this paper was comparing Coster and Phelps. He picked Coster to win. He liked the way Coster boxed, his good left jab, and his coolness. He brought up the names of some of the fighters Coster had beaten. Very few knockouts. The majority had lost to Coster on points. Coster was a skillful, clean-fighting boy who knew his way around in the ring. He never bragged. He played the rules.

But Phelps was completely different. He had been in the ring for only a short time but in that time he had won seventy-five per cent of his fights by knockouts. The *Times* columnist talked about his last fight. It was with a very tough local boy who was way up there on the contender list. Phelps was the underdog in the betting. I had seen that fight on Long Island. I had never seen a welterweight hit that way. Phelps knocked this other boy down four times in five rounds, each time with a short right cross you almost missed seeing it was so fast and short a punch. The boy stayed down the last time he was hit. But Phelps was still young and inexperienced and he was a bleeder. The columnist said he would be cleanly out-pointed by Coster. I hoped so.

It was time to go. I paid my check and went out. Mack was just unlocking the door of his shop. He looked at what I had to sell.

"What are they worth?" I asked him.

"You tell me, Blake."

"But I'm not sure."

"It's old stuff. You know that."

"Yes. I know that."

"It's good but it's hard to sell."

"I know. It is expensive stuff."

"Did this stuff set you back much, Blake?"

"More than I like to think about."

"Are you sorry?"

"Not really, Mack."

"I'm glad to hear that. A lot of people get very sorry about this sort of thing."

"Too many sorry people hanging around these days."

"I see that you didn't sign your name in these, Blake, like some people do."

"It's because I never got the idea they were mine. I'm funny that way, though."

"You know, it's funny how much sooner people will buy a book when it doesn't have a name in it."

"An index of literary taste."

"Listen, Blake. How about six bucks? Is that okay?"

"They aren't worth that much, Mack."

"Let me worry about that."

"All right. I've worried about it long enough," I said.

"You'll be buying it all back again one of these days, Blake."

"No. I won't buy it again."

"I think you will."

"You think I'm like the dog returning, is that it?"

"If you want to put it that way. Six bucks, then?"

"That's swell of you."

"I wish I could give you more."

"Please. You're killing me, Mack," I said.

He put the books on his desk next to another pile and gave me six dollars from some crumpled bills he kept in his side pants pocket. He asked me if I wouldn't have some coffee with him. I told him I would like to but that I had to beat it. I did, too. I had to do a couple of things at my place before Porter and Grace came by.

I walked back to my place.

CHAPTER XIII

Henry Porter was in the driver's seat. It was Grace then who had rung my bell.

"We'll go by way of the Lincoln Tunnel," Porter said, driving away from in front of my apartment. "I think that is the best way."

"I'm glad you got this idea, Blake," Grace said. "Anything to get away from that dreary office."

"That was the whole purpose of it." I said.

"You."

We drove to Eighth Avenue and then followed it north to Thirty-Fourth Street and the Hotel New Yorker, then off it and west to the Lincoln Tunnel. We drove fast into the mouth of the tunnel behind a Greyhound bus.

Then as we were under the water the pressure began in our ears, and going farther under in the tunnel, underground beneath the water, the pressure increased.

"Are we underground now?" Grace said loudly. "Under the water?"

"Yes," I said.

"It's funny how soon you get used to it," said Porter, referring to the pressure.

The pressure underground was heavy now and the stink of exhaust was all over us, coming back at us from the other cars. There was nothing to do about it. We drove fast. Then I saw daylight ahead. We came up out of the tunnel into the open, the highway smooth, clean concrete before us, and the New York skyline over to the left, the stink of the exhaust gone, the air clean, the sun warm, the underground pressure leaving your head as you swallowed and breathed in the fresh air.

Then we stopped in the line of cars at the toll booths. Porter reached into his pocket for the fifty cents for the toll.

"I've got it," I said.

"No. I have it, Blake."

"I insist." I gave him a fifty-cent piece.

"Okay," he said. "But can you afford it? I thought you were broke."

"He is very rich," Grace said.

Porter pulled up by the toll booth, and the guard there leaned out of the booth, holding on with one arm, the other reaching out, and Porter reached out his arm, their arms meeting, neither having to move from where he was, and the guard leaned back into the booth and rang the fifty cents up in the register, and we drove off.

Driving on the smooth, curving highway uphill and the Hudson River below us, the Grace Line docks across the river, and then the curving highway took us away and the river and the New York skyline were gone. Looking down on my left I saw the double-mouthed tunnel we had just come up out of, and the exhausted underground feeling was gone now as we drove toward Paterson.

"Do you know how to get there, Henry?" Grace asked.

I liked sitting next to her, soft-feeling and perfumed.

"Sure. All you do is follow this road."

I suggested that we stop soon and get something to eat. Grace said she was hungry, too. Porter said he would keep his eyes open for a place.

"What is your opinion of this Coster boy, Blake?" he asked. "Do you think he has a chance?"

"He's going to win," I said, trying to make myself feel as convinced as I said it. Then I told him how they stacked up in my mind. I made Coster sound terrific. The next welterweight champion. Grace squeezed my hand.

"My friend," she said.

"I don't know," Porter said from his driver's seat. "Coster doesn't sound too great to me. He hasn't beaten anybody big. And I get the feeling the guy hasn't the stomach for it. I don't think he is a real fighter."

"Oh, yes he is," I said.

"He is, too," Grace said.

I mentioned Coster's superior boxing.

"What a romantic you are, Blake," Porter said. "What good is the guy's skill going to do him if he can't hit? You're nowhere if you can't hit."

He was right but I did not want to tell him so. I did not want to give him that satisfaction.

"He'll surprise you," Grace said.

"Aw, he's a bum," Porter said, joking.

"I hope he beats Phelps to death," Grace said. "He is a sweet, clean boy."

"What good is his sweetness going to do him against Phelps's right? I'll bet Phelps knocks him out."

"You've got yourself a bet," I said.

We made it for five dollars.

The Jersey meadows were on both sides of us. They looked at first like wheat fields but looking closer you could see that what looked like wheat was only a kind of tall grass, and still looking you smelled the wet heavy bog smell rising off it. Acre after acre of it.

Grace moved. "Are you crowded?" I asked her. "I can get in the back seat if you are."

She said she wasn't. I told her to let me know when she felt uncomfortable. I said I would not mind sitting in the back. She smiled at me.

We came to Rutherford. It was an ugly town. Everything looked alike. We were on the main street and all the buildings were stores with large signs that looked funny because the signs looked bigger than the stores. The fronts were faked brick. We decided to drive through it and stop at a diner on the other side. We all agreed it was a crumby place to stop for anything. On the other side of town we spotted a diner called the Sorrento. This was the first Italian diner I had ever seen. It was white on the outside and neat-looking. We parked behind it next to a trailer truck and went in.

There were just three men in the diner besides us. They must have belonged with the trailer truck outside. They were having a big meal. They were all unshaved and tired-looking. It always made me hungry to watch truck drivers eat. They ordered so much and ate with such appetite. It made the food seem much better than it really was.

The man behind the counter stayed behind the counter and asked us what we would have.

"Beer?" Porter asked me.

"Yes."

"I'll have beer, too," Grace said.

Porter told him three beers, then we would order. The truck men looked our way. The counter man put the opened bottles of beer on the counter. I got up and brought them to the booth. We drank the cold beer fast. I drank out of the bottle. Porter and Grace drank from glasses.

"This is wonderful," Grace said. "I was dehydrated. It's just what I needed."

"The first beer is the only one that really tastes good," Porter said.

We ordered three meatball sandwiches and after that three slices of apple pie with cheese. Somewhere I had heard that apple pie was always good in these diners because it was the favorite dessert of the truck drivers who stopped by all the time. If it wasn't good they would not go there any more. This sounded reasonable to me.

Grace asked Porter for a nickel to play the small music box on the wall at the end of the table. She played "Baby, It's Cold

Outside." The music was low and soft. I liked it. It seemed to be playing just for us. When the record was over Grace asked Porter to play it once more.

"You're as demanding as a pregnant woman," he said, putting another nickel in the box.

"I am."

"You are?"

"Uh huh."

"How do you feel?"

"Pregnant."

"This is a bad kind of joke," he said. "Jokes like this have a way of catching up with you sometimes."

"Want to go now?" I said.

We paid the check and left.

Out on the highway Porter turned on the radio in the car. He dialed past several stations, past a symphony program, to a fairly good disk jockey's program. Grace was sitting closer to Porter now. It was getting hotter. The disk jockey played a couple of good Billy Eckstine records and a Billy Holliday record that was rather literary and phony and some girl whose name I did not catch singing to a bop recording. She did not sing any words but made bop noises. She did this to show that the words were of no importance. It was only the music that counted. The program seemed to be an almost all-Negro one.

Grace and Porter seemed relaxed with each other now. They were talking to each other. I watched the scenery.

We passed a big outdoor sign advertising baby food. The baby in the sign stared down at us. The whole thing seemed rigged. I could not help looking at Grace. She looked at me out of the corner of her eye. Then a little farther on we passed the wreck of a car that had gone off the road. Two policemen were examining the wreck.

"Good Lord," Grace said.

"It is amazing how people don't watch where they are going," Porter said. "You would think they'd be more intelligent about it."

"Maybe the driver had an unconscious desire to commit suicide," Grace said, and her tone was not kidding.

"Quite possible," Porter said. "That's a good observation."

"It isn't original with me," she said.

"It's still good," I said.

We drove through Passaic and Clifton and Paterson and came into the wooded and country parts of New Jersey. We stopped once to read the arrow signs at an intersection. Pompton Lakes was three miles away. Coster was supposed to start sparring at two-thirty. We would make it.

"I'm getting excited," Grace said.

"It's worth getting excited about," I said.

"I'm very anxious to see it," Porter said. "I've never been in a training camp before."

"I hope there isn't much of a crowd," I said.

"Okay, alienated," Porter said, laughing.

"Why do you sound as though you are condemning him? I'm alienated, too," Grace said.

"You're bragging," Porter said.

In a few minutes we reached the training camp. There was not a big crowd. A man in a sport shirt was standing at the gate. He told us to park the car behind the building at the end of the driveway. There were three cars driving ahead of us. We followed them. On our right was the outdoor ring, in the shade. The wood tiers like bleacher seats were built all around it. A few people were already sitting there. On our left was the main building where the fighters lived. An old country-style house. Several boxing-crowd-looking men were sitting on the porch.

We parked the car behind the building at the end of the driveway. Most of the cars parked around us were in the high-priced bracket. There were three black convertible Cadillacs. Grace admired them. Porter said they probably belonged to the big bookies. He made a couple of cracks about hoods and bookies, talking loud. I told him he ought to hold that kind of talk until we left the place. There were too many people around who would not like it.

"Blake's right. Henry," Grace said.

"These guys aren't that sensitive," he said. But he stopped making the cracks just the same.

We walked to the outside ring and sat down on one of the top wood tiers. No one was around yet but the few people sitting in the tiers with us. It was shady there. We waited, talking a little. Nothing happened. Coster did not come out. I told Porter and Grace I was going to walk over to the house and make sure he was training outside. I got down and walked across the driveway, where cars were still coming in, and asked a fat man with a loud Charvet tie who was sitting on the porch whether Coster was going to spar inside or outside.

"It's over there, Johnny," he said, jerking his head toward a narrow one-story wood building. He looked away from me.

I walked back and told Porter and Grace. As we were leaving the outside ring I saw some of the people watching us, and I told them Coster was going to spar in the building across the road. They all got up off the bleacher seats and followed us out and across the road.

"This Coster is smart," a man behind me said to me. "He knows he'd melt away in this sun." The man was wiping the perspiration from his face.

I said he was probably right. Porter and Grace were walking ahead of me. Grace had her arm in his. At the entrance to the little building Porter stopped to wait for me. A group of loud-dressed men were standing off the driveway, talking. They were bookies and fight managers and hangers-on. They were all well-built men. They looked Italian and Jewish. A couple of them held themselves compactly like fighters.

"This admission is a gyp," Porter said to me, nodding his head at the admission price painted on a card at the ticket taker's desk there.

The ticket taker looked at us. I shrugged at Porter instead of saying anything. We paid the admission and went inside the small building.

This was better than the outside ring. You were closer here to the fighters. All of the seats were ringside. We got three seats in the second row. I had never been this close. I felt almost inside the ring. The seats inside sat about a hundred people. Behind and to the left of us beyond where the chairs went was the exercise section, the light and heavy bags and the mats and standing around the heavy bag in shorts and wearing the leather head protectors were three kids. Coster's sparring partners. The head protectors made them look tough and vicious.

The ringside filled up. In the same row with us was a tall blonde, expensively dressed and wearing dark glasses. She was with a small deeply sun-tanned man who was smoking a cigar. He kept watching the door where Coster would come out.

Coster came out of the side door. The crowd went still when he came out. Then a few people clapped. He was with his trainer. He did not look at anyone. He walked through ringside to the ring. He stopped at the ring and waited for his trainer to put his head protector on. He was a handsome, calm-faced boy. His face was not scarred.

"He looks pretty good," Porter said.

"He looks marvelous," said Grace. "Doesn't he, Blake?"

"Yes."

Coster got in the ring. From the other side one of the three kids got in too. Coster's trainer was giving him directions, but we were not quite close enough to hear. Coster and the other boy did a little muscle stretching and shadow boxing, their backs to each other. The bell rang and they turned around and faced each other now in the middle of the ring, headgeared, moving cautiously, shoulders crouched, and the crowd, now quiet, watching. Coster boxed cautiously, jabbing accurately with his left and waiting for the other boy to come to him, blocking the other boy's less accurate punches. The other boy hit Coster twice in the body and Coster landed three solid left labs in the other boy's face. Coster boxed skillfully and did not try too hard.

"That's a lovely left," Porter said after the first round. "He's got a lot of style. I will say that."

"You're finally coming around," Grace said.

In the next round Coster hit his new sparring partner with a long right cross and when he hit the boy and the boy did not go down I could see that Coster did not have a real knockout right. It looked nice but it was not short and fast enough to be a finishing blow.

But his boxing made the other boy look bad. Coster always broke clean in the clinches, holding his gloves up to show that he was breaking clean and not hitting on the break which was against the rules. I liked this about him. He did fight fair.

The crowd around us talked more after this round. The blonde on my right leaned close to the tanned man she was with and whispered in his ear. They both laughed.

"He looks young," I heard her say.

"He is only about twenty or so," the man said.

"He is almost a baby."

"How do you feel?" I asked Grace.

"Safer," she said.

"I don't mean that," I said, seeing that Porter was looking away and would not hear us. "I mean how do you feel watching Coster?"

"Oh. A little nervous, but I love watching him. I can't quite get used to seeing him in the ring. He isn't the type. He's so un-savage."

"He isn't unusual that way. A lot of boxers are not tough outside the ring."

"Isn't it strange how they can be so brutal in the ring and then after it is over be chummy with the boy they fought? I don't know how they do it."

"I don't imagine it is too difficult to do."

Another boy came in the ring now with Coster. The bell rang and they started fighting. Coster was warmed up by this time and he was more aggressive. He went after the other boy. He kept using that good left jab, scoring with it. It was very good watching a boxer like Coster.

Coster was using his right now. He connected with two rights and missed with a left uppercut. The right cross was still long-thrown and it jolted the other boy but he did not go down. The crowd clapped when Coster feinted with his left and the other boy went for it and then Coster drove a hard right to the boy's heart. It was cleanly done. Grace clapped seeing him do it. I was too interested to clap.

In my mind I was putting Phelps in the ring with Coster now. The way I had seen Phelps fight out on Long Island. I was seeing Phelps throw that terrific short right cross.

"He doesn't fight enough in the clinches," Porter said. "He ought to be working more on the other guy's body."

"That isn't his style," I said. "He is not an in-fighter."

"But look at all the work the other guy is doing in those clinches."

"It is tiring him out doing it, too."

"I still think Coster ought to work more inside."

In the last sparring round Coster started the other fighter's nose bleeding with a stiff left jab. At the end of the round the crowd clapped hard. Coster's trainer took Coster's head guard off and rubbed him down over the head and face and all over his chest and back, and he climbed out of the ring with his trainer. Two photographers posed him and his trainer together. A small crowd was around them. Coster was smiling. He seemed quite good-natured.

"Shall we go over?" Grace asked.

"Sure," I said. "I'd like to meet him."

The photographers were taking final pictures. Coster seemed to be enjoying himself. Now his trainer moved him away from the crowd. He had still to do some calisthenics and punching on the light and heavy bags. Many people who were not interested in seeing him do this were leaving the gym. He was coming our way with his trainer. Grace waved at him.

"Hey, Jimmy," she said, loud.

Coster seemed not to recognize her at first but then he did and he smiled and waved and came up to us.

"Hello, hello," he said to Grace, taking her hand. "Gee, I'm glad to see you, Grace," he said, still not looking at me or Porter. "What are you doing way out here?"

"We're another fan club," she said.

She introduced Porter and me to Coster. Coster appeared glad to see us. He introduced us to his trainer who had been answering some questions a reporter was asking him about Coster. He said he was very happy to meet us. He put his hand on Coster's back to move him along to the training he had still to go through.

"Look," Coster said. "I have to do a little more work. Why don't you stick around until I finish? It won't be long. Then I'll buy you a Coke." He smiled at us.

We said we would wait. Now Coster's trainer walked him back to the heavy bag. They passed the blonde and the suntanned man. Coster's trainer smiled at them and spoke to the man. The blonde looked Coster up and down. We followed them back to the heavy bag and stood next to three mobster-looking men watching Coster work out on the bag.

"Imagine that the bag is Phelps," I said to Grace.

"Is he that tough?"

"No. Look. Every time Coster hits where he is hitting now, Phelps is getting it in the solar plexus."

"Now he is getting it on the chin, right?"

"Right."

"Do you want to see any more?" Porter asked.

"It doesn't make any difference to me," I said. "How about you, Grace?"

"I guess I have seen enough."

"We can meet him on the porch when he finishes," Porter said. "It's too warm in here for me."

As we walked through the gym, it smelling of sweat and resin and tobacco smoke, there began the rapid flat rhythmic sound of Coster hitting the light bag.

"That is a fine sound," Grace said. "It sounds like some kind of tap dancing."

"It sounds better than that," I said.

Most of the people who had been in the gym were driving away now in their cars. The men in the open convertibles were relaxed there in a way that made you think they spent most of their lives sitting in such cars, as other people sit in their living rooms. We walked on the side of the driveway, out of the way of the cars, toward the country-style house where the fat man had been sitting on the porch. He was not there now, but a man in a sweat shirt and sweat pants was there talking with one of the men who had the appearance of a bookie.

We were walking single file. Grace was walking slightly out in the road.

"Better not walk so near the traffic," I said, thinking of a lot of things as I said this.

She walked back on the side, and a car drove by us fast and coming too close to us. It was the blonde and the sun-tanned man in an open Cadillac. She was driving.

"That was close," Grace said.

"I'm prophetic," I said.

We walked up the steps of the old house. The two men looked us over.

"What's on your mind, Johnny?" the man in the sweat shirt asked me.

I explained that we were friends of Coster's and were going to meet him here when he finished working out in the gym. They looked more friendly when I told them this.

"We have to ask," the man explained. "If we didn't people would be walking all over the place. You know."

We said we understood. He went inside the house and came back with two chairs. We thanked him. The two men started talking again but I felt it was not the same conversation they had been having before we came up. We talked about the layout of the training camp and how hard you had to train to keep in shape to fight. Porter said just being around the place stimulated him. He said it made him feel he should get himself in shape.

"For what?" Grace asked him.

"What do you mean for what? Just to be in shape. Just to feel good."

"Maybe I'll join a gym," he went on. "How about it, Blake? Want to join a gym with me?"

"Let me think about it."

"You could use a few good workouts, man. Get you in fighting trim. We could do a little sparring."

"We do that now."

"I'm serious. Join up with me. I'd really like to do it."

"Do you think it would affect your prose style?" Grace asked Porter.

"Listen to that," he said. "An intellectual yet. Think about it, Blake. It could be a lot of fun."

I said I would have to find a way of promoting the money first. I would let him know. Actually I intended to let it ride until he brought it up again. There was nothing wrong with working out in a gym. It was just that I could think of lots of people I would rather do it with than Porter.

There was a breeze up now, country-scented. The bookie who had been talking with the sweat-suited man got up and said he had to go. He had a dead cigar in his mouth, chewing on it.

"Be good," the sweat-suited man said.

"Ha. At my age?"

He winked at us and said good afternoon, touching his hat for Grace, and walked off.

The sweat-suited man watched him walk in the driveway to the parking lot.

"He's worth three million dollars," he said to us. "Three million. You wouldn't think it to look at him, would you?"

We agreed that he did not look like three million dollars.

"He owns the Walker Hotel."

Apparently he was not a bookie after all.

"Up on Thirtieth Street," Porter said in his one of-the-fellows way.

"Some place, huh?"

"Terrific."

He opened the door of the house to go in. "Jimmy ought to be out soon," he said, and went in the house.

The man who was worth three million dollars now drove by the porch in a black Buick convertible. He smiled at us and touched his hat again, and drove away. In a few minutes Coster came out of the doors behind us. He was dressed in summer sport clothes. He looked like a high-school kid. He was carrying three open bottles of Coca-Cola.

"Sorry you had to wait," he said, with that young-kid smile. "Here you are," he gave us the Cokes. "See? I wasn't just talking."

He smiled all the time. In his clothes he looked much heavier, more like a middleweight than a welterweight.

"Are you going to see me fight?" he asked us.

"Of course we are," said Grace. "I wouldn't miss it for the world."

Porter asked him what he thought of Phelps. "I've never met him," Coster said. "But I've seen him fight. He looked pretty strong."

"They are all comparing him to the Fargo Express," I said.

"That makes it hard for a guy," he said. "He's compared to a great fighter like that and then people say he is no good if he doesn't right away become like that great fighter."

"Do you think you will fight Robinson after this?" I asked, making it sound as though we all took it for granted that he would beat Phelps.

"I'd like to. But I don't know. It's very hard to get a bout with Robinson. He won't fight unless he is guaranteed a big chunk of dough."

"He sounds pretty cagey," said Porter.

"He is," Coster said. "Robinson is very smart. He is a businessman."

"Have you ever seen him fight?" Grace asked.

"Oh, sure. I've seen every fight he's had around here. He's a great boxer. Really great. You should see him."

Then Porter asked him how long he had been fighting. Coster said he had been fighting professionally for a little more than three years. Before that he had fought in the Golden Gloves one year as a lightweight. He had won the Eastern championship. Now he was rated fourth on the list of contenders for the welterweight championship of the world.

Grace took a cigarette from her purse. She was looking for a match when Coster quickly took a silver lighter from his pocket and lit her cigarette. He explained that he carried the lighter around for just such times as this.

"Don't you feel scared when you are getting into the ring in front of all those people?" Grace asked him. "I should think it would be terrifying."

"The first few times you do," Coster said. "Then you get used to it. You always feel nervous when you first go in. But that goes away once you start fighting. At least, that is the way it works with me. You try not to show you are nervous."

"Can you tell whether a fighter is scared of you?"

"Oh, sure. You can tell."

"How?"

"Well, for one thing, he freezes up. Gets stiff and can't seem to move much. Or he sort of pushes his punches instead of snapping them. Then you can smell it. I don't know how to explain it very well. It makes you feel bad. Embarrassed."

"Can you tell very soon whether you can beat the other guy?" Porter asked.

"Most of the times. But sometimes you get surprised."

He laughed when he said this.

Porter looked at his wrist watch. "It's getting late. I think we had better stop bothering you, Jimmy."

"You're not bothering me. I like you being here. But I guess we had better break it up. We have to be going in soon for the weigh-in."

We all said it had been a pleasure talking to him and we wished him luck in the fight tomorrow night.

"I'll probably need it," he said. "Where are you going to sit?"

"Maybe in the ringside," I said, knowing we probably would not because the prices were too high.

"I'll look for you."

"All right."

"I'll see you all again, won't I?" he said. "Grace knows where to get in touch with me."

We said we would all get together. His trainer came out on the porch. "We better be getting ready, kid," he said to Coster.

"Right now."

We all shook hands and he waved so long to us as we walked down the driveway, and he and his trainer, his trainer with his hand on Coster's arm, went back inside.

"He seems unusually bright for a fighter," I said as we were getting into the car. "Why do you think he got in the fight game?"

"It is a good living," Porter said, now we were driving out of the camp.

"His father and his uncle make him do it," Grace said. "They run him. He really doesn't like to beat people up."

"What makes you think so?" Porter said.

"He has told me. It makes him feel bad if he really hurts another fighter. Whenever he knocks somebody out he always helps him back to his corner. And he stays there until the other fighter comes out of it."

"I prefer them the other way," said Porter. "He sounds too goody-good."

"It is funny," Grace went on. "Jimmy is always surprised when the other fighter fights dirty. He described it to me once as though it were a kind of betrayal."

"In a way it is," I said.

"What does he do with all his smash?" Porter said.

"His father takes care of it for him. Invests it. The first thing his father does after each fight is run to the box office to see how much the gate was."

"Some smart girl should snag him," I said.

"A lot have tried," said Grace. "But he is waiting for something special. He wants a smart girl who is good-looking and a virgin."

"He'll have a long wait," said Porter.

I switched on the car radio and got some music then.

CHAPTER XIV

That night I went to Mary Fenner's party and jam session. She lived in a place on West Park that had once been a manufacturing loft and had since been made over into an apartment. It was the largest apartment I had ever been in. It was so large that it had a ping-pong room in the back. I could hear the bop music all the way out in the street.

The door of the apartment was open and you just walked in. The musicians were playing in the front room. The room was crowded and rather dark and I could not immediately find any faces that were familiar. I walked along the side of the room toward the front where some people were getting drinks. The music was loud. I was trying to follow the improvisations of it and at the same time looking around the room. Several couples were standing at the table with the liquor. Then I saw Mary Fenner there.

"Hello, Blake, you old night wanderer," she said. "Do you want some whisky?"

"We can open this," I said, giving her the pint I had brought with me.

"We certainly can. Thanks for bringing it."

She fixed the drinks. Looking around the room, I saw some faces I knew, and waved my hand at them, and then I smelled the charge. Somebody up in the front of the room was blowing it. In the corner of the front of the room near the window a tall thin man was standing over a wire recorder that was taking down the bebop music. A hipster. Another hipster came up to him and I saw him hand the tall one the already lit stick of tea. He inhaled it, sucking in air with the smoke, holding it in, and gave the stick back to the other hipster.

"What have you been doing with yourself?" I asked her, drinking now.

"I've found a new riff."

"What is it?"

"Bicycling. Ever try it? It's wild, really wild, Blake. Look." She lifted her skirt. "I'm getting muscles in my legs."

"Are those muscles?"

"Go ahead. Feel them. Go on."

I felt her leg muscles. "You can take up track soon."

"Well, you have to do something, don't you?"

I agreed with her. I finished my drink, standing there listening to the jamming and looking around and talking with Mary. The music was fast. If you did not listen carefully it did not make any sense to you. Each player seemed to be playing something personal on his own that had nothing to do with what the others were playing, and the whole composition they were playing did not seem to have any pattern. But actually it did. If you listened carefully you heard each player play a variation on what another player had just finished playing, and then he would add something of his own and another player would pick it up from there, the piano playing continually holding it all together, and then they would all be together jamming.

A girl alone a few feet from us was staring at the musicians and keeping time with the music with both hands as though she were playing the drums.

I asked Mary if Decker, one of the musicians, had been touring with anybody's orchestra. I said I had not seen him around for a long time.

"He just got out of Lexington," Mary said. "He was busted and sent down there for the cure six months ago. Don't you think he's talented?"

"He's the best I've heard around here." Now they jammed, loud, and stopped playing. "Is he playing with anybody now?"

"With Tiny. Did you hear what happened to Tiny?"

I said I had not. I did not see him very often.

"Nobody understands it," she said. "Some agents raided his apartment the other day and caught him with two hundred caps of cocaine. Enough for a year. Anyway they could have sent him up for a couple of years. But they didn't touch him. All they did was confiscate his car because they found a hypo needle in it. Can you beat that?"

One of the musicians was scratching his legs. He rolled up his trousers almost to his knee to scratch. He was a junkie. They all scratched themselves this way. And he was wearing smoked glasses.

The smell of tea was all around me now. The talking in the room was louder because the music had stopped. A few dead-faced hipsters were standing near the piano, talking to the musicians. They were not talking loud. I saw Harry Lees sitting on a crowded couch with Grace. I told Mary I would see her later and walked to the couch.

"Where's Porter?" I asked Grace, sitting down on the couch. She looked a little tight. So did Harry. There was a pint bottle on the floor near his feet.

"In the back room somewhere, I think," she said.

"They're dancing in the ping-pong room," Harry said. Then he laughed. "Did that sound funny to you?"

"What?"

"They're dancing in the ping-pong room. It sounds as though I'm talking about a big brawl at the Vanderbilt's. They're dancing in the ping-pong room and duck hunting in the pantry."

"You're way ahead of me," I said. More people were coming in. Some of them were carrying bottles.

"Max brought his millionaire lady," Grace said. "Have you seen her?"

"No. Have you?"

"Yes. Max brought her over. She's nice. A little nervous though."

"Nervous and a little moist," said Harry. "Max is going to get her high on tea and then teach her how to parlay an image."

Records were being played in the ping-pong room where they were dancing. I was feeling high now on my second drink.

The musicians in this room started playing again. Someone on the couch next to ours kicked over a drink getting off the couch. Harry picked up his bottle and poured whisky in all our glasses.

"Drink it while we can," he said.

I saw a girl whose face was familiar looking at me from a small group at the side of the room. I was not quite sure who she was because of the darkness and the distance. Then I recognized her. It was Gloria. She smiled at me. I nodded my head in a hello. She came across the room.

"Are you busy, Blake?" she asked me.

"Sort of. Why?"

"Well, when you finish being busy come on over and have a drink with us. Will you?"

"All right."

I introduced her to Grace and Harry. Harry stood up when he was introduced, and said they had met, then I remembered. "I'll expect you, then," Gloria said. "Promise?"

"Yes."

She walked back across the room.

"She's quite a showpiece, isn't she?" Harry said.

"Watch your language," Grace said, mocking. "Is she a good friend of yours, Blake?"

"I know her fairly well. She's a model."

"Oh," Grace said. "One of those."

We listened to the music. The players did not seem to know we were even there. I smelled charge again. It was coming from the couch next to ours. Decker was soloing on the sax. He kept blowing up and down and getting more elaborate. Mary Fenner was sitting on a stool next to the drummer and talking to a Negro hipster.

"Would you like to dance?" I asked Grace when the music had stopped.

"You know I would."

Harry got up to look around and Grace and I went into the ping-pong room to dance. We had to squeeze by a couple who were standing in the doorway of the room. We stood behind them for a moment and watched the dancing.

"Why don't you ever speak to me when you see me?" the girl was saying.

"Because I'm afraid you don't want to speak to me," he said. "If I say hello to you first that gives you the chance to give me the brush-off."

"But I wouldn't. I've wanted you to speak to me."

"Well, that's the way I've felt."

We moved farther into the room. Some primitive music was on the machine. This was enough to tell me Porter was trying to take things over here, too. But then I thought what the hell. That kind of music is as good as any to dance to. I heard Porter's ha-ha laugh. He was dancing with a blonde Vassar girl I had met a couple of times. Grace and I started to dance.

"I see your boy is giving a dancing lesson," I said.

"She doesn't worry me," Grace said, following me smoothly on the crowded floor. "He doesn't like her much. He's just impressed that she went to Vassar."

Then I told her, speaking low and dancing as much to ourselves as I could manage, that I had arranged everything for Monday.

"You're a sweetheart, Blake."

"Porter still doesn't know?"

"No."

"You'll have to bring the money in cash. They won't take a check."

"Trusting, aren't they?"

"They can't risk anything."

"I guess they can't."

The record ended. Porter was pushing through the people to the record player. He saw us.

He said, smiling and slapping me on the shoulder, "Trying to steal my girl, huh?"

He went on to the record player and put on another primitive piece and came back.

"Did Grace tell you what happened?" he asked me.

I said no.

"I got a contract on an outline for a book. What do you think of that, man?"

"Congratulations."

"It's a wonderful break," Grace said. "He can quit that awful job now."

"I wish I could," he said, "but it's too risky to quit right now. I'll have to wait until the book becomes a sure thing. Dance this one, Grace?"

"Excuse me, Blake?"

"Go right ahead."

I left them dancing and went to the side of the room near the record player. I watched them. They were both expert dancers. They looked well dancing together. I looked around and saw Julia. She was talking with a too-well-dressed man who reminded me immediately of the sun-tanned man at Coster's training camp. He raised his hand to draw on his cigarette and I saw a diamond ring that was so big it almost looked fake. But I knew it wasn't. Julia was doing all the talking and he was listening and looking over the dancers. I walked over to them.

"Hello, doll," she said. She called many people doll. She turned to her friend. "Darling, this is Blake Williams. Blake, Martin Hyman."

"It is a pleasure to meet you, Mr. Williams," Hyman said, shaking my hand. He had a Jersey accent.

I said it was nice to meet him, too.

"This is quite a place here, isn't it, Mr. Williams?"

"Don't be so formal, Marty," Julia said. "Call him Blake. What the hell is this?"

He smiled.

"Some people don't like to be called by their first name on such short notice."

"I don't mind," I said. "Go ahead."

"See?"

"All right. Is this party in honor of something, Blake?"

"No," I said. "The hostess just wanted to throw a party."

"Well, I would say that that is a very fine reason for having it. Is the hostess here?" he asked Julia.

"She was the girl talking to the Negro boy. Remember?"

"Oh yes. She's a very handsome girl. Very handsome. She looks like a society girl."

"She was," Julia said.

"I don't understand, Julia," said Hyman. "What do you mean was?"

"I mean she got sick of living uptown with all the rich creeps, so she moved downtown."

"Oh. I see. She sounds very unusual."

Hyman used a faint men's toilet water, and as he lifted his left hand to smoke I saw that his nails were manicured. We watched the dancers. Porter and Grace were still dancing together. The Vassar girl danced by us and smiled at me slightly. Hyman stared after her.

"That girl has a lot of quality," he said.

I couldn't tell whether he was talking to me or Julia so I did not say anything.

"Uh huh," Julia said, glancing after the other girl.

Hyman suddenly looked down at my hand and at Julia's. "I think we could all stand a drink, don't you? Suppose I go in and get us some."

I said that would be very decent of him. He walked along the side of the room, keeping out of the way of the dancers and went into the front room.

"Well?" Julia said.

"Well what?"

"Why don't you ask me who he is?"

"Since you ask me, who is he?"

"He's a gangster. That is, I think he's a gangster. He's in some kind of syndicate that controls stores and night clubs and things like that. I just met him tonight. He's a friend of a friend."

"Is that a real diamond?"

"Yes. Isn't it amazing? He's very rich. Loaded. Absolutely loaded. He's very tough, too. You wouldn't believe it, but he spent three years in the penitentiary for shooting a man. A gang war, I think."

"Nice guy."

"But he really is, Blake. No fooling. He's very generous and *simpático*. Who cares what he does for a living?"

"I certainly don't."

"He's offered to set me up."

"You didn't turn him down, did you?"

"Well, not exactly. I told him I wanted to think it over."

"But what is there to think over?"

"You're kidding," Julia said. "Anyway, wouldn't it be sort of dangerous?"

"I can't say. I've never been kept by a mobster."

"Maybe I'd get shot or something."

"That's better than dying of boredom."

"You said it, doll. You said it."

Hyman came back now with our drinks. The music on the record player had changed back again now to plain swing. The session in the front room was not loud now.

"Well, here's luck, everybody," Hyman said, lifting his glass.

"Here's luck."

"I just met our hostess," Hyman said.

"How did that happen, Marty?" Julia asked.

"It was very simple. I was at the table, fixing these drinks and she just came up and introduced herself. She's a very gracious person."

She's not blind, either, I was thinking.

"So what did you two talk about?" Julia asked, with no edge in her voice.

"Well, we talked a little about this bebop stuff," Hyman said, "and I told her I didn't go for it much. Then she told me about an art gallery she was helping to set up. She invited me to come uptown and look it over."

"Did she by any chance tell you they were looking for backers?" Julia asked, still without an edge in her voice.

Hyman laughed and put his hand on Julia's shoulder. "As a matter of fact, she did. She was very straight about it."

"So what did you tell her, Marty?" Julia asked.

"I told her I would come uptown and look it over."

He drank from his glass. "I sort of like the idea. I've backed a lot of things in my time, but never an art gallery."

"I wouldn't be surprised if you got quite a kick out of it," I said.

"Neither would I, Blake," he said. "Neither would I. Maybe we can all go up together sometime."

"Maybe we can."

"I'm waiting for you to say you've always wanted to be a patron of the arts, Marty," Julia said, smiling.

"That's the funny thing about it' I never have. I've never even thought of it."

"Good for you."

Grace and Harry were dancing together. I could not see Porter anywhere. He may have been somewhere in the room but I did not see him. I felt tighter on my third drink. The Negro hipster was in the room talking to the Vassar girl. They began to dance. He was a nice looking boy. He had a slightly East Indian face. I tried to imagine what he would look like if he were white. He held the Vassar girl in a careful way as they danced. They were talking as they danced, each one facing a different way, and not turning their heads to look at each other as they talked. The bop session in the front room had stopped for the time being and the record music in this room now sounded louder. The air was smoky.

Hyman took out a gold cigarette case and offered Julia a cigarette from it. Then he held it out to me. I took a cigarette and Hyman lit Julia's and then my cigarette with a gold cigarette lighter that matched the case.

"You dance, don't you, Blake?" he asked me.

I said I did.

"Well, would you do me a favor and dance a little with Julia? I don't dance. I know it sounds funny but it's the truth. I never got around to learning."

I said I would be very happy to dance with Julia. Julia said I was doll again. I put her drink and mine on a small table next to the record machine. And then we started dancing. But I could not seem to get started with her. The music was too New Orleans for me to do much and Julia did not follow me well. We were both aware of it. I could not tell whose fault it was. I was not sure it was mine because I thought I was a fairly good straight dancer.

"There's Grace and Harry Lees," she said. "They look sort of noble together, don't you think, Blake?"

"They look all right," I said.

They looked our way and we smiled and nodded. Harry burlesqued his dancing for us. He looked pretty tight, but he held it well. He was very proud of this ability. It meant quite a bit to him.

"Where is that dog's body Porter?" Julia said. "Is he off exploiting somebody else?"

I said he was somewhere around.

"Did he tell you about getting a book contract?"

"Yes. Did he tell you?"

"Sure. He must have told everybody by now. You can't keep him down. Not that boy."

"He had an unhappy childhood."

"Who didn't? Everybody I know had a stinking childhood. So what? I don't see why that should excuse him."

"Don't get me wrong," I said. "I'm not an apologist for Porter."

"He wouldn't be for you, that's for sure. All that pal stuff is just a cover-up. The only person he's interested in is H.P."

"I didn't know you paid that much attention to him."

"I'm not really down on him. He gets under my skin sometimes. Who does he think he is?"

It occurred to me that Porter had probably slept with Julia and then dropped her.

The Negro hipster-intellectual and the Vassar girl danced near us, and then away.

"If he's a Negro, why doesn't he admit it?" Julia said. "As it is you don't know where you stand with him."

"Let's leave him," I said.

The music stopped. I was glad it was over. It was hot in the room. We walked back to Hyman. Before I could get to the little table he was picking up our drinks and handing them to us. The drink tasted very good and cool now that I was so warm. I drank it off.

"I feel like sitting down for a change," Julia said. "What do you boys say we go into the next room?"

"Anything you say, Julia," Hyman said. "Blake?"

"I'm with you."

We walked through the couples waiting for another record to be put on for dancing and then through the long corridor separating the rooms, and into the front room. The musicians were playing again, and now Decker was soloing on the sax. Most of the men had taken off their jackets and everybody looked tight. A couple were necking on one of the couches.

Decker finished his solo and then all the musicians jammed, coming in together. The tea smell was all over the room. In a far corner of the room one of the musicians was passing around a stick of tea with three people. They were all smiling at each other.

Hyman inhaled deep through his nose and turned to me. "I thought I was mistaken before," he said. "But somebody around here is smoking marijuana."

"Several people," I said.

"You wouldn't like some, would you?" Julia asked Hyman. "I know who has some here."

"No, thanks," said Hyman. "None of that stuff for me. It is pretty risky to fool around with that stuff. You can get in a lot of trouble with the police."

"You aren't afraid, are you, Marty?" Julia asked him. Hyman smiled at her. "I would feel pretty stupid if I was here when they made a raid, honey."

Gloria was standing near the liquor table with her friends. I thought I would go over and see what she had to say. I asked Julia and Hyman to excuse me for a few minutes, and walked to where Gloria was.

"Well, you finally made it," she said, and took me by the arm. She introduced me to the man and the girl she was with. She held me by the arm. "Blake," she said. "You need a drink," and she mixed me an other drink.

"I've met you somewhere before," Gloria's girl friend said. She had platinum hair. "I never forget a face."

"Where do you think you met him?" Gloria asked her, giving me the drink she had mixed.

"Do you know George Tyler?" the girl asked. "I think I met you at his house."

I said I did not know Tyler, so she could not have met me at his house.

"Are you sure you were never at any parties there?"

"Positive."

"That's funny. I'm almost positive I've met you somewhere. I never forget a face. Never."

"Neither do I," said Gloria, looking into my face. "Where have you been keeping yourself, Blake?"

"Nowhere special."

I was trying to decide whether I wanted to take her home tonight. I knew she wanted me to. Well, I would see. I was thinking about Grace, too.

"Let's get a breath of fresh air," Gloria said.

We walked through the crowded front of the room to the window. Someone began playing the piano, alone without the other instruments of the band. Cap Fields was coming away from the window with a girl. He and the girl were both giggling and he had his arm around the girl's waist.

He saw me looking at him. "Don't you shake your heads at me, man," he said and went on giggling. The girl laughed and looked at the floor, laughing still, the laughing seeming to go on without stopping.

Gloria and I stood at the open window. Outside a crowd was standing on the sidewalk across the street looking in. They were the Italians of the neighborhood and they had seen the people coming in here and had heard the jam session and they were now collected across the street looking in at us and listening to our party. There were men and women and even the local hoods, watching and listening to us.

"Quite a gathering," Gloria said.

"You mean out there or in here?"

"Both."

We talked about what we had been doing lately and about the party and the girl who was giving it, and about the musicians and what sort of people they were personally. Porter was nearby talking to Max's rich lady.

"They make me feel funny," Gloria said, looking at the crowd across the street. "I wonder what is going on in their heads?"

"That they are out and you in."

"That isn't all they are thinking."

"No. They are probably hating and envying us at the same time. They would like to be in."

One of the hoods in the crowd outside whistled at Gloria and shouted, "Hey babe! Want to dance?"

She turned her back to them.

"Want to?" I asked her.

"Stop twisting my arm," she said.

We left the window and went to the center of the room and began to dance.

"Are you taking anyone home tonight, Blake?" she asked me.

"I'm not sure yet."

"When you find out, let me know."

I was still not sure that I wanted to go with her. As we danced near the other side of the room near the couches I saw Grace with some people who were blowing tea. She took the stick of tea and inhaled sucking in a lot of air and gave the stick of tea to one of the musicians next to her. I did not want to see her do it again and I maneuvered us across the room. This was a strange way for her to get back at Porter. I told myself to mind my own business.

"Why are you so elusive, Blake?" Gloria asked me. "You don't seem to want to get involved in anything."

"You get involved and you get hurt."

"But nothing ever happens unless you get involved."

"I'm a little tired of things happening. I wish things would stop happening for a while."

"It couldn't be that bad."

"It isn't. I'm exaggerating."

"Hey, Blake."

It was Porter, tapping me on the shoulder.

"You don't mind if I cut in on this, do you?"

"Oh, hello, Henry," Gloria said.

"You seem to be doing it anyway," I said.

"Thanks, man."

"See you later, then, Blake," Gloria said to me.

I nodded my head. Porter danced her away. I walked to the side of the room near the bookshelves. Grace was laughing with the other people who were getting high on the tea. Everybody was laughing at once. Someone had probably said something that was slightly funny but being high on tea everybody thought it was terrifically funny.

Max came across the room. He kept his hands in his pockets and bent his head slightly, looking at the dancers. He stood by my side and we did not speak right away.

"What did you let him do that for, Blake?" he finally asked.

"Do what?"

"Cut you out with that Gloria. You should have held on to her."

I did not feel that I had lost anything much. "It doesn't matter to me if he dances with her."

"You know you don't mean that, Blake," he said.

He put his glasses on and looked across the room at Grace and the people she was with.

"Is that Grace I see passing a stick around?" he asked me.

I said that was the way it looked.

He took off his glasses and shook his head. "A good girl gone wrong. Too bad. Too bad."

I told him I was going into the next room.

"Before you go," he said, "I want you to introduce me to that platinum-blonde chick you were talking to."

She was still talking to the man she had been with when I had met her. I took Max over to them, and interrupted their conversation to introduce Max. I was slightly drunk and I introduced him as a movie producer who was in New York looking for talent. Then I left them and went into the back room. The dancing in this room was faster than it was in the front room. A couple were jitterbugging. The girl had taken off her shoes. The boy was spinning her around and under his arm.

Harry Lees was sitting on the side of the room and arguing drunkenly with a sharp-faced girl who was a magazine editor. I walked over. Harry was quite drunk. I could not understand how he managed to stay in the chair.

"Stop reading books and be a woman, for Christ sake," he said to the girl.

"Harry is giving me a blueprint for living," the girl said to me. She was well-dressed and you had no doubt the moment you saw her that she was successful in some uptown activity.

"He thinks a lot about such things," I said.

"Goddamn it," Harry said, loud, though with the loudness of the music it seemed natural and not shouting. "All I'm telling her is to stop being so goddamn smart and successful and start making some men happy. That's all."

The girl laughed, a sharp laugh that was a little like Porter's laugh. "I'm afraid you are rather worked up about it, Harry."

"Of course I'm worked up about it. Good God. Don't you know it is women like you who make men insecure? You're not a woman. You're a hawk. What do you want to be a hawk for?"

"You are really too worked up about it," she said.

"Oh nuts. Blake, what do you think?"

"I'm not thinking."

I did not want to get into this particular argument. It did not matter to me if the girl was a hawk or a magazine editor or the mother of five children. I just did not care. She was not my worry. Let somebody else worry about what she was. I turned away to watch the people jitterbugging. They were good.

Then, still watching the dancers, I heard the chair and Harry fall at the same time. I turned quickly. Harry had passed out in the chair and fallen with it to the floor.

Before I could get to him a fast-dancing couple danced by him and the man stepped on Harry's hand and his other foot hit Harry's head. The girl dancing saw this and shrieked and held her hand over her mouth and stared down at Harry.

"Oh, Christ," the boy said as I was picking Harry up off the floor. "I was on the guy before I even knew it."

He helped me put Harry in the chair that had fallen.

"Do you think he is hurt?" the magazine editor asked.

"His hand is probably bruised a little," I said, opening his shirt collar. He was out cold.

"What should we do?" she asked.

"Leave him here," I said. "He'll come out of it. He'll be all right."

"Good Lord," the girl who had been dancing said.

"I guess he will be all right now, huh?" her partner asked me.

"Sure."

"Come on," he said to the girl, and took her by the arm and they began to dance again.

"The poor guy," the magazine editor said. "He is such a sick person."

"He will be a sick person tomorrow."

"He is very sick right now," she said. "He is one of the sickest people I have ever talked to. He needs help. Badly."

"So do a lot of people."

"Most of them won't admit it."

"Maybe not to other people."

"Not to themselves."

"Oh yes they do."

She smiled and raised her eyebrows in a way that meant she did not want to argue the point I took another look at Lees. He seemed all right now. There wasn't anything else that could he done for him. At least that I could do. He was breathing heavily, head slumped down, chin on his chest.

I wanted another drink to keep what I had from wearing off. It would not make me feel any better but it would keep me from feeling that awful half-drunk feeling. I asked the editor if she wanted a drink.

"I don't think so, thank you," she said, smiling so well that I thought she must have thought she was being patronizing. She was staying sober and playing it safe. If she was sick nobody was going to find out about it. That was one way of working it.

I said I was going in for a drink. I walked through the dancers and out into the front room. The smell of tea was all over now, heavy in the air. I found a bottle with some liquor left in it and made myself a short drink. The room seemed bigger and darker now than it had been. But I thought that was because I was tight.

I walked over to the couches. Hyman and Julia were sitting together on one crowded couch talking to Mary Fenner and a hipster who had a reputation as a wit. Grace and the people she had been with were not around. She must have gone into the little room between the two big rooms. I heard loud talking and laughing coming through the partition of the next room. I decided that was where she had gone. I sat down on the floor.

"Are you having a good time, Blake?" Hyman asked me. He sounded sober.

"Great time."

"Give me some of your drink, doll," Julia said.

I gave her my drink. I told Mary Fenner about Harry. She said he could stay there in the back room, and that she would look in at him in a short while. She began talking to the hipster about James Joyce. He had just finished reading *Ulysses*. He was saying it was the wildest thing he had ever read.

"That cat writes like he was high," he said. "He really does."

Now Gloria sat down beside me.

"May I?" she said.

"What can I lose?"

Hyman watched and listened to Mary and the hipster. He often looked around the room. He was not drinking. He was being very alert.

"Did you find out?" Gloria asked me, referring to what she had asked me earlier in the evening.

I was about to make some kind of an answer when there was suddenly a lot of loud talking from the middle of the room where they were all dancing. Porter and the Negro boy were arguing.

"Don't give me that," the Negro boy said.

Porter hit him. The sound of it was a loud smack, a loud, solid smack. The Negro boy went down. Then there was shouting and pushing.

Hyman got up and pulled Julia with him.

"Come on," he said. "Let's get out of here. Come with us, Blake. This is a good time to go."

The Negro boy got up and swung at Porter and missed, and Porter hit him and then they clinched and people were trying to separate them.

"Want to go?" I said to Gloria. "Things look as though they are breaking up."

I stood up and pulled her up to her feet. Mary Fenner had gone over to the fighting. Hyman and Julia and Gloria and I went to the door. I did not like leaving Grace. But she could take care of herself. And besides, she was Porter's worry.

There was that loud smack again and I saw the Negro boy go down again. Everybody closed in on Porter and the boy, telling them to stop fighting. I felt for a second that we might be running out. But I really did not want to stay any longer. The place was getting messy and I was drunk and hungry and had seen enough of the party. The fun was ending.

"We can go to a place I know of uptown and get something to eat." Hyman said as we stood in the doorway, waiting for Julia to get her coat.

Julia came back now and we left the apartment. Outside you could hear the dance music from the ping pong room and the loud talking now in the front room where the fight was. The crowd was still standing on the sidewalk. They watched us walk to Hyman's parked car. It was a black Lincoln.

"This is not a very good neighborhood to have any trouble in," Hyman said when we were all in the car.

You are so right, I said to myself as we drove off. Then I heard the sound of thunder overhead.

CHAPTER XV

It was raining when we got to the uptown restaurant Hyman knew about. The doorman took the car to park it. The hatcheck girl and the waiter at the table we took both spoke to Hyman. Gloria and Julia excused themselves and went to the powder room.

"What will it be, Blake?" Hyman asked, looking over the menu.

"I don't know yet."

I was reluctant to order anything because I had very little money. I knew Hyman was going to pick up the check, but I still thought about the little bit of money I had.

"Get anything you like," he said. "The party is on me."

"There isn't much I want."

"Have a steak sandwich. They're marvelous here. What about it?"

I said all right, I would take a steak sandwich. The restaurant was air-conditioned and shadowly lit with indirect lighting. Music was being piped in. The talking in the place was soft and controlled. The waiters did not make any noise walking back and forth taking orders because the floor was covered with a heavy carpet. When the waiters spoke to each other they bent their heads together and almost whispered. I was relaxed in a way that I had not been relaxed for a very long time and I was trying to recall where and when I had felt this way before. I knew it had been a long time ago.

Gloria and Julia came back to the table. Julia looked around and then said, "The place makes me want to whisper. It's just like church."

"It is church," I said, it coming back to me where I had felt like this before. It had been in church when I was a kid. I felt the same slight awe that I had felt then, and I had the same desire to whisper. That had been when I was a kid. Now I was in the church of today.

"Then I had better get up and genuflect," Gloria said.

"You can do it on your way out," I said.

"If that's the way it's going to be," Hyman said, slapping me on the shoulder, "I'll go back and put on my hat. It's for the Jews, too, isn't it?"

"It's for everybody."

"Now what would you two girls like to have this high priest bring you?" Hyman asked. The waiter was at the table now, waiting to take our order.

"Something divine," Julia said.

"Ohhhh."

"All right. I'll do penance for that."

They told Hyman what they wanted and Hyman repeated it to the waiter.

"*Subito,*" the waiter said and went off.

"And he even speaks the new Latin," Gloria said.

The headwaiter passed our table and said good evening to Hyman, bowing slightly as he did so and smiling.

"You must be in pretty good standing, Marty. You know the bishop."

"He's an old friend of mine. I can get you any sort of dispensation you want. Just name it."

"I may take you up on that offer."

"I wish you would, kid. I certainly wish you would."

"I'd like a little holy water with soda," Gloria said. "Could you arrange that?"

Hyman snapped his fingers and the waiter came over quickly and silently on those heavy carpets. Marty asked us if we wanted some, too. I said no, thanks, not yet anyway, and Julia said yes she would like some. She said I was a lousy church member for not taking any holy water. The music being piped in now was a swing piece based on Tchaikovsky.

"And that's the new church music," Julia said. "It just about sounds like an organ, too."

"But where is the altar? There has to be an altar somewhere."

"Down there. The bar. See? Can't you see them kneeling? Look hard and it will seem as though they are kneeling."

"Of course. That's it. It's lit up like one, too. All those colored lights made by the light shining through the colored bottles."

"Every time they buy a drink it's like lighting a candle for themselves. Salvation."

"Here's our salvation now," said Hyman.

The waiter had brought the drinks. He put them in front of Hyman and Gloria and Julia and then left.

"You won't be saved," Julia said to me, drinking.

"I have a couple of charms up my sleeve," I said.

"I know you do," said Gloria, laughing, and drinking.

Now another waiter brought our food. The steak sandwich was nothing like the downtown steak sandwiches. Here they were Delmonico steaks on four triangle-sliced pieces of toast. I had never tasted better steak. I ate it, remembering that the price on the menu was four dollars a sandwich. Hyman ate the way most Americans are brought up to eat switching his fork to his right hand from his left hand when he finished using it for cutting and picking up the food. Gloria and Julia and I ate the other way, keeping the fork in our left hand to eat with and not switching it. I tried to remember when I had stopped doing it the way Hyman was doing it now.

The piped music had been shut off and a radio turned on. Vic Damone was singing.

"There's the litany," I said.

"That's one I know all the words to," Julia said.

Hyman stopped eating for a moment and put his knife and fork leaning on his plate. "You know something," he said. "I've never been in one of your churches. Never. And I've always wanted to go."

I asked him why he had never gone. It was simple. All you had to do was walk in. You could do it any day at St. Patrick's.

"I've been scared to do it," he said.

"I'll take you in, Marty," Julia said. "Any time you want."

"You know," Marty said to me, "the part that interests me most is confession. Have you ever been to confession, Blake?"

I said that I had not The church I had gone to when I was a kid was a Protestant church.

"Think how good it must be to tell somebody all the wrong things you've done," Marty said. "And nobody does anything to you. You get it all out. You don't have to keep carrying it around with you."

"Are you carrying around so much?" Gloria asked him.

"Not as much as you probably think," said Marty, smiling at her. "But enough. There are a lot of things I would like to get off. I think just talking about them the way you do in confession would make me feel a lot better."

"Then why don't you join the church?" Julia asked him. "You can, you know."

"But he's already a member in good standing of this church," I said. "Way up in the hierarchy."

"But there's no confessional here."

"Sure there is. The bartender. Everybody confesses to him."

"I can't do it that way," said Marty. "I know a lot of people do. But I can't. Besides, he wouldn't keep it to himself the way a priest is supposed to."

"Well, there's always psychoanalysis."

"So I've heard. But I don't need psychoanalysis."

"That's another religion."

"What about it, Blake?" Marty asked. "Do you believe it does you any good?"

"It depends a lot on the person being analyzed."

"A guy I know was psychoanalyzed," Marty told me. The girls were talking between themselves now.

"A very big guy around town. A big operator. Anyway, he got psychoanalyzed because he thought people didn't like him. He thought nobody who counted respected him because of the business he was in."

"How is he now?"

"He gets around a little more in certain circles. Maybe psychoanalysis did that."

"So long as he gets around more."

Hyman took out his gold cigarette case and lit up, leaving his case on the table. We had all finished eating. Gloria and Julia were still talking between themselves about the way a model has to dress. All the tables in the restaurant were filled now. A complete sellout for this mass.

"What do you believe in, Blake?" Hyman asked me.

"Not an awful lot."

"Don't you have any sort of religion?"

I thought about it before answering him. He watched me, drawing on his cigarette.

"I believe in eating and sleeping and sometimes I believe in myself," I said.

"Don't you believe in people?"

"Very seldom. Mostly only when I am enjoying myself with them."

"What about after that?"

"Then they're out for themselves. And you have to watch out for yourself."

"I used to believe that," he said. "But I'm changing."

"I still believe that," I said. "Everybody is out to save himself. And when he has to he will do you in to save himself. I've never seen it fail."

"Somehow I don't believe you really feel that way. Completely, anyway."

"Sometimes, when I'm confused, I don't."

"What about love? Do you believe in that?"

"I'd like to believe in it. It seems to be a way of sharing your fear with another person."

"And what about politics? Don't you think one party is better than another?"

"I don't care about politics. If you really want to know, I think most of the people who have all this so-called political consciousness are all kidding themselves. They do it because they can't do something else they really want to do."

"It's funny," Hyman said. "I used to feel exactly the way you feel now."

"What does that prove?"

"Probably nothing."

The waiter was taking the dishes away. Hyman asked Gloria and Julia if they wanted coffee, and suggested they have some cognac with it. So we all had cognac and coffee. The headwaiter came to our table and bowed a little and asked Hyman if everything had been all right. He said it had been excellent, excellent, and we agreed with him. The headwaiter smiled and went away.

"What have you two been talking about?" Julia said to Hyman.

"Religion."

"Religion? I hope you finished talking about it."

"We have," I said.

The coffee-and-cognac combination smelled better than it tasted. At least, to me. Gloria said something about having an early appointment tomorrow morning. Then the waiter brought the check. Hyman paid it with three ten-dollar bills from several others he kept in a gold money clip. The waiter brought his change on a small silver plate. He waited for Hyman to pick up his change and to leave him a tip. Hyman left a large tip in the plate.

"The collection plate," he said, as we got up from the table.

The waiter thanked him and took the plate away. On our way out the headwaiter very politely said good night to us, first to Hyman. And the hatcheck girl did the same.

It was still raining outside, but not as hard as it had been. The doorman went for Hyman's car. We stood under the awning. The falling rain was making two sounds. It was making one sound falling on the canvas awning over our heads, and it was making another sound falling on the black asphalt of the street. We stood there under the protection of the awning and I listened to the two different sounds the rain was making.

"Don't you hate rain?" Gloria said.

"I don't hate it," Julia said. "I like it. It makes everything clean again."

"It depresses me," Gloria said.

"Got any feelings about the rain, Blake?" Hyman asked.

I did not want to tell anybody how I felt about the rain. It got messy when you started comparing notes. Everybody had his own way of feeling, and that was the end of that. So I said that I was indifferent to the weather. I thought, still standing there under the awning, how I liked the smell of the rain better in the city than in the country. The smell of it cleaning off the streets.

"Nobody has said they like the sound of it on the roof when they are in bed," said Gloria, moving to one side as two people got out of a cab and went into the restaurant.

"Thank God for that," Julia said.

The doorman drove the car up in front of the awning and got out and held the door open for us to get in. Hyman tipped him half a dollar, and we drove off, downtown. Hyman was a good driver, and riding in the Lincoln was quite pleasant. He drove to Gloria's place.

"I'll get out here, too," I said when he pulled up at the curb.

"I've had a very good time," Hyman said. "The whole evening has been fun."

We said we had had a good time, too. I meant it. I thought he was all right. He was not square. Not like Goodwin.

"Take it easy, Blake," Hyman said.

"You too," I said.

He winked at me. We all said good night, and Hyman and Julia drove away. Gloria and I walked quickly through the rain and into her brownstone walk-up. She started up the stairs. I stayed down.

"I'll be seeing you," I said.

"Aren't you coming up?" she asked, turning around.

"No. I'm staying down. I'm going along home. I've got a couple of prayers I have to say."

She wiped the rain from her face with a handkerchief.

"Do you have to go home to say them?" she asked me.

"Yes."

"Most people would sin first," she said, standing there above me.

"I'm different."

She shrugged.

"All right then, you old home-lover."

"So long, Gloria."

"Good night."

I went back outside and walked home through the rain.

CHAPTER XVI

The next morning I got up at about ten-thirty. Saturday. This was the day of the Coster-Phelps fight. I got dressed and went downstairs to have some breakfast. I picked up my mail first, three letters, and then bought a paper at the stand on Spring Street, and went into the lunch counter around the corner.

I ordered grapefruit juice and coffee and a cinnamon bun. There was a letter from my sister, one from the William Alanson White Foundation, and one from somebody in North Carolina. I read the one from my sister first and then, drinking my grapefruit juice, I read the letter from the William Alanson White Foundation. I don't know how they got my name, but they wanted me to contribute to a fund they had that provided psychoanalysis for needy neurotics. That was a good idea. The poor people were entitled to neurosis as well as the rich. It was an idea that might sweep the country. Maybe somebody could get elected on it. But the fund would have to go along without me. Could you spare a dime for a poor old neurotic, mister? No, I could not.

The letter from North Carolina was about a vacation. Would I like to spend my vacation in one of a few adorable cottages on the farm of Burt and Martha Gaines? I would have the swellest time, they said. The whole letter was written in tiny tots prose. I turned to the sport section of the paper.

Phelps was a seven-to-five favorite. The man in the *Times* said he was going to go on to win the championship and bring some badly needed life back into boxing. He would eventually take the championship because he could hit harder than anybody around. Then there were some quotes from Phelps's manager. I finished reading the paper and paid my check and went back to the apartment. The street was already crowding up with the fat Italian women doing their shopping for the day. The boys from the social club had not yet arrived.

I was reading the want ads and trying to think of how I could make some money when the phone rang. It was Harry Lees. He wanted to know if I would have lunch with him. I said all right. I asked him how he felt.

"I'm dying," he said.

"Don't die before you buy me lunch."

"You are a callous son of a bitch."

We said we would meet at a Spanish place called Oviedo on Fourteenth Street and Seventh Avenue in about an hour and a half.

"Listen," he said, before hanging up. "You're going to the fights tonight, aren't you?"

"That's right."

"Well, is it all right if I come along?"

"Of course it is."

"Thanks a lot, Blake."

I called the Garden and asked if they had any side arena seats left. The man in the ticket office said they had but that they were going pretty fast. I figured I would pick the tickets up after lunch. I shaved and after that I wrote a note to a friend in Baltimore who was related to the manager of a fashionable East side hotel in New York. I wanted him to arrange an introduction because I had for a long time thought seriously of working in a hotel. It was clean work, you did not have to tell lies, I thought, and the people were interesting, I imagined. Anyway, I wanted to look into it. Being a hotel clerk was nine times better than being an advertising-agency copywriter. That was the worst.

Another friend had asked me to recommend to him sections of certain good books to reprint in a magazine he had recently become the editor of. There would be some money in it for me.

I thought offhand of three books that might produce something. Rereading parts of these would kill the time before lunch. I went to look for the books among those I still had left on my shelves.

At twelve o'clock I put on a tie and went out. I was hoping Grace had got home all right from the party. And I was speculating on what had been said between Porter and the Negro boy that started the fight. Outside the social club boys had begun to stand around. One of them was reading a scratch sheet. The street had that clean fresh vegetable smell. The bookies were hanging around in front of the bar at the corner. I cut over to West Broadway to get a change of scenery, and walked up that street to Eighth and then Eighth to Fifth Avenue.

Harry was sitting at the bar in the Oviedo when I got there. The juke box was playing flamenco music. The singing was a kind of controlled hysteria that made me think immediately of a Jewish cantor.

"I think I'm dead," said Harry as I sat on a stool next to him at the bar.

"You look pretty bad," I said, "but not that bad." I ordered a glass of beer from the bartender. Harry was drinking whisky and water.

He looked at himself in the mirror of the bar, turning his head from side to side. "Is this the face that burned the topless towers of Ilium? No."

"Let's sit down at a booth," I said. "Drinking at a bar this early in the day brings up all my guilt."

We took our drinks from the bar and went in the back to a booth. An old waiter put a table cloth down for us and took our order. He had a heavy Spanish accent. It was a relief from all the other accents I had been listening to.

"I did pretty well last night, didn't I?" Harry said.

"You just went to sleep."

"A fine time to go to sleep. Pass out you mean. Incidentally, did I hit anybody, Blake? My hand hurts like hell."

I told him what had happened. He looked at his hand. It was slightly bruised. I asked him if he knew whether Grace had got home all right. He said he guessed so. He thought he remembered seeing her leave quite late with Porter. He said she seemed to be acting sort of funny.

"I went home with a blonde model," he said.

"Good for you."

"Not so good. Wait till I tell you. But after lunch."

The waiter brought our food. We ate quickly. The food was spicy and rich. All the music coming from the juke box was Spanish. It was a pleasant change from Vic Damone and the others. Not that I didn't like them. But a change was good. All the people in the restaurant looked and acted gentle. This was a nice change, too. The women seemed shy. But maybe that was just the way they seemed to me.

We had strong black coffee and then Harry paid the check and we went out, the high hysterical—but exciting this early in the day—flamenco music following us out. I told Harry I had to go to Madison Square Garden to pick up the tickets for the fight tonight.

"I'll go along," he said. "I don't have anything special to do. But let's not go on the subway. My stomach isn't strong enough yet for that. Let's ride the Fifth Avenue bus. Okay?"

"It is all the same to me."

We walked to Fifth Avenue and caught a bus going to Riverside Drive via Fifty-Seventh Street, and got seats upstairs.

"Max and I took the platinum-blonde home," Harry said. "To his place."

"Why the two of you?"

"Don't know. It just worked out that way."

"And?"

"Well, it turned out that she didn't go too much for Max. She didn't want to do anything with him. But she did like me. That was fine. But Max was very pissed off. So do you know what? He wanted to watch us."

"No kidding?"

"That's right. He wanted to watch us. He wouldn't let us alone. He got nasty when I told him to go away. He wouldn't go. So she finally said to hell with that kind of stuff. She told Max he must he crazy. Then she left."

"What did you say to Max?"

"What could I say about it? After all, it was his place. I guess he was hurt pretty much because the girl didn't go for him. He told me he was sorry about what happened."

"He meant he was sorry for himself."

"What do you think of that? Isn't that something, though?"

"It doesn't surprise me too much," I said.

"Jesus," he said, shaking his head, "he can do anything. Anything. The guy is completely underground. Could you do that, Blake?"

I said I did not think so. But I had never been given the opportunity.

"Well, I couldn't. I'm not saying I wouldn't get something out of it. I'm just saying I couldn't do it. My Renaissance blinders."

We got off the bus at Fifty-First Street and walked west through Rockefeller Plaza to Eighth Avenue and the Garden. The walls of the ticket office upstairs were lined with full-length photographs of all the best fighters. Harry gave me his money and I bought four tickets, side arena, for Grace and Porter and Harry and myself. Harry and I stayed a few minutes and looked at the portraits of the fighters.

More than half of the fighters were Negroes. There were photographs of Sugar Ray Robinson, Sandy Saddler, Willie Pep, Rocky Graziano, Tony Zale, Marcel Cerdan, Ezzard Charles, Jersey Joe Walcott, Lee Oma, and Coster and Phelps. For some reason there was no picture of Joe Louis.

Harry asked me if I had seen any of them in the ring. I said I had seen all of them except Oma. I was not sorry about having missed Oma. Then he asked me which one was the best of the lot. I said that everything considered the best of the bunch was probably Sugar Ray Robinson.

"These dark boys seem to run the ring," he said, as we left the ticket office. "Why is that?"

"Probably because this is one of the few ways they can get into the big time," I said.

"A pretty rugged way of getting there."

"Aren't all the others? You just get beaten up in a different way."

We decided to walk back to Fifth Avenue where we would stroll with the afternoon crowds for a while. We had to walk through what Harry called the hot-dog belt to get there. Once we were on Fifth we walked north toward Fifty-Ninth Street. It was warm and bright along the Avenue and the crowds were all handsome and handsomely dressed and walking slowly.

"This is my favorite part of town," said Harry. "The part of town that is like Europe. It's just like walking down the Corso in Rome. Or the Champs Elysées in Paris."

"You mean it's un-American?" I said, joking him.

"It is, almost. You ought to go to Paris some time, Blake. Or Rome. You'd like those places."

"I will one of these days."

"Don't put it off too long," he said. "Something happens if you do."

I asked him how his hangover was.

"It's gone," he said "I feel human now, thank God."

Someone on my right was speaking French rather loud and in front of us now was a small woman in an expensive-looking print dress walking two Bedlington terriers. The loud-spoken French was passing me. It was a stocky man in a black suit and small black-rimmed eyeglasses gesticulating with his hands as he talked to a young woman who walked with her eyes on the ground and she was saying, *"Oui, oui,"* as her companion talked. Then out of the corner of my eye I saw someone I had at one time worked with, going the other way. We saw each other and we both looked away. We were waiting for the other to speak. This was the easiest way out, not to speak. We had been on uncertain terms when we worked together. This happened every time I walked on Fifth Avenue.

"Look at the way the model walks," Harry said, nodding his head to the left in front of us.

The model was tall and had black hair and was chicly dressed and she carried the model's hatbox swinging at her side.

"It's a fascinating style, isn't it, Blake? Hermetically sealed. A combination of seductiveness and defensiveness. Look at the tightness of it. The style is sexy and yet so tight it keeps anything from happening. Does that sound precious to you?"

"No. It's pretty good."

The model disappeared in the crowd ahead.

"That's a very revealing thing," Harry said. We crossed Fifty-Sixth Street through the jammed cars waiting for the light. "The way you walk shows a lot about you. Like your handwriting."

"Go on."

"Take the Europeans and the Americans. The first thing you notice about the European men is the way they walk. It is a steady precise sure walk. They are pretty sure of themselves and their walk shows it. They walk as though they own the place. Then look at the Americans. Most American men have an exaggerated style of walking. As though they were unsure of themselves and want to hide it."

"What about American women and European women?"

"It's about the same. Generally speaking, that is. The European women have a very feminine and charming walk. They walk as though they were trying to please you. They seem sure of themselves as women. But the American woman has a half-masculine, half-feminine walk. As though she were trying to look a little tough."

"You seem to have them cold," I said.

"Professor Lees," he said. "The man who has everything cold. Free lectures on modern civilization."

We had reached Fifty-Seventh Street. The Fifth Avenue walking crowd was now crossed by the crowd of people walking along East and West Fifty-Seventh Street. The Fifty-Seventh Street crowd was slightly different from the Fifth Avenue crowd. It was faster-walking and looked more American and less stylized. We crossed to the other side of the Avenue, the east side, and began walking back down Fifth.

At Fifty-Sixth Street we paused for a second to let an old woman pass who had been helped out of a long black Packard by the chauffeur now holding her arm as she walked through the crowd to a luggage store.

The bell of St. Thomas Church began to toll. We were close enough to it for me to feel the sound vibrations on my skin. People walking around us looked in the air to see where the tolling was coming from. It was a very powerful tolling.

"Some bell," said Harry. "Probably tolling for me."

"What's the matter? Are you afraid of dying?" I had started asking the question in a joking way but by the time it had got all the way out I felt serious about it.

"I don't think so," he said. "I'm just afraid of how it might happen. Like being hit by a car or something on that order."

The big bell tolled on.

"God, what a sound," said Harry, putting his hands over his ears. "I'll bet you can hear it all the way downtown to the circle."

The bell stopped tolling, but the heavy metal sound stayed in the air after the tolling had stopped, and I could still feel the vibrations of it on my skin.

Harry asked me if I felt like taking in the movie at the Museum of Modern Art. It was *Casablanca.* I said I couldn't make it. I had some work at home I had to finish. I had never especially liked the crowd that went to the movies there. There was something about them. Harry said he was going.

"I have to kill the afternoon somehow," he said. He said he would walk down to Forty-Second with me, then walk back.

We stopped to look at the book displays in the windows of Scribner's Book Store, then again to look at the Dream House on exhibit at Forty-Eighth Street. You could win the house by taking a chance of some kind. Harry turned back at Forty-Second Street.

"See you tonight then," he said, making it sound like a question.

"Sure," I said, it sounding like a reassurance.

He walked back uptown and I waited in front of the Public Library for a bus to take me back downtown.

CHAPTER XVII

Grace and Porter and Harry and I were going to have an early dinner together before the fights. The fights started at eight-thirty with a four-round preliminary bout. The main event went on at ten o'clock. I put on a clean white shirt and went out.

We were going to eat at George's Restaurant at Bleecker and Seventh. The food here was good and it was not expensive. I walked there by the way of the park. The rim of the fountain circle was crowded with sitters. The same people were there who had been there yesterday and the day before and the day before that. All of the benches were taken up, too. Several men were standing around two old Italian men who were playing checkers on a bench.

Grace and Porter were sitting in a booth when I got to George's.

"All set for the fight, man?" Porter asked when I sat down.

"Trained to a peak."

"Your boy is going to need all the help he can get," he said.

"Don't worry about him."

Porter laughed loud.

"He'll be laughing you know where when the fight is over," Grace said.

"It should be a great fight."

The waiter came to our table and I ordered a drink. He asked us if we wanted to order dinner yet.

"Sure," Porter said. "I'm ready."

"Let's wait for Harry," I said. "He'll be along any minute."

"He's already late," Porter said.

"We'll wait anyway," said Grace.

The waiter said all right and went for my drink. Grace and Porter were drinking beer and a martini. Grace was drinking the martini. Porter did not say anything about his fight with the Negro boy. There was really no reason why he should have. But I thought he might just the same. We talked about the fight and Porter switched the conversation to what he had been writing lately. I really did not care much what he had written but he talked about it insistently. He talked very sure about how good the stuff was. Grace was reading the newspaper.

"Max and some girl are coming, too," Grace said, looking up from her newspaper.

"Fine," I said.

"They may meet us here," Porter said. "Here comes Lees, now."

Harry said hello and sat down at the booth with us. We were the only people in the restaurant who were eating. There were two other people sitting at the bar. Harry looked around the almost empty place.

"This place must be run on a Guggenheim Fellowship," he said.

The waiter came with my drink. Harry ordered a drink and we all looked at the menu and ordered dinner. The drink was lifting me up from all the dull reading I had been doing in the afternoon.

"Who is your money on, Harry?" Porter asked.

"Coster."

"So you're betting on the all-American boy too?"

"I gather you're betting on Phelps."

"Sure I am."

"Didn't he beat his father half to death or something when he was a kid?" Harry asked me.

"Something like that."

"He sounds so obnoxious," said Grace.

"He'll win, though," Porter said. "Wait and see."

The waiter brought Harry's drink, and Harry thanked him.

"Look at that," Porter said. "The guy even thanks waiters."

"Why not?"

Grace was looking at the paper. "Listen to this," she said. "Some man just killed four people not three blocks from here. It says that an unidentified man walked up to a crowd of people sitting on the steps of a tenement apartment, and started shooting at them with a pistol."

"Just like that?"

"Yes. He killed four of the people and then disappeared during the confusion. Nobody had ever seen him before."

"This place is getting worse all the time," Harry said. "It's enough to make you think of moving uptown."

"It's terrible," Grace said. "Nobody is safe around here."

"It could have happened anywhere," said Porter.

The waiter brought our dinner. The food was hot and rich-smelling. Fried shrimps, chicken hunter style, veal stew, and broiled lamb chops, and a large salad for all of us. All of us except Porter ordered an-other drink during the meal. Porter told us about having to go to Philadelphia Monday for three days on an account he was handling. He did not like the idea of leaving New York.

"I know a couple of people in Philadelphia," Harry said. "I'll give you their names and addresses and you can look them up. You can have a good time with them."

"Okay," said Porter. "But I don't know whether I'll have much time to play around. I'm going to try to get some of my own work done while I'm down there."

"I'll give you the addresses anyway," said Harry. Max and his girl for the night came in as we were drinking our coffee. The waiter brought two chairs for them and they sat down on the outside of the booth. Max introduced the girl I remembered seeing her walking in the park quite some time ago. Porter acted very friendly to her. Grace watched him as he did this. The waiter took their order for coffee. Max said they had already had dinner.

"Can we get tickets up there, Blake?" Max asked me.

"The mezzanine and side arena seats are probably gone by now," I said. "But there must be a lot of balcony seats left."

"The balcony? Can you see the fighters from there?"

"Sure."

"You don't look like a boxing fan," Porter said to the girl whose name was Victoria.

"I'm not really," she said. "I've never even seen one."

"That puts you in Harry's class. Neither has he."

"Okay, Mr. Jacobs," Harry said.

"Who is Mr. Jacobs?" Victoria asked.

"The man who runs the boxing racket," said Grace.

"Oh," said Victoria and smiled.

"Listen to that girl," Max said, reaching across the table and touching Grace's hand. "Listen to how sharp she's getting."

Porter started telling Victoria about boxing matches, and about the one we were going to see to-night. I looked at Grace. She was watching them. She looked at me and I winked at her, and she smiled. Max was looking around the restaurant at the other people, casing the place. Porter was telling Victoria about the time in the Army when he had sparred with a fairly well known middleweight and the middleweight told him what a great left he had.

The waiter brought the check. No one paid any attention to it.

"We'd better get going if we expect to make the prelims," I said.

"Are they going to be any good?" Porter asked.

"Its hard to tell. But I would like to see them, anyway."

"Aw, the first one will most likely be just a couple of crumbs," he said. "We can miss it."

"Maybe you can," I said. "But I want to see all the matches."

"So do I," Grace said. "Let's pay the check and go."

"All right. If you want to see a couple of crumbs."

"Yes. let's see them all," Victoria said, seeming very happy about her first fight.

"Baby, you've got that old killer instinct," Max said.

We got up and paid the check and went out. Harry whistled a cab down, and we drove off to the Garden. Six people made it a tight fit. All the way up to the Garden I could feel one of Grace's legs pressing against mine.

"Are you nervous?" I asked her.

"Just a little," she said.

"It will be a very good fight."

There was a big crowd at the main entrance of the Garden when we got there. Very few women were in the crowd. But there were some. We waited for Max to buy his balcony seats. He finally did get two but they were high up. I told him he would still be able to see well. He said he should have brought his binoculars. He seemed unhappy about not being able to sit with us and having to sit way up in the balcony.

"We'll see you during intermission, Max," Porter said.

Then we all went in with the crowds. Max and Victoria went up one flight of stairs and Grace and Porter and Harry and I went up another toward the end arena. A bell rang far inside the Garden. The first bout was starting.

CHAPTER XVIII

The first round of the first bout on the card was almost over when we got to our seats. Porter tipped the usher who showed us where our seats were. The fighters were Puerto Rican lightweights. They boxed fast and cleverly but did not damage each other much. In the last round one of them was knocked down twice. The decision went to the boy who had scored the knockdowns. It was a good boxing exhibition.

The second prelim was between two white welterweights. One of them looked unusually young to me. About eighteen. He must have been older than that, but he did not look it. The other boy looked much stronger. The young boy came out of his corner nimbly and you could tell by the way he handled himself before they even started fighting that he was a boxer, not a slugger. The other one came out wide open rushing across the ring his arms held low, no guard up. The young one nimbly jabbed a left at him and then the strong boy started swinging roundhouse rights and lefts, knocking down the other's guard, and a hard right and a left and the young boy fell. He took a count of nine. As soon as he got up off his knees the strong boy was at him again and all he could do was try to guard himself but the other was too strong and those roundhouse rights and lefts dropped him again.

He got up at the count of three instead of taking a nine count because he was stunned. The strong boy rushed him again and backed him into the ropes, the young boy not throwing a punch, just holding his gloves up trying to protect his head, and the strong boy was hitting him with rights and lefts, and now he was crouching against the ropes trying to protect himself, just crouching there, the other one hitting him with everything, and the referee ran over and came between them, helping the young boy up from his defensive crouching and stopped the fight.

The crowd roared and whistled and clapped.

"That was awful," said Grace, making a face. "Awful."

"The kid looked terrified of him," Porter said.

"He was too young for a guy like that," I said.

"Well, novitiate, how do you like it?" Porter asked Harry.

"It's tremendous. Absolutely tremendous."

"Oh, I thought that was a terrible match," Grace said. "It was so unfair."

"It was a lousy match," I said.

"You two," Porter said.

The white-coated vendors were walking around through the crowds selling beer and ice cream and copies of *Ring Magazine* and soft drinks. Harry yelled to the vendor who was selling beer. Grace and Porter did not want any. Harry and I had a bottle. Grace asked Porter to get her a copy of *Ring*. Porter waved the vendor over. There was an article on Coster in the magazine. Grace passed the magazine around for us all to look at. She was very pleased about the article.

"I'll bet half of Long Island is here to root for him," Porter said.

"Naturally," Grace said. "He is their boy."

"He has a fine build, hasn't he?" Harry said, giving the magazine back to Grace.

"Beautiful," she said.

"It takes more than beauty," said Porter.

"Why don't you lay off the guy?" I said, tired of his riding Coster.

"That was a general philosophical statement," he said.

"I wonder how Max and his girl are making out up there," said Harry.

"Don't worry about him," I said. "He'll get along." I knew he would, too. If anybody would, Max would. And Porter would, too.

Harry took two small Robert Burns cigars out of his lapel pocket and asked me and Porter if we wanted one. I had my hands full with the bottle of beer, so I said no. Porter said no, too. I said I would like one later if that was all right.

The semifinal bout was between two Negro heavyweights. Dick Hagen and Joe Walters. They got a big hand from the audience. They were both superbly built. Hagen had been one of Joe Louis's sparring partners and he had the same smooth quiet suddenly exploding style that Louis had. I had seen him fight before. Both boys were very good.

"These jigs look good enough for a main event here." It had occurred to Porter, too.

"They are," I said. "The story is that none of the big boys want any part of them. Nobody will give them a match."

"They really look big-time," Porter said.

Hagen gave you the feeling of being something very unusual, the way Louis did. It was something he created just by moving around. You could not take your eyes from him. He had a style of authority. It was the way he felt about what he was doing and he made you feel the same way. You knew he had it as soon as you saw him move around in the ring. There was no confusion or hysteria in him. He did not do anything wrong.

In the first two rounds the other fighter, Walters, made most of the motions, did most of the fighting and seemed to be forcing Hagen back. But Hagen was not getting hit. He moved very little but always enough to get out of the way, and he did not waste any energy. When he threw a punch it was swift and it always landed. Walters was fighting fast and Hagen was fighting little. Then the style of it changed.

Walters was still doing most of the fighting, throwing most of the punches, but he was moving back, Hagen after him. Hagen was not throwing any more punches than he had been. He was still blocking and weaving but now he was following Walters. Somewhere during the fight the positions had changed. It had happened but I had not seen it, and I don't think anybody else had, either. It happened too fast and too beautifully to be noticed above what else was going on in the ring. But now Hagen was slowly, weavingly after Walters who was fighting furiously.

This was the way Louis did it. I had never seen anybody else create this same kind of action in the ring. You knew that something final was going to happen in just a little while.

Hagen caught up with him in the fourth round. It had been only a matter of time. Walters was doing all the fighting, it seemed, and Hagen ducked a hard fast left hook to his head and then, weaving fast, hit Walters in the solar plexus with a left hook. Walters' guard went down just a little, and Hagen, in a continuation of the same motion that began with his ducking the left hook, crossed with a right against Walters' jaw, and Walters was down. Hagen moved into a neutral corner. The referee counted Walters out.

The crowd gave Hagen a big hand.

"My God, that was lovely," Harry said. "The guy almost scares you."

"Terrific hitter," Porter said.

"After that I need a drink of something," Grace said. "Let me have a sip, please, Blake."

I handed her the bottle of beer. I had a slight heavy beer feeling now. The smell of Harry's cigar was very strong. It was good if you were doing the smoking, otherwise it was not too pleasant. I asked him if I could have the cigar he had offered me. He gave it to me. Grace gave the bottle back to me and I put it under the chair.

"Do you want to stretch?" Porter asked Grace. "Max and Victoria might be walking around."

"You go ahead if you want to, Henry," she said. "I can wait until after the fights to see them."

"Suit yourself. I'll be back shortly."

The announcer was telling of the fights that were going to be put on in the near future in the Garden.

"Everybody seems to be a crowd pleaser," Harry said, kidding about the announcer's build-up of the fighters. He yelled to a passing beer vendor and got another bottle. I was too heavy with the one I had already drunk to want another. In the row of seats below us were four young hoods. They were talking loud and tough about fights they had seen and who they thought were the best fighters of all time. They looked around at us a couple of times.

"You never see them alone," said Harry, looking down at them.

"Forget about them, Harry," I said. "They're nowhere."

"They're all over."

"How much do the fighters get who don't fight main events?" Grace asked me.

"Depends," I said, knowing she was purposely changing the subject. "Anywhere from a hundred and fifty to seven hundred and fifty dollars. Sometimes more if they are really good."

"How much do they keep?"

"About two-thirds."

"Who pays the doctor bills?" Harry asked.

"I think the manager."

"And who buries them?"

Just then the announcer began introducing well-known fighters who were watching the fight from ringside. Four of them were lined up already in the ring. All of them were holding their hands clasped in front. Then as the announcer introduced the first one the crowd started whistling and shouting because first Coster and then Phelps were coming down the aisles from their dressing rooms into the ring.

We jumped up now and clapped. Porter came back and he clapped a little, too. Coster was smiling. Phelps was shadow boxing a little as he walked down the aisle, dancing on his toes and punching into the air, limbering up. He did not pay any attention to the crowds. They came into the ring and we sat back down.

"I can hardly stand it," Grace said.

They were in their corners and the newspaper photographers were taking their pictures, the flash bulbs exploding brilliantly and for a second hurting your eyes. As their trainers rubbed them down the announcer was introducing the other well-known fighters. Sugar Ray Robinson, Henry Armstrong, Billy Graham, Tony Pellone, a well-known Argentine heavyweight, Rocky Graziano whom the crowd clapped wildly for, then Robert Villemain and finally, waiting for him to come to the ring from very far back in the ringside, Willie Pep, the unbelievably polished featherweight champion. After he was introduced each fighter went to the corners of the fighters about to fight and shook hands and wished them good luck.

"There is a walk for you," I said to Harry about the way the visiting boxers walked on the sides of their feet and swung their shoulders from side to side.

"It is indeed," he said, drinking from the bottle of beer. "I'll have to include that in my collection."

"I wish they would start," said Grace, leaning forward in her chair.

The announcer was in the middle of the ring, reading the weight and home town of Jimmy Coster. There was a great amount of cheering. Grace jumped up and clapped. Then the announcer introduced Phelps. There was not as much cheering for him as there had been for Coster. Porter clapped very loud for him. Grace gave him an exaggerated dirty look.

"Take it easy, kid," Porter said to her. "You'll blow your top if you don't calm down."

The two fighters were in the middle of the ring with their managers and seconds as the referee with an arm on the shoulder of each fighter was explaining the rules that they had heard explained so many times before. Break clean from the clinches. Phelps was moving his shoulders restlessly. Coster standing calm. Phelps's trainer was massaging his back muscles. Break clean. The referee was telling them to shake hands now and to come out of their corners fighting. Coster reached out to shake Phelps's hand. But Phelps just touched Coster's outstretched glove instead of shaking it and turned away.

Both boys went back to their corners, Phelps shadow boxing as he walked, Coster moving his shoulders in limbering up for the first time, their trainers and managers talking to them as they, back to back, holding on to the ropes, knelt down and stood up and knelt down and stood up to stretch their tight muscles. The bell rang.

Phelps hit Coster a hard left in the midsection and followed with a right to the heart that you could hear landing and Coster clinched. The referee separated them and Coster broke clean, holding his arms up to show he was not hitting on the break. Phelps swung a left hook and missed and Coster encountered with two sharp jabs to the face and Phelps came back with a right cross that landed high on Costers head, jolting him. They clinched. The referee separated them. Phelps hit on the break, hooking into Coster's midsection, and the referee warned him about it. Coster boxed him, landing some good jabs but taking a lot of body punishment for the rest of the round. Phelps was pushing the fight.

"What a dirty fighter," Grace said. "Did you see the way he hit Jimmy when they broke?"

"He's trying to win any way he can," Porter said. "He isn't in there for his health."

"What a dirty fighter."

"Does something happen when a fighter does what he did?" Harry asked me. "Fouls?"

"He may get the round taken from him."

"That was Phelps's round, wasn't it?"

"It looked that way to me," I said.

In the second round Phelps worked on Coster's body, hitting him with hard rights above and below the heart that we could hear land because they were solid and not glancing blows. And Coster boxed him, hitting him with left jabs, landing a couple of times, working on his face, on the thin scar tissue around his eyes where he would bleed easily. It was clear what Phelps was doing. He was hitting Coster around the heart to make it hard for Coster to keep his left up guarding his chin. Phelps missed with a wild left hook and Coster countered with a left jab and at the same time Phelps slipped and fell down.

The crowd kept shouting at this first fall. But Phelps got up immediately and the referee wiped the resin from his gloves on his shirt and Phelps then went after Coster again. He landed two good body punches and they clinched. Phelps was using all the tricks he knew in the clinches, coming up with his head against Coster's face, heeling, and wrestling him around. The referee broke them.

Already there was a red area around Coster's heart where Phelps had been hitting him. Coster jabbed him three times with his left and grazed his head with a right cross. Phelps came back with a right cross that caught Coster on the temple and staggered him, making him stumbled back a little, and he clinched as Phelps followed him. The crowd was wild with shouting and whistling and all over the Garden people were no longer sitting down but standing up to watch.

Phelps was out to kill him.

"Coster had better stay away from him," said Porter. "Phelps hits too hard for mixing it up to be safe."

Grace did not say anything. She watched the ring.

"That's right," I said.

In the third round Coster's fine left jabs opened an old cut over Phelps's left eye, and there was now bright blood on the side of Phelps's face from it. Coster was hurting Phelps's eye with those jabs, and it was swelling. But Phelps kept after his body, hitting him with short fast rights to the heart and hooking him steadily in the midsection with his left. Coster boxing expertly and making Phelps miss lefts to the head, but taking those punches to the body. Phelps missed a couple, crowded him to the ropes, worked on him in the clinch, then broke suddenly before the referee came to them, and with a short sudden left to the jaw dropped Coster.

Grace jumped up. The crowd was jumping up and shouting.

"Get up, Jimmy," she shouted. "Get up. Get up." She looked frightened.

The referee was counting over Coster. Coster was slowly getting up on to his knees, shaking his head to get rid of the effect of the left that had dropped him.

"Come on, Jimmy," I shouted. "He didn't hurt you. Come on, boy."

Grace grabbed my arm now, looking scared. "Oh, God he has to get up," she said.

"Take it easy. He'll get up," I said.

He was on his feet at nine, the referee wiping his gloves off and staring into his face to see if he was out on his feet and fighting only with his reflexes.

"God, what punch," Harry said almost in a whisper.

Now Coster, hurt but still in there, kept Phelps away as Phelps rushed him for the knockout, by jabbing with his left and moving all around the ring never standing still so he could be hit, and he made the cut on Phelps's eye bleed more, and managed to land a right cross that made Phelps fall into a clinch. Coster was all right now. This time he protected himself better in the clinch, but kept the clinch as long as he could to get the round over with. There was blood on both fighters from Phelps's eye cuts and a slight cut in the corner of Coster's mouth. The blood was on their chest and shoulders, too, from the blood-splotched gloves.

Coster's seconds were working hard on him in his corner, rubbing him down and clearing his head with smelling salts and giving him water to rinse his mouth with, and giving him quick advice for handling Phelps. Phelps's manager was fixing the cuts on Phelps's eyes with adrenaline.

The crowd was restless for the knockout. Everyone was talking very loud.

"Don't take this so seriously," Porter was telling Grace who had calmed down some. "It's only a fight. They are getting paid a lot of money to do it."

"All right, all right," she said.

"Coster is making him look silly as a boxer," Porter said. "This boy is just a dumb slugger. Your boy may cut him to pieces."

"I just hope he wins," she said.

"He will," I said. "He'll stay away from him and box him silly."

She squeezed my arm and smiled at me.

"This is weird," Harry said, shaking his head.

Coster cleanly and coolly outboxed Phelps in the fourth round. He kept him at a distance and made Phelps box him. His left jabs opened the cut over Phelps's left eye again, and Coster started working on his right eye. Phelps rushing him once missed and slipped again, turning all the way around this time, his back to Coster and leaning against the ropes, and Coster stood away from him and let him regain his balance and turn around. A few people applauded when he did this.

"He's so decent," Grace said.

Then Phelps hit him with a long low right in the stomach and the referee warned him about low punching. Phelps got in three good blows to Coster's heart but taking more jabs to the face before the round ended. And both of Phelps's eyes were bleeding from cuts.

"He'll kill him, he'll kill him," one of the young hoods in front of us shouted to his friends.

"This is a good place to sell tickets to a lynching," Harry said, slightly tight on the beer.

"Getting queasy?" Porter asked him jokingly, reaching across us and slapping Harry on the knee.

The bell rang for round five. Phelps in a weaving crouch, Coster upright and holding his left lower now. Those punches to Coster's heart were beginning to tell. They were slowing him down. He moved on the flat of his feet. He hit Phelps twice with a left jab in the face, Phelps crouched and weaving in front of him, slipping two more left jabs, then hooking quickly to the body and crossing with that right to the heart that now pushed Coster back and you could tell that he was tired, how much the body blows were hurting him. They fought hard in the clinch, Coster opening both cuts over Phelps's eyes. And both fighters splotchy with the blood of their cuts.

It looked as though Phelps was holding and hitting in the clinch. Holding his left on the back of Coster's neck to keep him from riding the punch, taking the full force of it instead. The referee broke them and spoke to Phelps. Phelps's face was covered with blood. The referee came between them once, holding Coster off, and looked at Phelps's cuts to see if they were bad enough to make him stop the fight. They were not. He waved them back to fighting.

Coster boxed him, cutting away at his face. Phelps crouched and weaving, looking for an opening. Costers left getting lower. Then Phelps weaving low feinted with his left, Coster moved his arms slightly, and Phelps crossed with a short right chop past Costers lowered left to the jaw, hitting with the force of his twisting shoulder, and dropped Coster, Coster collapsing suddenly with his arms to his sides.

The crowd was on its feet, shouting and whistling. We were on our feet, too. Coster did not take the full count. He raised himself up at the count of five, the referee wiping his gloves on his shirt and looking into his eyes for the staring glaze, and Phelps came at him and instead of boxing and moving away from him Coster stood there and slugged it out with Phelps.

He rocked Phelps with a left hook and a right cross to the head, but Phelps countered with a left to the midsection that made Coster bend, and then Phelps hit him with a short right cross, his whole torso moving with the blow, and Coster dropped.

Coster's mouth piece fell out and the referee was counting over him. Phelps in a neutral corner, his face streaming with the bright blood from his eye cuts, his chest blotched with blood where he had been hit by Coster's bloody gloves. Coster was pulling all of his strength together to get up, and then he was on his knees, resting there on his knees and hands, shaking his head, the referee swinging his arm down in the count. And at nine he staggered up onto his feet.

"Stop the fight! Stop the fight!"

Phelps rushed across the ring at him. Coster held him off with a long left jab that twisted his face and threw a right cross that was high. Phelps hit him with a left hook to the head that snapped his head back, and the crowd on its feet, screaming, and then a hard chopping right cross, and Coster staggered back and Phelps swung through Coster's half-guard and hit him with another right cross and a left hook that spun him around, and Coster fell against the ropes and then crumpled to the floor.

The referee rushed across the ring to Coster and helped him up, stopping the fight at this knockdown, and with his left arm motioning to Phelps that it was all over, the fight finished, the fight his.

"Oh, God. Let's go," Grace said. "I can't stand it."

The ring was full of people. Flash bulbs were exploding. They were working over Coster in his corner bringing him out of it. Phelps's handlers were excitedly congratulating him.

We pushed through the crowd to the nearest exit. I felt lousy.

"It was a tough fight, all right," Porter said. Very tough. I didn't think Coster was that rugged."

"The poor guy, the poor guy," Grace said.

"I don't even know how I feel about it." Harry said. "I don't know whether it disgusted me or whether I liked it."

I threw the stub of my dead cigar away. The taste was cold and bitter in my mouth. The nasal voice of the announcer was coming over the loud-speaker but we were too far away now for me to understand what he was saying. There was just the nasal sound, far away, as we walked out.

"That Phelps is a wild man," Porter said. "What will happen to Coster now, Blake?"

"Who knows?"

"Let's go somewhere and have a drink," Harry said. "I can still see the blood on those guys."

We were standing in front of the Garden now.

"I told Max we would wait for them out here," said Porter.

I had forgotten all about them.

"You certainly seem concerned about those two." Grace said to Porter.

"What do you mean? I told them we would meet them. Don't let the fight get you down."

"All right," she said. "I'm sorry."

"I know how you feel," he said, taking her arm. "I'm sorry about Coster. I really am."

"Okay."

"I wish he had won," Porter went on. "He looked like a good kid."

"This will knock him to pieces," said Grace, looking at me. "He'll feel he let everybody down."

"Is that really the way he will feel?" Harry asked her.

"Yes. He'll worry about all the money his friends lost betting on him."

"What a guy."

"He should quit now," Porter said. "He has made a pile. Why should he stick around and get beaten punchy?"

"He isn't through yet," I said.

"Hey, Blake. You owe me five bucks."

"I know it." I took the money from my pocket and handed it to him.

"Forget it," he said. "I was only kidding. I was not serious about the bet, anyway."

"I was though."

He shrugged then and took the money.

"It is only one fight," I said to Grace.

"You don't think he is finished, do you, Blake?" she asked.

"No. Of course not. There will probably be a return match. He can beat this guy."

She smiled. "I'm taking it too seriously."

"That is better than not taking it at all," I said.

"Listen to that old Blake philosopher," Harry said. "Jesus, I'd like a drink."

"There they are now," Porter said.

Max and Victoria came up now. "It was almost epic," he said. "That Coster looked murdered."

"Stop it," Grace said.

"I'm sorry, baby. I'm sorry. Forgive me." He put his arm around Grace.

"Come on," I said. "We can go to Mickey Walker's down the block."

"Wasn't it something?" Victoria said about the fight. "I've never seen anything so brutal in my life."

"You loved it," Max said.

CHAPTER XIX

The cold bitter taste was still in my month when we sat down in a booth at Mickey Walker's Bar. I wanted something to wash it away. An old waiter took our order. He had a broken nose and looked like an ex-fighter.

Porter was talking to Max and Victoria about fighting. Grace put her arm through his and he said that it was uncomfortable because they were so crowded in the booth. She took her arm away.

"There was the funniest man behind us," Victoria said. "He kept yelling instructions to the fighters. I thought he was going to climb down into the ring. He was a scream."

"He had bets riding on those fighters," Max said.

"Robinson would kill both those guys," Porter said.

"I don't know," Max said. "That Robinson is getting sort of old."

"He isn't that old."

"Who is Robinson?" Victoria asked.

Grace looked at me and shrugged.

"Robinson is a Negro who is now the middleweight champion," Harry said.

"All that blood didn't upset your stomach, did it, Harry?" Porter asked.

"Not a bit. Did it upset yours?"

"It's a very ungentlemanly sport," Porter said.

"Are you still on that? Your imagination is at a new low ebb, Porter."

Porter laughed ha-ha-ha.

"This punchy waiter must have forgotten our drinks," Max said, looking for the waiter.

"Here he comes now," I said, seeing the waiter appear from behind a group of men standing at the end of the bar.

The waiter did seem a little punchy as he put our drinks down. His eyes had a peculiar slowness about them.

"Found a job yet, Blake?" Max asked me.

"Not yet," I said, drinking the rye-and-soda and tasting the bitter cold taste wash away.

"Listen, man," he said, smiling, "you'll never get a job. Why don't you give it up and marry some nice girl who can support you?"

"He's going to marry me," Grace said from across the table. "Didn't you know that?"

Porter laughed loud at this.

"That's right," I said. "Grace and I are getting married. Then we're going to raise pastramis. I've always wanted to have my own herd. And Grace can bake the rye bread."

"Not a bad idea," Max said. "Maybe I'll work as a slicer for you."

"Yes," Porter said, turning to Grace. "Why don't you and Blake get married? He would make you a good husband. Regular, loyal, traditional, middle-class. He wouldn't brutalize you."

As he said this I tried to imagine what it would be like to be married to Grace. I imagined some marital scenes that were quite desirable. Then I thought about the operation. That made me nervous. I drank down the rest of my rye-and-soda. "Don't give me too much encouragement," Grace said. "I might really do it."

"Let's all do it," said Harry. "Let's all have another drink."

He shouted to the waiter to bring us another round. Max was caressing Victoria's hand. Two whores were drinking at the bar by themselves.

"How are you getting along with your millionaire girl friend, Max?" Porter asked him.

"Fine, fine. She is just like a lamb with me. She does everything I tell her to do."

"Do you give her a rough time, professor?"

"I make her toe the line, if that is what you mean."

"Listen to that."

The old waiter brought the second round of drinks.

"What a racket you have," Porter said.

"Don't be so salty, man," Max said. "I'm not getting anything for nothing. I work for it."

"Sure you do."

"This subject is beginning to drag me," Max said, shaking his head. "Talk about something else, will you."

"Did you hear about the new nationality Blake discovered?" Harry asked.

"No. What is it?"

"The anti-Semite. His father was English and his mother was an anti-Semite."

"Did you think that up?" Max asked. "It's pretty good."

"It's great, Harry," Grace said.

"Are you half-English and half anti-Semitic?" Victoria asked me.

"That's right."

"Say something else that's funny, Harry," Porter said.

"All right. Henry Porter."

"That's not so funny."

"Oh yes it is. Funnier than you think."

"You're in your cups, old sport."

"And who is in yours?"

"Did anybody here see the new Hamlet?" Victoria asked.

"I saw it," Grace said.

"Wasn't it wonderful?"

"I'm crazy about Henderson," she said. "He could play Tom Thumb and I would go to see it."

"Somebody told me he was a queer," said Max.

"People are always saying things like that," Grace said. "You didn't believe it, did you?"

"Why not? What's wrong with being a queer?"

"Are you defending them?" Harry asked.

"I merely asked what was wrong with being a queer? Somebody tell me."

"Everything," Harry said. "Just the idea is obnoxious.

"Why?"

"Because it is."

"Be specific." Max said.

"I don't have to be. It's just obnoxious, that's all."

"We're talking in circles."

Max turned away from Harry and looked at Victoria. "So you like Hamlet? Well that's fine. I'm glad to hear that."

"You are pulling my leg."

"I wish I were, baby."

"Tell her about Hamlet, Max," I said. "Give her some inside information."

"Listen to that man, will you," Max said "He is riding me."

"Yes," said Grace. "What's the real story on that Hamlet?"

"You are all ganging up on me."

Harry wasn't saying anything. He had been looking in his glass nearly all this time. Porter was saying something serious now about Hamlet. He had it all figured out. Grace was listening with the others and had her hand on his arm. It wasn't that he was wrong in what he was saying. It was that he sounded so damn sure of it. He made it sound so uninteresting and psychoanalytical.

While he was talking Harry motioned to the old waiter to bring him a drink. When the waiter brought it he did not bother to mix it with the water. He drank it straight from the shot glass.

"Is anybody going downtown?" he asked.

"We're all going in a few minutes," I said.

"I want to go along now," he said. "I didn't get enough sleep last night. And I've got a filthy headache."

He got up and put some money on the table. "This ought to cover me," he said. "Sorry to beat it this way."

"Stick around, Harry. Don't run off," Max said.

"I really don't feel like it. Well, see you later."

"So long."

"Good night, Harry. Hope you feel better."

"See you."

"What is the matter with him?" Porter asked.

"He said he was sick," said Grace. "Didn't you hear him? People feel sick once in a while."

We had another round of drinks and after that we left Mickey Walker's. We walked back past the Garden to Fiftieth Street to get a downtown subway. The crowds were all gone from around the entrance of the Garden and the ticket windows were closed and barred. An old man was standing against the side of the deserted arcade talking to himself. The street had a heavy end-of-the day smell.

We turned off at Fifty-First Street and walked downstairs and underground to the subway platform. We were all going home. We had tried to think of something else to do because it was not very late, but we could not think of anything that seemed very interesting.

"I wish I never had to ride on a subway train," Grace said, now we were waiting for the downtown train. "I hate it. Down here."

"It is pretty bad," I said.

"It's strange," she said to me. "But I haven't completely re-acted to the fight yet. The shock of it froze me up. And I haven't thawed out yet."

"I know. Perhaps it will hit you tomorrow. It sometimes takes that long. Sometimes longer."

Our train came now and we got on it and looked for seats. There were none together, so we sat apart.

CHAPTER XX

I killed Sunday by sleeping late and working a lot, a long walk down the East River, a double-feature movie, then supper alone, and in bed early.

Monday morning after breakfast I took the work I had been doing uptown to my friend at his office on Forty-Third Street and Fifth Avenue. His secretary showed me into his office as soon as she had told him I was there. He was working at a big desk in his shirt. But he still looked very dressed. He had not opened the collar of his shirt. He looked cool although it was warm in the office.

"Tell me what's new in this garbage can of a world, Blake," he said when I had sat down.

"Almost nothing," I said. "How has it been with you?"

"You can see it before you," he said and waved his arm over the books and papers piled on his desk. "My life is just a series of condensed manuscripts."

I gave him the work I had brought with me. He looked at it quickly and then put it in a basket on his desk. He said he would read it over tonight at home and then tomorrow would have his secretary send me a check.

"Can I let you have some of it now?" he asked, putting his hand in his pocket.

"No. That's all right. Tomorrow will be fine."

He leaned far back in his desk swivel chair and put his hands behind his head. "God, what a rat race," he said. "There must be some way for a man to make a living and not be disgusted with himself. There must be."

"What about bricklayers?"

"Nope. I don't think that's the answer. The bricklayers hate themselves because they're not making enough money and because they think they work too hard."

"Why don't you become a gentleman farmer then?"

"I've thought of that," he said, coming forward now in the swivel chair. "But that wouldn't work, either. After a while I would start spending all my time trying to think up some way of working less and making more money."

I asked about his family and when he had finished telling me I got up and said I had to be running along. I had to meet Grace in a little while, and I was beginning to be jumpy thinking about the operation.

"Come out to the country some weekend, Blake," he said. "Do some swimming. We never see you any more."

"I will," I said. "I'll give you a call soon."

"I wish you would. You'll have the check tomorrow or the next day at the latest."

"Thanks a lot."

I left his new office and outside said good-by to his pretty secretary and caught the elevator down. I was going to meet Grace at 12:15 on the corner of Sixth Avenue and Ninth Street. Under the bank clock there. Then, walking along Fifth Avenue to the bus stop, I remembered that it was right across the street from the women's prison. God. Why had I picked that place? What a place to be meeting at this time. But there was nothing I could do about it now. I did not have to wait long for the bus.

I got a seat by myself at the back of the bus and looked out of the window at the women who had come uptown to shop and waited for the ride to be over.

Grace was already waiting under the clock when I got there. I thought I might be late, but I looked at the clock and saw that she must have got there early. She turned around now and saw me walking toward her. I drew back in a mock gesture of surprise at seeing her there, and she laughed slightly at it.

"You look great," I said.

"That's it," she said, taking my arm. "Build me up."

"You're pretty well built already."

"Oh, you."

"How would you like to take a cab ride to Brooklyn? It's a lovely ride."

She laughed a little but I could see she was nervous and worried. I thought my joking might be offensive under the circumstances, but it seemed to me that if we were serious about what was going to happen it would be too grim.

"Sure," she said. "I like to ride in cabs."

I hailed a cab and told him to drive us to the corner of Jones and Schermerhorn in Brooklyn. This was two blocks from the doctor's office. You never drove right up to the place. At least, with this one you didn't. Grace kept her arm in mine in the taxi. She was smoking a lot, lighting one cigarette from the one before. Now she reached for her bag.

"Here," she said, handing me an envelope. "I better give you this now."

I looked into the envelope even though I knew what was there. It was the two hundred dollars for the abortion. All new bills. She must have taken it out of the bank this morning. I put the envelope in my inside coat pocket.

"Did Porter leave?" I asked.

"Uh-huh."

"It's going to be all right. You're not scared, are you?"

"A little."

"There should be some trick that would keep a person from being scared."

"Like holding your breath for hiccups?"

"Yes. Or drinking sugar water."

"Do I looked scared, Blake?"

I looked her full in the face. Then I shook my head.

"Terrified," I said. "Absolutely terrified."

She smiled.

"So early in the day, too."

Then she said, "Keep talking to me, will you, Blake? That will take my mind off it."

I looked ahead through the glass separating us from the cab driver and looked into his mirror to see him looking back at us, and he looked away, out of the mirror, when he saw me looking back at him.

"Let's see," I said, trying to think of something to tell her. "Did I ever tell you about the time I was riding in a cab with Alec Templeton?"

"No. Tell me all about it."

"Well, I was interviewing Templeton for the newspaper I worked on. After the interview in his hotel he and his wife had to meet some people for a dinner before the concert. He invited me to go along, During the ride in the cab we talked mostly about him and I saw that the cab driver was listening with a lot of pleasure. Anyway, when we got out of the cab the driver said, 'Well, Mr. Templeton, I'll be seeing you tonight at the concert.' 'Oh I'm very glad to hear you can make it,' Templeton said. 'I have to be there,' the cab driver said. 'I'm the second violinist in the orchestra.'"

"Honestly?" Grace asked.

"Yes. The guy played the violin at night and hacked during the day."

"That was a fine story," she said, still holding her arm in mine. "Talk to me some more. You're doing beautifully."

"I used to know a gentile girl who went out only with Jewish men. I couldn't figure it out. Finally I asked her why she did it."

"Why did she?"

"It was a very good reason. She told me she liked Jewish men best because they give her the feeling that they always have an erection when they are with her."

"It must be very flattering to her."

"It's an interesting angle. I wonder if other women feel that way about Jewish men. Do they?"

"I've heard they treat their women better than gentile men treat theirs."

"Maybe there is something to that."

We were driving over the Brooklyn Bridge now. Only a few minutes more and we would be there. The envelope inside my jacket pocket was pressing against my side.

"Look, Blake, look. Look at the big boat."

On our right, heading slowly toward the Hudson River, was a gaily colored ocean liner. Her decks were crowded with passengers watching the New York shore line.

"It's beautiful, isn't it?"

"Yes."

"Think how wonderful it must be to be on it, going somewhere. Wouldn't you like to be going somewhere on it?"

"Uh-huh. Where would you like to be going?"

"Anywhere. Everywhere. France, Spain, Italy. Maybe even Africa."

"They tell me Africa is very nice." There was a long splitting blast from the ocean liner. "South Africa especially. Beaches fifty miles long."

"Wonderful. Let's go to Africa, Blake."

Another splitting blast from the boat.

"All right," I said. "Any time you say."

"Do diamonds wash up on the beach?"

"Of course. You hire native boys to pick them up for you."

"Let's go tomorrow morning."

The driver pulled up to the curb and flipped down the flag on the meter box.

"Here we are," I said.

We were at the corner of Schermerhorn and Jones Streets. I helped Grace out of the cab and then paid the driver, and we started walking to the doctor's office two blocks away. Grace was holding on to my arm. Now there was another blast from the boat, though farther off and not as splitting as before. Neither of us said anything as we walked. We turned down the street where the doctor's house was in a row of brownstones. It was a quiet street and there were young maple trees newly planted along the sidewalk.

"It's going to be all right, isn't it, Blake?" Grace said finally as we neared the house.

"Don't worry. Nothing is going to go wrong."

She looked down at the sidewalk. "It's just like killing someone."

"Don't look at it that way."

"I can't help it. That's what it is."

"There are better ways of looking at it," I said.

She looked into my face now. "You won't tell anybody, will you, Blake?"

"What do you think I am?"

"Promise?"

"You know I'm not going to tell anybody, Grace."

"You never will, will you?"

"Never."

We walked up the steps of the doctor's brownstone. I rang the doorbell. In a few seconds a heavy, middle-aged woman in a nurse's uniform answered the door. I told her my name, and she showed us inside and through the corridor and into a small sitting room that was empty.

CHAPTER XXI

We sat down in the maple-wood easy chairs. The nurse went into another room and closed the door behind her. I smiled at Grace. She tried to smile back. A large reproduction of a Van Gogh painting was hanging above a false fireplace. It made the room look like almost any living room in almost anybody's house. I looked at the Van Gogh and waited for the nurse to return.

"They probably like Muzak too," I said.

Grace smiled a little. The nurse came back.

"Will you come with me please?" she said to Grace.

I stood up as Grace did.

"I'll be here," I said.

She nodded her head. She went through the door with the nurse, and the nurse closed the door. I sat back down and picked up a copy of *Life* that was lying on a coffee table. In a few minutes the nurse came back alone. I knew it was for the money.

"It's all here," I said, taking out the envelope and handing it to her. "Two hundred."

"That's right," she said. "Thank you." She went back through the door.

I read through the copy of *Life* three times waiting there for Grace. It was the current issue. I noticed that the third time through it. Then in my mind I went back over the fight. The accounts in the newspapers had been accurate enough but they all missed something about the fight. I saw Coster and Phelps fighting now, round by round. I tried to imagine how Coster should have fought Phelps to beat him. But whatever I contrived, Phelps was still in there with that terrific right and fighting as though he had nothing to lose. Coster was making him look foolish with his sharp classical boxing and his politeness but he still went down all those times, finally to have the referee stop the fight. Another victory for the underground.

I imagined myself sailing on a boat like the *Queen Elizabeth* to South Africa and lying all day on a beach fifty miles long and looking out over the blue water at a school of porpoises that were playing games in the water solely for my amusement. I tried to imagine those native boys running up to me with diamonds falling from their hands, but I could not quite bring that picture off.

I tried not to think about Grace being operated on in one of the rooms around me. But it was in the front of my mind all the time and there was no getting it out of my mind. I could not help thinking of all the stories I had read in the newspapers about girls dying of abortions, of infections, or bleeding.

Once the hemorrhage started you could not stop it and it was only a matter of time before you were dead.

Then I thought about Porter. And as I was thinking about him the door opened and Grace came out with the nurse.

The nurse was holding her arm. Her face was white and sick and she had been crying.

"Everything is all right now," the nurse said to me. I took Grace's arm and thanked the nurse and the nurse smiled at me and then walked in front of us to the outside door and she and I said good-by to each other. Grace did not say anything. We stopped on the sidewalk outside the brownstone house.

"I hope it didn't go badly," I said.

She shook her head slowly.

"Stay right here," I said. "I'll run down and get a cab."

"I can walk with you."

"No. Stay right here. I'll be right back."

"Hurry then."

"I will."

I walked very fast, almost ran part of the way down to Jones Street. I was lucky to get a cab right away. We went back for Grace. I helped her in and gave the driver my address, and we started back to Manhattan. Grace leaned her head against my shoulder and I put my arm around her. I asked the driver if he would take it easy and he said he would be glad to.

"Well, it's all finished now," I said.

"I know it," she said, her head on my shoulder. "I feel horrible."

"Are you sick?"

"I didn't mean that."

"Think about all that some other time," I said. "Don't kill yourself thinking about it now."

We rode through Brooklyn not talking until we came to the Brooklyn Bridge. When we were on the bridge Grace raised her head from my shoulder and looked out of the cab window down at the river.

"The boat is gone," she said.

"It is probably just docking."

"I wish we could have seen it again. It is such a beautiful boat."

"You can see it the next time it comes in."

"Yes. I guess I can."

"I'll take you to see it."

She leaned her head back on my shoulder, and then we were across the bridge and the river and driving up Third Avenue.

"Blake, I'm going to be sick."

I told the driver to stop the cab. He pulled over to the curb and I helped Grace out and turned around and in a couple of minutes I was helping her back into the cab.

"I'm awfully sorry, Blake. This must be terrible for you."

"It isn't bothering me at all."

We came to my place and I helped Grace out and we went up.

CHAPTER XXII

In my apartment I took Grace into the bedroom and she lay down on the bed. I pulled down the window shade.

"I can't tell you how I feel about your doing this, Blake."

"You're embarrassing me."

"Let me kiss you."

I bent over her and we kissed, and I asked her if she wanted anything. She said no. She said she wanted to try to sleep for a while. I told her I would be in the next room, and went out closing the door behind me so that she could sleep.

I took a copy of Dostoyevsky's letters from the bookshelves and lay on the day bed and began looking through it. In nearly all of the letters I read he was asking people to forgive him. Sometimes it was not quite clear what he wanted to be forgiven for having done. He always called himself wretched and unworthy in his letters because he had just lost his last fifteen kopeks gambling, or because he was always breaking his word and because he had such a filthy temper. So much guilt.

Then I remembered that there was a quart of beer in the icebox. I got the beer out and settled down for some more reading. But the letters soon became monotonous with all that guilt and I looked through the books for something more diverting. I picked Conrad's *Victory* which I had never gotten around to reading even though it had been in the house for more than a year. I liked reading and drinking at the same time. Heyst struck me as very, very pathetic. All those people down on him just because he was different. I began to wonder why he did not knock himself off. The beer made me sleepy and slightly tight. I finished it off and stopped reading and went to sleep.

I woke up in about an hour hearing Grace walking around.

"Do you know that you snore?" she asked. She was wearing my bathrobe.

"It runs in the family," I said, getting up. "My father was a great snorer. His father, too."

"What about your mother's side?"

"Very quiet-sleeping people. Some of them don't even breathe."

My head was heavy from the beer. I always felt peculiar after sleeping that way during the day. Grace sat down and lit a cigarette. I got up off the day bed and went into the bathroom and rubbed cold water on my face. That took some of the heaviness away.

"Could I interest you in a little food?" I asked her.

"Very little, I'm afraid."

"I'll go down and get some sandwiches."

"There's some money in my purse, Blake."

"I have some."

"Take some from my purse. Don't be so proud."

"All right."

I took a dollar from her purse in the bedroom and went downstairs to the delicatessen across the street. It was very pleasantly cool in the store after the dead, hanging, afternoon heat outside. I bought two big Italian sandwiches on half loaves of Italian bread with salami and mortadella and Swiss cheese, and a bottle of beer and a bottle of ginger ale for Grace.

"This is the best sandwich you taste," the old Italian man behind the counter said to me when he wrapped the sandwiches up.

"I hope so," I said.

There was a big bowl of olives and onions and something else chopped up on the counter. It smelled strong and very good so I told the old man to give me a ladle full.

"Are these the best olives I'll ever taste?" I asked him as he was wrapping the mixture up.

"The very best," he said, smiling.

I went back upstairs with the stuff, twisting through the crowd of social-club boys standing in front of my entrance. I put the sandwiches and olive mixture on plates in the kitchen and poured the ginger ale and brought it all into the other room and put it on the coffee table.

"What service," Grace said.

"You're spoiling me." I asked her if she wanted beer instead of ginger ale.

"I can't. The doctor said no alcoholic beverages for a couple of days."

"This stuff tastes better with ginger ale anyway," I said.

"Smell the garlic."

"I like it. Don't you?"

"Yes, but I'll smell for weeks."

"So will I."

We began to eat. The ginger ale was cold and tasted springy after the heaviness of the beer I had drunk. The sandwiches were a little clumsy to eat because of their size. Grace took a couple of bites then suddenly put her hand to her head and closed her eyes.

"What is it?"

"I just felt dizzy for a moment."

"Come on," I said. "You'd better lie down."

"I'll be all right."

"Lie down here on the day bed then."

"I'm sorry."

I helped her to the day bed and propped her up with the pillows there. I was afraid something might be wrong. But I did not want her to know that I was scared.

"Are you all right?"

"It's gone now," she said. "It was just a little dizziness."

"Look. Don't be afraid to tell me if you're sick. We can call a doctor."

"No. I'm all right. Honestly. I'd tell you if I were sick."

I sat back down and finished the sandwich and ginger ale even though I was not hungry anymore.

"I'll eat something later, Blake," she said. "Save it for me."

I took the rest of the stuff back to the kitchen and put it in the icebox. Then I went in and turned the radio on. The only program that was at all tolerable was on WQXR, which I seldom listened to.

"Don't let me keep you from doing anything," Grace said when I had sat back down. "You don't have to worry about me."

"I haven't anything better to do right now," I said.

"All right then. Would you read to me?"

"Sure."

I read to her from *Victory*. I had almost finished a chapter when the phone rang. It was Max. He felt lonely. He said nobody was around. He wanted to know what I was doing. I told him I had to go up town to see somebody in a few minutes. Maybe I would see him tonight at the Sporting Club Bar. He said all right.

"Max?" Grace asked when I came back.

"What did he have to say?"

"He wanted to come up."

"And you told him you were going out. You are so nice to me."

I read some more from *Victory*. Poor Heyst. Everybody suspected him of doing his partner in. It was fun reading out loud. I had not done it in a long time. But after two chapters we both had enough of it, so while Grace lay there on the day bed listening to the radio, I undressed in the bathroom and took a shower. In the shower I let myself feel how much I liked having Grace in the apartment with me. I was not as worried as I had been about her being sick. And I kept wondering what she saw in Porter.

When I came out of the shower Grace was reading an old copy of *Time* that I had left half under the day bed. "Why don't you go to a movie? Don't stick around here just because of me."

"I like it here," I said.

"No. It makes me feel guilty. I insist that you go to a movie. Now go on. I'll be perfectly all right here."

"You won't mind?"

"I'll feel much better if you go to a movie."

"Okay. I'll call the Waverly and see what's playing."

I got the ticket office of the Waverly on the phone and the lady there told me that the *Treasure of the Sierra Madre* and *Manhandled* were playing. It sounded like a good bill. I had not seen either picture. Several people had told me I had to see the treasure picture, that it was the best thing to come along in years.

"If anything happens while I'm gone call this doctor," I told Grace as I was putting on my jacket.

I wrote down the name of a doctor I knew quite well and his phone number. I still owed this doctor twenty dollars.

"You're a great worrier," she said. "But I like it."

"I'm glad somebody does."

"Go to the movies now."

"All right. I'll see you in a couple of hours."

"Fine."

"So long."

"So long, honey. Don't worry now."

I went downstairs and walked up to the Waverly Theater.

CHAPTER XXIII

The *Treasure of the Sierra Madre* was excellent, but the other picture dragged so I left in the middle of it. The soggy heat unmoving in the streets pressed all over me as I left the air-conditioned lobby of the theater. I bought an afternoon paper from the stand just outside the theater and walked to the Sporting Club Bar for a cold glass of beer before going back to the apartment.

Not very many people were in the bar. I ordered a glass of beer from John and began reading the paper. John asked me if he could look at the inside section of the paper for a second. I gave it to him. I liked him better than any of the other men who worked there. He did not act as surly as they did.

Then Max and Harry came in.

"The place is a morgue," Max said.

"What a pleasure it will be to get away from all these weary prose-lined faces for a while," said Harry. "I really need some sunshine."

"Let's cop that booth," Max said.

I said I could only stay for one beer because I had to get back to my place to finish up something I was working on. I took my beer from the bar and we went to a booth. John came around from the bar, bringing the inside section of the paper back to me, and took Max's and Harry's order for beers. Max took part of the paper and began looking through it.

"Here are pictures of the fight," he said.

I did not particularly want to see them.

"Poor Coster," Max said, looking at the shots of Coster stretched on the floor.

"What do you recommend for him now?" Harry asked.

"He'll be all right after a while," I said. "It was the first time he was ever knocked out."

John brought the beers now. Harry paid for them.

"It's the first time that counts," Max said to me.

"When is there going to be another good fight, Blake?" Harry asked.

"I think the next good one will be the Robinson-Graziano fight."

"Who do you think will win it? Robinson?"

"Easily."

"We're going up to the Cape this week, aren't we, Harry?" Max asked.

"Yes. I'm going up tomorrow to get the house ready."

"So you're going to put your house in order?" Max said.

"I wish to Christ it could be done that easily."

"Who are you taking up?" I asked Harry.

"I don't know yet," he said, looking into his beer glass, "I haven't asked anybody."

"Maybe I can promote a chick for you," said Max.

"I wish you would. I don't seem to be so good at it."

"Got any preferences?" Max asked, beginning to make a joke of it.

"No. So long as they are white."

"You don't like the dark stuff?"

"Afraid not," Harry said.

"Maybe you're too color conscious," I said.

"There's nothing I can do about it."

"Well, you know these New England types. Blake," Max said.

Then we laughed. I finished my beer and said that I had to be leaving.

"Stick around, man," Max said. "The place is a desert."

"I really do have to finish some work," I said.

"Have one more beer anyway, Blake," Harry said.

"I'd like to, but I have to get home."

"All right. Then go home."

I said I would see them around, and I left. Grace was lying on the day bed when I came into the apartment. I saw immediately that the ashtray on the coffee table in front of her was full of cigarette butts. She must have smoked half a pack of cigarettes in the time I had been gone. I asked her how she felt.

"A little rocky," she said. "But it will go away. Was the show good?"

"One of them. The treasure picture."

"What was it about?"

"Some guys who spent a lot of time digging up gold only to have it blow away in a wind storm."

"Sounds delightful. Don't you like happy pictures, Blake?"

"Sometimes."

I gave her the paper and told her the fight pictures were in it.

"Oh, God. Take it away. Please. I couldn't stand to see them."

"I know how you feel," I said.

"Wasn't it a shame though?"

"Yes. It was rotten."

"Hand me one of those cigarettes, please, Blake."

"I know this sounds stuffy," I said, "but aren't you smoking too much?"

She smiled. "You're right. Old Doctor Blake."

I told her I had run into Max and Harry and this started us on a conversation about them. As she talked I became aware of the fresh perfume she must have put on not too long ago.

"I don't understand it," she said. "Harry shouldn't have any trouble getting a girl. He's good looking and intelligent. What's wrong?"

"A lot of things, I gather," I said. "One of them is he doesn't believe very much in himself."

"He needs a woman who'll make him believe in himself."

"Where does he get her?"

"Somewhere. He has to keep looking. I wish I knew of one I could steer him to."

This was as good a time as any to ask her.

"Tell me something, will you, Grace?" I said. "What do you see in Porter?"

She did not answer me right away. She looked around the room and not at me.

"Maybe you would rather not talk about it," I said. "It really isn't any of my business."

"I'm very confused about it, Blake?" she said finally. "He's changed since I first knew him. I don't know just what to do about it."

"Perhaps he is a lot nicer when he is alone with you," I said.

"He is. Outside he gets sort of hysterical."

"That isn't all he gets."

"I know. It's a problem with me. I'll have to solve it very soon."

"He's quite a boy," I said.

"I feel dependent on him. I don't know just why. I can't explain it."

"Well, maybe you will find out."

"I think I could go for something to eat now."

"I'll go across the street for some spaghetti. We can have some spaghetti with a bacon and egg-yolk sauce, and a big salad."

"Sounds tremendous," she said. "I'll make some coffee."

I went downstairs and across the street and bought the spaghetti and bacon and the stuff for a salad. Some of the men from the social club were having a crap game in a doorway near the street light two fat women were sitting on a doorstep watching the game.

Back in the apartment Grace was boiling the water for the coffee. I told her to lie back down on the day bed, that I would fix everything. She said she wanted to help but I knew she was not supposed to walk around much. She turned on the radio and sat down on the day bed, propping herself up with the cushions.

"Oh. I forgot to tell you the phone rang while you were gone," she said.

"It could not have been anything important," I said. "But if it is they will call again."

"Doesn't it worry you to miss phone calls like that?"

"It used to. But not any more."

I tried to think of who it might have been. The most likely people probably would call again. The spaghetti was soon ready and the salad took just a couple of minutes to put together. I carried all the food into the next room and put it on the coffee table.

"Where did you learn to make this kind of spaghetti?" she asked me. "It's wonderful."

"An Italian waiter I used to know told me how."

"Do you like the Italians, Blake?"

"I like you."

"I don't mean me."

"I don't know enough of them to really say."

Grace did not say anything for a moment, then she said, "I often wish I weren't a wop."

"You're not a wop."

"Oh, yes I am. Every Italian in this country is a wop. The people in this country think there is no such thing as a decent Italian. They're wops and ginzoes."

"Are you so sure of that?"

"Yes. And so are you. Everybody thinks the Italians are dirt. They class them with the Negroes."

"Only the stupid people do," I said. "And besides, they think that way only about the kind of Italians around here."

"You're wrong, Blake. Do you know what it is like to try to get into a country club if you're a wop? They wouldn't touch you with a thirty-foot pole."

"I don't know. I really can't argue about it."

"It's worse than being a Jew. At least anti-Semitism is aboveboard. But nobody even talks about anti-Italianism. Democracy. What a laugh. You would think the wops killed Christ." And she added, "You don't know how lucky you are being an Anglo-Saxon."

"I'm sorry, Grace. I did not know it was that way."

"I'm sorry I got excited, Blake. Let's drop it. It's too depressing a subject. The salad is wonderful."

I went into the kitchen and brought out the coffee. There was a news commentator on the radio now. I dialed him off and got some music.

"Would you like to have kids, Blake?"

"Sure I would," I said, putting cream in both our coffees.

"I don't think there is any point in a man and woman being together very long unless they have kids. Do you?"

"It's quite a project to have kids these days."

"What makes you say that?"

"Oh, all the insecurities. Jobs. Money. People breaking up. The kids getting the worst of it."

"Don't you ever expect to have kids?"

"I think about it sometimes. But it takes a lot of nerve to go through all that business. I'm not sure I could swing it."

"I think you could, Blake."

"Thanks. But I'm not so sure."

"I think if you really want to have them, you will."

"You're probably right," I said.

I turned off the lamp near me so that it would be cooler in the room. I felt comfortable and relaxed now. The meal had not been too bad. It could have been worse. I would have wanted it fancier for Grace. When I ate alone it did not matter much what the food was. I was thinking about how much nerve I had as Grace finished her coffee.

"You know what really scares me?" she said after a couple of minutes.

"Tell me."

"People not liking me. I'm always afraid people don't like me much. I want lots of people to like me."

"That's the way everybody else feels."

"I'm sure it is. But when I'm around people I always feel they have some kind of strength I don't have. Some kind of an edge on me."

"Well they don't."

"I wish I could believe that."

"Work on it. It comes after a while. It really does." What the hell are you being so philosophical for? I asked myself. Who do you think you are? The Rockefeller of experience? Why don't you set up a foundation?

We listened to the radio for a while. When we got tired of that I suggested a game of gin rummy. Grace was a very good player. She beat me two games running.

"Nuts," I said, after the second game. "I give up."

"You weren't concentrating, that's all."

"That's what you think."

"It must be late."

"Sort of. Do you want to go to sleep?"

"I think I had better. I'm whipped."

"Hypochondriac."

She thought that was funny. After doing a few things she was finally in bed.

"I feel bad kicking you out of your bed," she said.

"If we talk about that much more I'll begin to feel bad, too," I said.

"You're terrific, Blake. Kiss me good night?"

We kissed. I liked it but just the same I felt funny doing it. For all of the obvious reasons. We said good night and I turned the bedroom light out and started closing the door of the bedroom.

"You don't have to do that," she said through the darkness.

"Do what?"

"Close the door."

"I thought you might want it closed."

"Not all the way. I like to hear you."

"All right."

I left the door open a little and went into the next room and undressed in the semidarkness there. I put a couple of sheets on the day bed and then turned out the lights and lay down. I lay awake hearing Grace breathing. After a while her breathing changed, meaning she must be asleep. That relaxed me, knowing she was asleep.

CHAPTER XXIV

The clean morning sun slanting through the Venetian blinds woke me up the next morning. It was Tuesday. I bathed my face and neck and brushed my teeth, and went downstairs for the mail and the morning paper. I always hoped my box would be full of letters. There was nothing in it this time. I walked around the corner and bought the *Times* and read the headlines as I walked back up the street already noisy with the women shopping at the push carts.

Grace was awake when I got back upstairs. She was still in bed. I asked her how things went.

"Great doc," she said, yawning.

Then I saw the circles under her eyes and knew she must have had a bad night. Well, she could stay in bed all day and that would bring her around some. I went into the kitchen so that she could get out of bed. In a little while we were having orange juice and coffee and a soft-boiled egg each. Her appetite was better.

I gave her part of the paper, and I looked through the want ads. Nothing very good there. Many "cute" ads for advertising copywriters. For "live wires."

"What are you going to do today?" Grace asked.

"Get a haircut for one thing. After that I don't know."

"Don't worry about staying around here, Blake. I'm much better now. There is a lot I can do to keep busy."

"I don't like the idea of leaving you alone," I said. "Something might come up."

"No it won't, I'm sure it won't now. You don't have to be a nursemaid to me all day, Blake."

"I'm not nursemaiding you."

"Yes you are. But you don't have to now."

"All right. But I want you to take it easy while I'm out. Understand?"

"I will."

We had a second cup of coffee. Then I told Grace I would see her for lunch and went out to get a haircut. I walked over to Sullivan Street and up Sullivan to the park. It was so young-green and fresh-feeling in the morning park and already sitting on the benches among the young mothers and their children were the local bums, reading the newspapers. It seemed early for them, but there they were. I had seen them many times but we never spoke. Perhaps we should have. I guess I felt superior to them.

Then up to Eighth Street. I looked into the window of a silversmith shop to see if a friend of mine had got to work yet, but there were no lights on in the shop. From the outside the place did not look prosperous. But it really was. That was a lesson in something or other. Along Eighth to Sixth Avenue and through the heavy traffic there and on to Greenwich, and looking up the small-windowed steepness of the Women's Prison but seeing no one looking out. Maybe they were having their morning civics class.

"You are the first this morning," the barber said as I entered the small shop and sat in one of the big chairs. "Nobody's been in yet."

"It is early," I replied. Already I felt the peculiar drowsiness that I always felt in a barbershop no matter what time of day it was. I tried to keep it from getting any stronger. I don't know why I did not like it.

"Don't take too much off," I told him.

"I know. I never take too much off."

He did though. In the barbershop drowsiness I thought of Samson in Gaza. Then the barber rubbed perfumed witch hazel on my neck. There was nothing I could do about it. I paid and tipped him and left. The drowsiness left me when I started walking outside. I thought about what I could do now and after turning down several things in my mind decided to run up to Stillman's Gym to watch the boxers train. I had plenty of time. I got on an Eighth Avenue sub-way and went uptown.

When I got to Stillman's Bobby Brown was sparring with a Negro boy in one of the two rings. They were good welter-weights, both of them. Most of the seats at the ringside were taken. The managers and trainers and bookies and hard-faced young boxers were standing behind the ringside seats. Directly across from where I was standing, on the other side of the two rings, several boxers were shadow boxing and doing push-ups and being wiped off with towels by their trainers.

In the other ring two white heavyweights were pushing each other around. Neither one looked very good. They were big and strong but they were slow and clumsy. In two or three years they would be slightly punchy. Now Brown dropped the Negro boy with a left hook, and the bell rang and Brown helped the Negro boy get up from the floor.

"I like that Brown," a man next to me said. "He is a very good hooker. A little more polish and he'll be right up there."

"Oh, he's good," someone replied. "Brown is a tough boy. All he needs is a little more polish. But he'll get that."

Two other sets of fighters came into the rings now after their names and weights were announced over a loud-speaker in the gym. One of the fighters was a Mexican boy who was already becoming a punching bag. He was game and strong but he had been hit too often in the head and now his reflexes were going. The boy boxing with him looked very good against him.

"They ought to sell that poor bastard to a glue factory," a man standing next to me said. I guessed he was talking about the Mexican boy.

"Or send him back to Mexico," I said.

"It's the same thing," he said.

The bell rang and they stopped fighting. A trainer with a sweat shirt on leaned through the ring and spoke to the boy fighting the Mexican. He made motions showing his boy the way he should hit when they were in close. The boy nodded his head. The bell rang and they were fighting again.

The Mexican boy's nose bled all through the round. Then the fighters in both rings left the rings and two new pairs of fighters came in. I stayed to watch a couple of middleweights who were hard hitters and not too bad as boxers. One was Georgie Flood. I made a mental note to watch the papers to see how he did in his fights.

I bought a Coca-Cola and drank it watching Flood and left the gym when I had finished drinking it. In the corridor of the gym were several posters announcing different fights to be held soon at local clubs. They had not yet got around to taking down two posters of the Coster-Phelps fight.

Back downtown in the apartment I put the lunch groceries I had bought in the kitchen and went into the front room where Grace was sitting reading, now dressed.

"You had too much taken off," she said, looking at my haircut.

"It always happens."

"Men always get the worst haircuts. They all look as though they were in the Army."

"They would look strange if they didn't get their hair cut this way."

"They would look prettier if they didn't," Grace said.

"That's just it."

She asked me what I had bought for lunch. I told her and she said it sounded very good. She asked me if those hotdog carts ever came around the streets. I said they did on Saturdays. I had not seen them during the week. She said she loved hot dogs with mustard and sauerkraut and relish.

"I can't stand it," I said. "Let's eat."

"I'll fix it. You've done enough around here."

In a few minutes she had made sandwiches of the cold cuts and had put the potato salad on dishes. She opened the quart of beer too. I drank a glass of it, fast, before eating.

"All we need is some grass and we would have a picnic," she said.

"And ants."

"Ants? All picnics don't have ants."

"All I've ever been on did."

"Let's not have any ants at this picnic."

"Okay, romanticism. Anything you say."

Afterward Grace washed the dishes and I finished drinking the quart of beer. Then we sat around and talked an she told me about her job and how much she disliked it and that she was going to look for another one soon. I wrote a couple of letters taking a long time on each one because I did not have much to say in them. We played a couple of hands of gin rummy. We took a game each. Then Grace said she wanted to lie down for a while.

"Everything is all right, isn't it?" I asked.

"Yes. It's just that I could use a little sleep right now."

She went into the bedroom and drew the blind. I started reading *Victory* again and in a little while I knew she must be asleep. I finished a couple of chapters in the book and became restless. There was nothing to do except take a walk and sit in the park. From the way Grace was breathing now I was fairly certain she would be sleeping for at least an hour. Just in case though, I wrote a note saying I had gone out for a walk and left it on the coffee table, and went out.

I walked first to the circle when I got to the park. The rim of the circle was crowded with sitters. Some children were playing in the center where the fountain was. That fountain had been dry a long time. I watched the children play for a few minutes, looked around to see if there was anyone I knew and wanted to talk to on the rim of the circle, and, seeing no one, I went into the park itself and picked an empty bench in the shade and sat down where I could see the people walking in the lanes in the park alone or with their friends, and those they loved.

Then Cap Fields came up.

"What a day, man," he said, sitting down with me. "What a day."

"You look beat," I said, kidding him. "At the end of your rope."

"At the end of my rope is right, Jack. I'm really hung up."

Then stopping for a moment, "Say, what a great pun that was. Rope. Hemp is rope. Tea from hemp. Great. Get it?"

"Yes," I said. "It's not bad. But what is hanging you up?"

"That's it. No rope. No charge. Nothing. I don't even have a Benzedrine inhaler."

"Can't you promote any?"

"Don't think I haven't tried. Nobody is around. And on top of all that my chick took a powder on me."

"How come?"

He shrugged.

"My story wasn't sensitive enough for her, I guess. She was a real aesthetic chick. She met a poet and went off to Fire Island with him. He had a very sensitive story."

I told him I was sorry to hear it, and asked him what he was going to do with the summer.

"Get out of town, I hope," he said. "I don't think I can make this town another summer. Friend of mine wants me to go down South to a Jewish training farm with him."

"What's that?"

"It's a place where they train Jewish people for work in Israel. Army work and reconstruction. Stuff like that."

I said I could not easily see him on a training farm or going to Israel.

"I can't either," he said. "But maybe I'll go anyway. Who can tell? You never know what might happen."

"No. You don't."

He said hello to a couple of people who walked by and it seemed to me that they paused in their walking and saying hello to see if they would be invited to sit down with us. But Cap made no such gesture, nor did I because I did not know who they were, and they went on.

"Very draggy, those two," Cap said. "Good people to stay away from."

"Thanks. I'll remember that."

He lit a cigarette and after he had taken a few puffs he said, "I have to get something to quiet myself down. I'm jumping all over the place."

I said sure. He got up and said he was going to have a beer somewhere. He apologized for being too jumpy to stay with me longer.

After Cap had gone I sat there watching the people in the park for about fifteen minutes more and then I left the park and walked up Greenwich Avenue for the second time that day, this time to the library.

In the library I went to the magazine rack in the back and got a copy of the *Atlantic* and sat down at one of the long tables to read it. Two seats away from me an old man was snoring loud. I read an article on Bikini and a couple of short stories that were almost interchangeable. After the *Atlantic* I looked at the *Nation,* the old man's snoring making it impossible to concentrate on anything. Then I left that noisy table and walked up front and looked quickly at the shelves of recently published books, opened one and leafed through it, and put it back and went out.

Now the soft-edged late-afternoon light was in the streets, and it was quieter than it had been earlier, and cooler.

Back at the apartment I looked in my mailbox but it was empty. Grace was just waking up when I came in.

She yawned loud in exaggeration. "I've had the finest sleep."

"You needed it."

I dropped the note I had left on the coffee table into the waste basket. Grace came into the room now and took my face in her hands and kissed me on the cheek.

"Nice cheek. Smooth."

"It is, huh?"

"That's what I said, huh."

She went into the bathroom and took a shower. I listened to the radio while she was showering. When she came out she sat on the day bed across from my chair and lit a cigarette. I took one too She looked better now.

"I think I will go home tonight, Blake," she said.

"You don't have to."

"You're sweet. But I feel all right now. And I've been in your hair long enough."

"I haven't got any hair for you to be in," I said. "You haven't been any trouble," I added after a moment.

"I knew you would say that. But I think I'd better go anyway."

"All right then. Are you going to stay around for dinner?"

"Do you think I want to eat alone?"

Later, after we had had dinner in the apartment from stuff I had gone to buy, she asked me if I would get a cab for her. I phoned for one. I was very sorry she was leaving this night instead of tomorrow. But I was not going to persuade, or try to persuade her to stay over.

"What can I say Blake?"

"Why say anything? I'll see you then when we go to Harry's place?"

She said yes.

The downstairs bell sounded. It was the cab. We kissed so long, and I walked downstairs with her and saw her into the cab. She waved from the window of the cab as it drove off, and I waved back, watching the cab drive out of sight.

CHAPTER XXV

A little later on that night I went to the Sporting Club for a drink. I stayed just long enough to finish the drink. I did not talk to anyone at the bar, as I sometimes did when I was there alone. A girl who was always there was now sitting in a booth with four people and talking loud about how she had been donating her services to raise money for Israel. She was a gentile girl who for some reason was trying to become Jewish. She frequently spoke with a mock Jewish accent.

I left the Sporting Club and walked three blocks to a new bar on Houston Street where there was an unusually large and clear television screen. I watched three innings of a game between the Dodgers and the Phillies. There was something irritating about not being able to see the whole game going on at once. About seeing it in sections.

Then I took a walk along Houston Street for several blocks going east and cut back to my place.

While I was undressing the phone rang. It was Joan. She was going away for the rest of the summer, to a place in Massachusetts and she was calling to say good-by. We talked for a couple of minutes but there was really nothing we had to say. We finally managed to say good-by. Well, that was over with.

I went to bed in the big bed that Grace had been sleeping in. It felt exciting sleeping there now. I imagined it was still warm from her body.

The check from my uptown friend was in the mail the next morning, Wednesday. After breakfast in my place I went downtown to report to the unemployment office, and after that was over with I went to the bank at Sheridan Square where I cashed my unemployment checks—one of the minor officials in the bank O.K.'d the checks so that I could cash them there. But he did this only after a long conversation about cashing checks that were not drawn on this particular bank. He made me feel un-wanted.

I finally got out of the bank with the money in my pocket. I needed a couple of new shirts, so I went uptown to buy them while I still had the money. After I bought the shirts at a shop on Madison Avenue the day seemed to become part of the night before, without end. I went to a Broadway theatre to see a movie from a novel I had liked, and that took three hours, with a stage show I hardly remembered after it was all over, and I had lunch in a famous oyster house where they also served hot meat sandwiches, and I walked up Broadway to Fifty-Ninth, came back downtown to the Museum of Modern Art, looked at shows on all three floors and afterward sat outside in the gar-den among the Calder mobiles and had a glass of iced coffee, watched two pickups in the hour I was there, came back down-town on a slow Fifth Avenue bus, feeling the evening endless before me, showered at my apartment, then read *Victory* for as long as I could stand Heyst and his troubles, and now hungry, started calling up people who might be available for dinner with me.

I called all of the people I saw more or less regularly and finding none of them home I called some people I had not seen in some time for the simple reason that they did not particu-larly interest me, but now I wanted very much to have dinner with somebody. But they were either out or they already had dinner dates, and some of them seemed quite surprised to be hearing from me. I even called Gloria. But she was out. Then I would have dinner alone. But I put it off.

I went out and walked up to Sixth Avenue and Bliss Street to a better-than-average bar and had two drinks at the bar and after my second drink, feeling tight, the drinks being real drinks, Manhattans, not beer, and feeling better, they brought the hors d'oeuvres around on a big platter and because I was tight on two drinks I helped myself generously to the sardine and lox and chicken liver on toast, and had a third drink.

This was much, much better—the third drink. Everybody at the bar but me had someone to talk to, everybody except an old woman who was talking to the not-listening bartender and getting drunk on old fashioneds. I looked around for a woman who might be on the make but none was there, they were all talking to somebody already. Then I left that bar and went to a corner newsstand to buy a paper to read while I was having dinner so that I would have something to do, eating alone, and not be hung up with my hands on the table before me trying to feel and look composed and happy. Then dinner. Dinner in a place where I walked down a flight of stairs, almost stumbling on the last step because it was partly hidden from view. I took as long as possible eating dinner. Read the paper through, even parts I ordinarily skipped. Looked several times at a woman sitting alone a couple of tables away but I could not think of a way of approaching her there in the restaurant so I forgot about it, or at least told myself I had forgotten about it.

Felt people looking at me sitting alone but I tried to ignore this. Everybody at the other tables laughing and drinking and talking and with someone, seeming to be having a good time. Then felt the waiter waiting for me to pay up and leave so that two people could take my table who were now standing at the entrance talking and watching those people who seemed about to leave. I paid up and left, leaving my completely read newspaper on the table for the people who would take my place there. They could have it.

Outside now thinking of a place to go where something might possibly happen. Walked through the park, now in semi-darkness and cool with the semidarkness, voices coming from along the sides of the walks away from the lights where you could just see the people sitting on the secluded benches. Through the coolness of the park down to another bar I had not been to in a long time where nothing had ever happened to speak of but where something might now happen, although this night was no different really from the other nights. Feeling a slight unevenness in my as-much-as-I-could-control it walk. Feeling a slight unevenness in my head too but enjoying that.

Walking several blocks to this bar, across Sixth Avenue and down West Fourth Street and then down Lane Street toward the river. I knew the waitress at this place. She did a little hustling on the side but only with businessmen who did not mind spending money on her. She was nice.

"Long time no see," she said. "Or something like that. I thought you moved away."

"I did. I just came back to lay a wreath."

"The place isn't that bad."

"I didn't mean that. Will you have a drink?"

"Thanks. I will. Scotch. Can you afford Scotch?"

"Of course."

We had a drink together and then she went away and into the restaurant part to wait tables. The bar was noisy and crowded with Irish and Spanish seamen and the juke box was playing so loud in the smallness of the bar that I could barely hear any of the conversations around me. It was just as well. After two drinks the place got noisier and duller and I nodded my head good-by to the waitress who was looking into the bar from the restaurant and went out and walked to another place not too far away. In that bar I had carefully avoided looking at the clock because when I felt the way I did then it was very bad to look at clocks.

In this next bar I did see someone I knew, a painter-sculptor with his girl but they were on their way out to a friend's house so we just said hello and good-by. Two drinks at this bar. Getting drunk. Looking down the bar at all the people wondering if somewhere there was an interesting conversation, or a potential pickup. Saw nothing and when I finished the drink I was on I left.

Then I walked unsteadily back toward the Sporting Club Bar. I saw a crowd at the corner of Sixth Avenue and Fourth Street and I went to it. Members of the local Sacco-Vanzetti

206 c Chandler Brossard

branch of the Communist party were giving speeches, one man standing on a stepladder platform where an American flag was hanging. He was talking about our government's relations with the Soviet Union. Then some boys started booing him and as they were booing him a woman started shouting from near the stepladder.

"Get down off that platform, you Communist son of a bitch," she yelled, and walked out of the crowd and to the stepladder. It was a lesbian and she was drunk. She swore at the speaker again and the boys clapped and egged her on.

"You dirty lying yellow bastard. Get down off that platform. Get away from the American flag. We don't want bastards like you in this country," she shouted.

Some of the people in the now quite large crowd laughed and the boys clapped and whistled and the les kept interrupting the speaker. The speaker tried not to notice her but finally he began asking her to stop heckling him, saying that everybody in this country had freedom of speech.

"Can't you be decent and go away?" he asked her from his platform.

"Be decent, my ass. Get down off there you f . . . ing Commie."

The speaker's two fellow members, a man and a woman down below, looked nervous and afraid, the boys shouting against them and nobody in the crowd showing sympathy.

"If you don't get down off there, you bastard, I'm coming up," the les shouted. "You stinking bum. You bastards want to spoil this country."

"Look," the speaker said. "I don't want any trouble with you. Now why don't you behave yourself?"

The les started up the stepladder of the platform. One of the boys went to the platform and laughing back at his friends took the American flag from the platform and shoved it into the hands of the woman Communist. She kept it in her hands and spoke to her friend and they seemed to be arguing now. There were no police around to protect this meeting. I was quite drunk now and felt unreal about what was going on in front of me.

"Get away from here, you crumby bastard," the les shouted, now on the platform with the speaker who had given up his speech. The les started swearing and shouting about the Communists and taking her clothes off to humiliate the man.

The crowd laughed and the boys yelled and whistled. I was dizzy and unable to move.

"You Jew bastard," the les shouted. She took her shirt off and threw it into the crowd and there she was with only a black brassiere on her top. The crowd clapped.

"Don't get me wrong," the les said to the crowd, "I'm not against the Jews. My wife is Jewish."

Then she grabbed the man and tried to throw him off the platform. She stopped that, and said if he didn't get down she would take off all her clothes. She took off her brassiere. The crowd yelled as she stood there her bare breasts big and white in the light from the street lamp.

"You are scum," the speaker said to her. "Stupid, vicious scum." Then he turned to the crowd. "Won't someone please help me get rid of this woman so the meeting can go on?"

No one moved.

"Want to make everybody slaves," the les shouted.

She started taking off her skirt. The speaker looked at her and then shrugged and jumped down off the platform. The les stayed up on the platform, barebreasted, and told the crowd what she thought of Communists in this country.

I walked away. I walked unsteadily up Sixth Avenue and then cut into a side street and walked to the Sporting Club Bar. The unrealness in me persisting. The bar was jammed. I pushed through the people to the bar.

"What do you say, Mister Blake?" Mike asked at the bar.

"It's a long story," I managed to reply.

I knew now that I could not really carry on any sort of a conversation with anybody, or too successfully pick up anybody, that all I could do was watch. You had to get your kicks some-how. Many touristing uptown people there.

The juke box was playing Khatchaturian's Saber Dance sung by the Andrews Sisters. It sounded like the swan song of my decade. After that there could be nothing. I saw several people alone the way I was. And I saw two people I had seen before that night at the other bars. I knew that if I went to another place I would eventually see one or the other there, too. I did not like to look at them. I looked only at the people in groups.

A glass smashed to the floor and at my side the surly young Italian waiter was moving quickly through the crowd to clean up the broken glass. Then I saw a too-intense-looking man going from group to group staring into their faces and trying to get into their conversations but they very soon gave him the brush-off or some of them did not even listen to him and he went away, looking into other faces, turning abruptly if a face looked invit-ing, going up and down the entire place that way. He must have seen me looking at him because there he was next to me.

"Do you know Bernie Marks?" he asked me, staring into my face. He looked slightly insane.

"Well maybe this description will help you remember him. He wears black-rimmed glasses and—"

"But I don't know the guy," I said.

I turned my back on him. He was too far gone for anybody to help him. I asked Mike for another drink. I turned around and the slightly insane-looking man was gone. He was standing at a booth trying to get into a conversation. He gave me a very bad feeling.

I finished my drink. The good effect of the drinks had worn off and now I just felt heavy and it was getting late and I was tired of standing around alone, so I left. On my way home, walking unsteadily and heavily, I went by the Mills Hotel with the drunks passed out lying on the sidewalk and in the door-ways, their empty pints of cheap wine lying near them, and the smell of piss and wine and body dirt all around them, some standing together very drunkenly trying to talk, holding on to each other for support, and walking by them I thought of my old man so long ago. The old man drunk and dirty and rolled of his money after being away for days, and crying and not knowing where he had been. The old man trying to argue with me when he was drunk like this, trying to tell me what I should do with myself, and I trying to listen and pleading with him to go to bed and not get drunk any more. Knowing the people in our neighborhood had all seen him staggering drunk through the streets, and hating that knowledge.

Then a young drunk came off the side of the hotel building and staggered in front of me and asked for some money.

"To get something to eat," he said.

I gave him a quarter.

"Why don't you ever say you're going to buy a drink with it?" I asked him. "You don't want to get anything to eat."

"Ah, thank you, Johnny," he said. "Thank you a million, Johnny. You're a pal. My name is Quinn," and he took some crumpled papers from his pocket to identify himself to me. I started walking away.

"God bless you, Johnny," he shouted after me. "God-bless you. Buddy Johnny."

Then I was past the Mills Hotel feeling a sort of soberness now, but still walking unsteadily. Finally at my apartment, and upstairs. I did not bother to turn the lights on. I undressed in the semidarkness of the front room and then went into the bedroom and fell on the big double bed. I lay there naked and unsleeping looking up at the ceiling, the room partly lit by the moon, and listened to the social-club men on the street talking about baseball.

After a while there came the steadily grinding noise of the trash-collecting truck chewing up the refuse of the day, the refuse that had been left in the street.

The grinding up of the refuse went on and on. I began to feel a little sorry for myself and thought of loneliness and what it does to you. What a terrible thing it was. But I knew that it was no use feeling sorry for yourself that way, now permitted by the alcohol, because it just made things worse. Everybody was alone and everybody was going through the same thing, all of the time, and if you didn't beat it, loneliness, if you were not able to live with it and keep it down, if you were not able to stop yourself from doing all sorts of things you really did not want to do only because you were lonely, then it had you beat and that was the end of you.

Nobody was going to help you not be lonely, and I knew— lying there listening to that grinding up of refuse—that the more you showed your loneliness the less people wanted anything to do with you, and once that started, once people saw you doing things because you were lonely, once you were tapped as a lonely person, you were finished.

The grinding up of the refuse went on and on, and finally I fell asleep.

CHAPTER XXVI

The day we were all going up to Harry Lees's place on the Cape I met Porter and Grace, after Porter had called me, in Grand Central Station, just after breakfast. He said Max was going to meet us up there. He had bought my ticket for me already to save time.

"Pay me later for it, sport," he said.

"No. I'll pay you what I owe you now."

I paid him what the ticket cost and we went out into the waiting room and stood by the gate of the track our train was leaving on. Grace looked much better now. I tried to act as though I had not seen her since the night we had all gone to the fights.

"What have you been doing with yourself?" Porter asked me.

"Working," I said.

"Glad to hear it, man. Do you good. Your morale was getting pretty low there."

"Oh, God," Grace said, "let's leave morale alone for a while."

Then she said, "It's really swell that you are going with us, Blake. Train rides are always better if there are lots of people along. Don't you think so?"

"Yes."

"Come on," Porter said. "The train is ready."

We walked down the steps with the crowd and to the train, and after walking through four cars of the train we came to a car that was new and air-conditioned, and we got seats there. The other cars were old and dirty-looking. We pushed the back of one seat forward so that both our seats faced.

"Doesn't it feel funny not to be facing the direction you are going in?" Grace asked me, after the train had started.

"Slightly," I said.

"It gives you a kind of advantage," said Porter, looking up from the book he was reading. "At least you can see where you have been."

The conductor came up our aisle now and punched our tickets. I expected him to say something about the way we were sitting, but he did not. After a while I got tired of looking out of the window at the Connecticut scenery, and I began to read *Victory*. Grace was reading a fashion magazine. We did not talk much during the trip. We stopped at Bridgeport and New Haven and New London. After we pulled away from Falmouth the conductor came through our car announcing our stop. Porter left his seat to get a drink of water.

"Hello," Grace said, pushing her foot against my leg.

"Hi. Porter seems refreshed by his little trip."

"So was I."

Porter came back carrying a cup of water.

"You looked thirsty," he said, giving the water to Grace.

She drank half of it and gave the cup to me. I wasn't thirsty but I liked the idea of sharing the water with her, and in front of Porter. The train jerked to a slow stop and we were at Brant Landing. As soon as we got off the train we saw Harry Lees looking into the crowds for us. He saw us and waved and walked toward us.

"Max is coming on a later train," Porter told him.

"Okay," Harry said. "We'll take one of these cabs to the house."

We got into a black sedan whose driver seemed to know Harry.

"It's only a short ride from here to the house," Harry said.

"I can already smell the ocean," Grace said, breathing deep. "It's marvelous."

"Isn't it?" Porter said. "Like breathing for the first time."

We drove through the small seaside town with its one-story buildings and its summer residents walking around in sports and bathing clothes and then beyond the town toward the ocean and the houses on the beach. We came onto the road running along the back of the beach and suddenly there was the ocean before us, a salt breeze blowing in steadily from it.

"We are here," Harry said, as the driver pulled up behind a new two-story beach bungalow.

We all contributed and paid the cab driver and went inside. The house was pleasantly furnished and comfortable-looking. Very clean. Harry told us we would use the bedrooms upstairs, and we followed him upstairs to them. Each bedroom had twin beds. Porter and Grace put their stuff in one bedroom and I took one by myself. Harry's room was downstairs.

"I'll fix you a drink," Harry said. "Make you forget the train ride."

I was alone now in my room. I changed clothes, putting on a pair of old khaki trousers and tennis shoes, and went into the bathroom to wash up. I heard Porter and Grace talking in their room. I finished washing off the train dirt and went downstairs.

"The place looks great," I said to Harry when he brought out the drinks.

"I'm going to spend the summer here," he said. "Just go to New York on weekends."

"Sounds like you've got it beat," I said.

"Does it?"

"A good deal of it anyway."

The whisky drink in the morning and the sharp salt air and the feeling of lightness and space that was really the best part of the seashore, were all making me feel new and excited and glad I had come there. Porter and Grace came in now. They were in their bathing suits. "God, what a figure," Harry said, looking at Grace. "How do you rate this, Porter?"

"You've got me," Porter said.

"Really first class," Harry went on.

Grace laughed. She took one of the highballs from the table and sipped at it. Porter did the same, but after a swallow he put the glass back on the table.

"Well?" he said, looking around. "What are we all waiting for? Let's go in."

"I feel like sitting around for a while," I said. "Why all the rush?"

"Come with us, Blake," Grace said.

"You go ahead. I'll be along later."

"I'm not going in until this afternoon," said Harry. "I have to fix some broken plumbing."

"Let's leave these corpses, Grace," Porter said.

"You'll come later?" Grace asked me as they were going out.

"In about twenty minutes," I said.

Grace and Porter went out and we watched them walk down the beach to the ocean. Porter spurted suddenly down the beach, running into the water then diving into a breaker as it rose up rolling to the beach.

"It really bothers that guy when people don't want to do what he wants them to do," said Harry, sitting down.

"He's just young and compulsive," I said.

"Is that it?"

"I don't know what it is, Harry."

"I'm going to say something funny. Why not call a spade a spade?"

"But I don't know whether that is his trouble."

"I think his camouflaging of it is."

"Don't begrudge the guy his camouflage. I have one. So do you."

"Not like his, Blake. You know what that guy's trouble is? He's spiritually incommunicado. You can't get to him. He won't let you."

"To hell with Porter."

"Okay. Do you want another drink?"

"No, thanks. I'm going in for a swim after this one."

Harry made himself another drink. I looked out of the open front door at Porter and Grace. He was trying to ride the breakers.

It was too rough to swim very much. You had to go out beyond the breakers.

Grace looked toward the house and waved at me. I waved back, and turned away from the door.

"Who else is coming, Harry?"

"Max and whoever he brings along. I couldn't get anybody. As usual."

"Always putting yourself down. Well, I'm going to get into my trunks."

"You can wear my beach robe if you want to, Blake."

"Thanks, old sport."

"You're welcome, old sport."

I got into my trunks upstairs and put a towel around my neck and went back downstairs. Harry was looking out at the ocean.

"Don't you want the robe?"

"I don't think I'll need it."

"That sun is hot. You'd better take it, Blake."

"The towel will be enough, Harry. Besides," I said, "I'm not used to the luxury of it."

"Okay."

The phone rang as I was leaving the house.

"That must be Max," Harry said.

I walked along the concrete strip in front of the house, hearing Harry talking to Max on the phone, and onto the warm sand and down the beach to where Porter and Grace were sunning themselves.

"You finally made it," Grace said.

"The water is cold," Porter said. "But it's wonderful when you get used to it."

I dropped the towel on Grace and stood there watching the breakers forming and rising and piling in and then I ran very fast down the beach and into the surf, through it still running, and dived under a breaker as it broke over me, the shock of the cold water suddenly and completely all over me, now being carried backward to the beach by the piling breaker, falling back on the sand where I was dumped by the rolled-in breaker, and getting my breath.

"Get in there and fight," Porter shouted.

I went in again. I dived into the breakers for a few minutes, diving beneath them and other times jumping up to their crest, twisting my back to them as they broke so that I would be swept back to the beach by their breaking, constantly spitting out the salt water, and then I felt exhausted from the hard swimming, and so I came slowly in and walked, dripping and gasping and surf-spent, up the beach to Porter and Grace and lay down on the towel Grace had spread out for me.

"I'm beat," I said. "Absolutely."

"You'll feel like a million in a little while," Porter said.

"Wipe yourself dry and I'll rub some lotion on your back," Grace said to me. "You don't want to get burned."

I sat up after I had got my breath and wiped myself off and lay on my stomach and Grace rubbed me all up and down with the suntan lotion. She started to put another coat on.

"Hey," Porter said. "You'll use it all up. Save some for me, baby."

"There's enough to go around," she said.

She finished rubbing the lotion on my back and legs. Then I rubbed it over the rest of my body and lay back down. The sudden exhaustion had left me and I was just pleasantly tired, almost sleepy. Grace rubbed the lotion on Porter. When she had finished she began rubbing it on herself.

"Let me," I said.

"Will you?"

I rubbed it over her back and shoulders. I wanted to keep on rubbing her. I gave the bottle back to her and lay now face up, eyes closed against the hot sun.

"I could stay here for the rest of my life," Grace said. "Just lying here and listening to the surf and sunning myself."

"A lot of people do, in a manner of speaking," Porter said. "But they get mentally flabby."

"Who cares? Who wants to be so smart?"

"There's nothing wrong with being smart," Porter said.

"Oh yes there is," Grace said. "Plenty."

"What would you rather be? Sentimental?"

"I wouldn't mind," she said.

After we had rested in the sun we played catch on the beach. We were the only people on this stretch of the beach. It ran empty and smooth-packed for several hundred yards on each side of us before there were any other people.

"I'm not up to playing ball," Grace said in a couple of minutes, and lay back down on the towels.

I got tired of it, too, and Porter and I stopped playing and went back into the surf. Each of us by himself. I was rolled back to the beach several times by the breakers, and then I came out.

"I'm getting hungry," I said to Grace.

"Me, too. Let's have something good to eat, Blake. A big salad."

"Something more than that. I'm very hungry."

"All right. I won't let you starve."

Porter came out and we walked tiredly back up to the house. He said something about the surf but I was not listening to him.

CHAPTER XXVII

Max was drinking with Harry in the front room. We said hello to him and went upstairs to shower off the sticky salt water and to change back into our clothes. I showered first and went downstairs. Harry gave me a highball.

"Lunch is already fixed," he said. "We can eat any time."

"Where is your chick?" I asked Max.

"At her dentist's."

"You mean her analyst's?"

"Yes. Maybe she will come up tonight. I don't know."

After the swim and the running and the shower the drink was just what I wanted. Porter came down. He looked more dressed than the rest of us.

"Man," he said to Max. "You should dig that surf. It is really something. Knocked out."

"I will later. It won't go away."

"Would you care for a drink, Porter?" Harry asked.

"No, thanks, Harry. I don't like to drink at lunch time."

We finished our drinks waiting for Grace. She was down in a few minutes. Max looked her over carefully.

"I can never get it through my head that you are a wop," he said.

"Well, I am."

"I just can't believe it. You're too beautiful, and too smart to be one."

"You know better than that, Max," she said.

"Have a drink, Grace," Harry said.

"I'd love one."

Harry mixed Grace a drink, and we went in the kitchenette to eat. It was a simple lunch. Salad and cold cuts and fruit, already laid out on the table.

"But I was going to prepare this, Harry," Grace said.

"I had nothing better to do," said Harry. "You can fix the next meal."

"You can cook, too," Porter said.

"I can, too, old sport."

"Let's eat," I said.

Porter started a literary conversation with Max that lasted until we finished lunch. Max did not say much. After lunch Porter talked him into going for a walk with him down the beach. Grace did the dishes, and Harry and I sat in the front room. He mixed himself another drink. I told him I did not want another right away.

We talked about jobs in New York. I was getting sleepy. The surf noise was having that effect on me. Then Grace came in from the kitchen.

"I'm going to nap for a while," she said. "I feel so deliciously sleepy. See you later," and she went upstairs.

"You like her a lot, don't you, Blake?" Harry said.

"Yes."

"I'm very glad. You are much better than Porter."

"Thanks."

"It is so unusual when you really like somebody," he went on. "When somebody really likes you. You know something? You are about the only friend I have, Blake."

"You must have more friends than just me."

"No I don't. I really don't. Maybe it is my fault. I'm not sure. I have begun to feel that personal relations are nonexistent these days. Almost nobody has them any more. They are outdated. Everybody is out for himself and to hell with personal relations. You know?"

"You're right."

"It seems that the only people who have so-called personal relations are the noodles. It is a phenomenon of our time. The brighter people get, the less importance they seem to attach to friendship. As old Porter would say, it is part of our cultural configuration."

Harry poured himself another drink. I was sleepier now but I knew that Harry wanted to keep talking for a while. The least I could do was listen. I guess I really was his best friend. I did not want to admit it, either to him or to myself, because it was like something that was too difficult to handle. And I felt slightly cowardly about that.

"I keep wondering what it is about me that keeps things from happening," Harry said.

"It need not be anything about you, Harry. It may be just the way things are set up."

"Have you ever been terrified of anything for a long time, Blake? I mean scared sick?"

"Not for a long time."

"I have. You know what it is? I'll tell you. You are the only person I would tell. And I would not tell you unless I were drunk."

He looked past me out to the ocean before going on.

"I'm afraid of being queer," he said.

"Queer?"

"That's right. A fairy. I'm terrified that people might think I am a fairy. And that I might really be one and not know it."

"I don't think you are queer," I said, and I meant it.

"Maybe you don't. Blake. But it has been suggested to me. You know, whenever I go into a bar alone I can't stay there alone for very long without getting a sick feeling that people are looking at me and thinking I'm a fairy. All my life I've been scared like this. Particularly when I am with women. I am lousy with them. As you know."

"But you don't act like one, and you don't go with them."

"And the funny thing is," he said, "I don't like queers. And I really don't feel queer. That is, I like women. But I am still scared all the time."

"Maybe you are really scared of something else."

"I'll tell you something else. It might make you sick. Do you know why I was not in the Army?"

"No. Why?"

"Because I told the Army psychiatrist that I had had fairy relations with men."

"Had you?"

"No. But I was scared. I had to do something. I was afraid then that if I were taken into the Army I would crack up. I did not think I could make it. Do you know what else I did? All during the physical examinations I carried around with me a letter from a doctor saying I had an anxiety neurosis. So they would not induct me. And I was shaking all the time. Now I despise myself for it. You can't imagine how I feel about doing that."

"It must be horrible."

"And there was more, Blake. I would give my right arm if I could undo it." He stopped for a moment. "You must think I am pretty slimy now, don't you?"

"No. Forget it."

"Maybe I'm nuts."

We sat there in the front room not talking for what seemed a very long time. I did not know what to say to Harry after that. I sat there not speaking and looked out at the surf. Then Harry started crying, sobbing loud. I started to go over to him to say some-thing that might help. But he got up and walked out of the room and into his bedroom and slammed the door.

There was nothing I could do. I knew that. But I stayed downstairs anyway, just stood there. Then I went upstairs to my room and lay down, hoping I could sleep. I did after a while.

I woke up hearing the surf and lay on the bed listening to it before getting up. I did not know how long I had been sleeping. Then I began recalling what Harry had told me. And as I was doing this Grace came in.

"What time is it?"

"Late, late," she said, smiling. Then she looked at her wrist watch. "Four o'clock."

She sat down on the side of the bed.

"Your face is already a little red," I said.

"Is it?"

"Yes."

I pulled her down to me and we kissed.

"Ah, you darling Blake."

"I shouldn't do this."

"No. I want you to. Kiss me again. You darling."

Later we heard Porter and Max come in downstairs and we got up and Grace went into her bedroom and then downstairs before me. I followed her down. Porter was laughing at something Max had said.

"You capped me, man," he said. "You capped me."

"Where is Harry?" Grace asked.

"He went to the store to get some beer," Porter said. "We met him coming in."

"Come on, Blake," Grace said. "Let's play games."

She got out the cards and I put up the card table. I dealt a gin-rummy hand and was sorting my cards, promising ones, when Harry came in.

"Sleep well?" he asked, going into the kitchen with the beer.

"Very."

"The sleeping is very good up here."

He came back with some glasses and poured us all some beer.

"Beer," Max said. "Wish I had some charge."

"Why didn't you bring some up with you?" Harry asked him.

"Couldn't locate any. My connection said the town was clean."

"Well, you won't die."

Harry watched us play cards. I was sorry that he had unloaded to me. Not because it changed my opinion of him, which I was sure it had not, but because of the way he felt having told it. I was building up a good hand. I felt I could win. Max finished his beer and turned on the radio. He could not find anything good so he said he was going upstairs to sleep. Porter said he was going to do the same thing.

Grace and I finished our game with Harry watching us. He left us, and I won the first hand of the new game.

"You've got me," Grace said.

"I have?"

She looked at me and smiled and looked across the room to see if Harry were watching us, and he wasn't, and then she made a kissing gesture.

"Anybody want to take a walk before dinner?" Harry asked. "We might hear those mermaids singing. You haven't lived until you've heard those mermaids."

"Let's live then," Grace said, and we both got up.

Harry carried a glass of beer with him when we went out. We walked through the soft sand to the smooth-packed sand near the water. The tide was coming in. The breeze was cool and salty and smelled thin and clean as it blew in off the ocean. We walked down the empty, clean beach toward the jetty bouldering out into the ocean about half a mile down. A row of beach houses began at the jetty. A few people were on the beach in front of the houses.

We did not talk for quite a while. Until we came near the big bouldering jetty.

"Where did Max meet this girl who was supposed to come up?" Grace asked.

"He met her through a girl I once picked up at the Museum of Modern Art," Harry said.

"Really? But isn't that a strange sort of place to pick anybody up?"

"Not at all," Harry said. "The place is like a cultural call house. Some people just go there when they're on the make."

"I didn't know that. Did you know that, Blake?"

"Yes."

"Have you ever picked anybody up there?"

"Uh-huh. A couple of times."

"Is it difficult?"

"Not very," I said.

"What sort of girls are they?" Grace asked.

"The sort that like pictures," said Harry.

"Seriously."

"They're all right. Nicely dressed. Good-looking. Sort of intelligent. All alike."

"You know," said Harry. "The *modern* girl."

"That's amazing," said Grace.

Then we were at the black bouldering jetty, the waves smashing into it, the salt water spraying over the top. Two men were surf casting there. We walked on for about a hundred yards more and sat down high up on the beach, in the soft sand.

"It would be nice if you two were together," said Harry. "Why don't you be together? You should be."

"Let's not talk about it, Harry," said Grace. "There is so much to settle."

"Yes. Let's drop it," I said.

"All right. But what I said still goes."

We sat on the beach for about forty-five minutes. I wished I were there alone with Grace. But it was nice being there anyway, with the clean calmness of the beach and the ocean. Then we started back to the house. I saw that the two surf casters had not caught anything.

At the house Porter and Max were still upstairs. Grace went into the kitchen to see about dinner. Harry said he had some letters to write. I read. Porter came down in a few minutes, and playfully slapped me on the back.

"There are some fairly good things in that," he said about the book I was reading.

"It isn't bad at all."

"He has a certain style."

"So do you."

"What do you mean?"

"Everybody has a certain style about him," I said, getting out of saying what I really meant.

Max came down the stairs yawning. He looked out at the ocean in the twilight, and went into the kitchen.

"Hello, baby," he said to Grace. "What are you cooking up. Are you cooking up something good?"

"Wait and see."

"Where did you get all this suspense?" Porter asked her from the front room.

"I've had it all along."

Harry came in from writing letters in his room. He asked Max and Porter if they had slept well. They said yes.

"What do you do in this place?" Max asked. "What do you do? You swim and eat and lie around."

"Isn't there anything doing in town?"

"Not much," said Harry. "There is a bar with television. We can go there if you like. We can go there after dinner and then come back and have a night swim."

"Are there any women at this bar?" Max asked.

"Local stuff sometimes."

"Sounds promising."

We had pork chops and fried potatoes and a mixed salad for dinner. We had cold beer with the meal and then we had Camembert cheese and pears. Porter told us about a girl he knew who had just started going with a man who was a lush. But she did not know yet that he was a lush. Porter thought it was very funny that the girl did not know this when everybody else did.

"I hope you aren't going to tell her," Grace said.

"She'll have to find out sooner or later."

"It shouldn't hurt her too much," Max said. "She should know that everybody's life is sordid."

"Good old underground Max," Harry said.

"What's the matter?" he said. "Do you want everything to be nice?"

"Does it have to be sordid?" I said.

"It always seems to be. Harry wants life to be charming. Don't you, Harry?"

"Basically I guess I do," Harry said.

"You overvalue charm," Max said. "Charm just gets in the way. Like bric-a-brac."

I got up from the table and suggested that we walk to the bar now. I wanted to hear what other people talked about. What they got their fun from. We went out to the road behind the house and headed for the bar about a mile away. Grace walked with me, Harry and Porter and Max walking up ahead.

CHAPTER XXVIII

The bar was a small place with one row of booths besides the bar itself and a juke box in one corner. The juke box was playing as we came in. Two local-looking girls were standing by it, selecting records. The television screen was dark.

We were all going to sit at a booth but Harry said we would have to serve ourselves if we sat there, so instead we sat at the bar. Max watched the two girls at the juke box. We ordered beers. Harry insisted on paying for them. We drank the beers and talked and listened to the juke box. The two girls who had been at the juke box were now dancing with each other. Max said it was a dirty shame that two girls had to dance together.

When the record was finished Max went over to the girls. They were drinking Coca-Cola from bottles they kept on top of the juke box. They smiled shyly as Max talked to them, and when the music came on again he danced with one. The other one sat at a booth alone and watched them.

"There is something depressing about these small dark bars," Porter said. "I don't like them."

"This place is all right," Grace said. "You just have an edifice complex."

Harry and I both laughed at the pun. You could tell that although Porter thought it was funny too, it had got under his skin. You really could not rib him.

Porter began telling us about some people he had met in Philadelphia. They were in radio. They had invited him to visit them at a place they had on a lake somewhere in New Jersey. Porter had been very taken with them. He told us about a woman scriptwriter who had made passes at him.

"They were all live wires," he said. "Particularly this woman who does radio scripts. She makes five hundred dollars a week. She was panting down my neck all the time I was at this place."

"For Christ sake, Porter," I said. "Don't you have any better sense than to keep talking about it? Doesn't it occur to you that it might bother Grace?"

"That's all right, Blake," Grace said. "Let him talk. I don't care."

"What the hell," Porter said. "What difference does it make? We don't have a lease on each other. Besides, old sport, aren't you getting a little too solicitous about Grace?"

"Maybe I am. You just don't have any goddamn sense."

"Don't quarrel," Grace said, putting her hand on my arm. "Please."

"You had better tend to your own garden, Blake," Porter said.

"What a jerk," I said.

"Don't talk that way to me."

"Stop it. Both of you," Grace said.

"We'll have another beer," said Harry.

Harry asked the bartender to bring us some more beers. I wanted to punch Porter in the mouth. I should have. It would have made me feel great. The bartender brought us the beers. Porter was watching Max and the girls as though nothing had happened.

Grace looked at me and frowned, meaning to drop the whole thing. I did not say anything. Max was dancing with the same girl. The other girl was sitting at the bar talking to a man and a woman who looked like husband and wife. Harry tried to make conversation. He said he wished modern communities would adopt the primitive custom of having a scapegoat to unload all its sins on and send into the wilderness and thus purify everyone in the community.

"What do you say we go for that swim?" someone said.

"I'm ready," I said.

Harry said he was, too. Porter said he wasn't sure he would go swimming, but he wanted to leave the bar just the same. He called over to Max and told him we were going. Max said he was going to stick around for a while. He was with the same girl. We left and walked back down the road to Harry's place.

Porter decided he did not want to go in swimming with us. But he said he would watch. We got into our swimming suits and walked down the dark beach to the hard-packed sand. The white-capped breakers made a running weaving line all the way down the dark beach.

"How about swimming nude?" Harry said. "I've never done it."

I said it was all right with me.

"I hear it is the best way," said Porter.

We took off our suits in the darkness of the beach and then ran down to the water and dived into the white-capped breakers. The cold night ocean all over my completely naked body. This was different from any other time I had ever been in water. I dived and rolled naked in the dark surf and yelled to Harry and Grace how good it was, and then in a few minutes came out, walking wet and nude-white and breathing hard up the beach.

We dried ourselves and put on our suits.

"Wouldn't it be fine if you could swim that way all the time?" Grace said. "Never having to cover up."

"Terrific," Porter said.

"It makes you feel so clean and healthy," said Harry.

"I don't think I could do it," said Porter.

"Try it some time."

"Maybe I will. But I'm not really sure I want to."

We went back to the house. None of us felt like taking a shower this time. We would take it in the morning. We changed into our clothes and sat in the front room and drank highballs that Harry fixed for us, and listened to a radio quiz program coming from New York. Most of the questions were easy. That program was soon over, and we heard a special radio adaptation of a well-known short story.

"What a coincidence," Harry said. "George Franks wrote the adaptation of this story."

"That guy," said Porter.

"What do you mean 'that guy'?" said Harry. "You used to be pretty friendly with him."

"Not now. I don't need that square any more."

"Jesus Christ," I said.

"What is the matter, Blake?" Porter asked me.

"Nothing at all."

"You are a confused moralist," Porter went on. "You don't know the difference between a practical relationship and a sentimental one. You think all relationships should be sentimental. Well, my relationship with Franks was practical. I needed him to get something I wanted. I got it and now I don't need him any more. What is your objection to having a practical relationship, or friendship? You all knock yourselves out trying to get sentiment from what is really a practical situation, only you don't know it."

"You are probably right about it, Porter," I said. "But I sure as hell don't admire you for it."

"Everybody is expendable to you," said Harry. "How do you do it?"

Porter laughed. "What a bunch of corny sentimentalists."

"Porter," said Harry, "you're confirming a suspicion I've always had that the real ambition of every guy in New York is to be a smooth heel."

Porter shrugged. Grace and I looked at each other. No one spoke for a few moments. Then Harry looked at Porter.

"Tell me something," he said. "Are you a Negro?"

Porter's expression tightened. Grace was staring at them, sitting up now in her chair.

"What do you care?" Porter said after a moment.

"Everybody I know cares. Why don't you settle it once and for all? Are you or aren't you a Negro?"

I felt sorry for Porter. The poor son of a bitch. I wanted to interfere so that he would not have to answer the question. But he would have to answer it sometime and it might as well be now.

"Don't let it bother you, Lees," Porter said.

Harry looked into his highball glass. Grace nervously lit a cigarette. The radio drama sounded loud now that no one in the room was talking.

"What about you?" Porter asked Harry. "What are you?"

"I'm going upstairs," said Grace. "I don't want to hear any more of this," and she left the room.

"What would you like to know, Porter?" asked Harry. "Why don't you answer my question?"

"Let's talk about me," I said.

"The trouble with you, Lees," said Porter, "is that you've got no balls." Then he got up, smiling nastily, and went upstairs.

"Go to hell, Porter," Harry yelled after him. Harry and I sat downstairs, drinking and listening to the radio and hearing beneath the sound of the radio the rushing sound of the surf.

"How do you think Max is making out?" I asked.

"Who knows?" said Harry, but not immediately. Smiling sickly, he shook his head and said, "Well, that didn't settle much, did it?"

"It will be settled eventually, I imagine."

"What about me," he repeated. "That is a very good question. What about me."

"Let it go. You will go crazy if you keep thinking about it, Harry."

"All right, Blake. Would you care for another drink?"

"Why not?"

"You think I shouldn't have asked him, don't you?" he said, mixing the drinks.

"Yes. I wouldn't have done it. But it had to be done sometime."

He gave me my drink, turned off the radio, and sat down.

"*Merde*," he said. "*Merde, merde, merde.*"

CHAPTER XXIX

After I had gone to bed I heard Grace and Porter quarreling in their bedroom. I could not make out what they were saying. I could just hear the quarreling. Then I went to sleep, quite tired from the swim in the night surf.

I got up late the next morning. I took a shower before going down for breakfast. I passed Porter's and Grace's bedroom, and they were not in it. Downstairs in the kitchen Grace was making coffee. Max was reading the paper at the table.

"Where is your boy?" I asked Grace, pouring myself a cup of the freshly dripped coffee.

"He left."

I drank a glass of orange juice, and it cleaned out my mouth.

"He went back to New York?"

"Yes. He left early."

"Why?"

"You know why. Everything."

We sat at the table. I asked Max if he were not having breakfast, and he said he had already had it.

"How did you do last night?" I asked.

"Not so bad. It could have been worse. What about you?"

"We had a good swim."

"You must have had something else, too. Isn't that why Porter left?"

"Yes," said Grace. "That and other things."

I poured myself a second cup of coffee and had a slice of buttered toast.

"What happened in the argument?" Max asked.

"Harry asked Porter if he were a Negro," I said.

Max laughed.

"Is that all?"

"Just about."

"Well, I guess Porter is still a little sensitive," he said.

He put his cigarette out and got up from the table.

"Arguments, arguments. I'm going in for a swim. Coming?"

"After a while," I said. "I'm going for a walk. Want to go with me, Grace?"

"Sure."

"That reminds me," said Max. "There was something on the radio about a plane crashing on the beach last night not too far from here. We could walk down and have a look at it."

"What a morbid idea," said Grace.

"Maybe I will go with you later," I said.

Max went upstairs. I remembered hearing Grace and Porter quarreling last night but I decided not to say anything about it. If she wanted to tell me she would. I was not going to press her. She said she had found Harry asleep in the front room this morning. He must have drunk quite a bit after I left. He had gone into his bedroom to finish sleeping. Grace shook her head about him.

"Come on for the walk," I said.

Going through the front room I noticed that the bottle Harry had been drinking from last night was now empty. It had been drained. Grace must have seen that, too. We went out of the house into the sunlight and cleanness of the morning beach, and walked down the beach toward the black bouldering jetty.

"I'm leaving early this afternoon," Grace said.

"Why don't you go back with us tonight?"

"Because it is better that I go back early."

"Will you call me tonight?" I asked her.

She took my hand. "Of course I will."

"Okay. It's a promise. Tell me," I said, "is Porter a Negro or isn't he?" I had to have it confirmed.

"I don't know myself, Blake."

"You aren't protecting him, are you?"

"Protecting him?"

"All right. It was a bad word. Keeping his secrets then."

"No. But it is silly that everybody is so concerned about this. It doesn't make any difference to me."

We walked down the beach past the jetty and turned around and walked back to the house. Max was already in the water. In the house Harry was having breakfast. Grace and I went upstairs to put on our bathing suits. We came out of our rooms into the corridor at the same time. She waited for me and I took her in my arms. After kissing, we went downstairs.

"You look a lot better, Harry," Grace said.

"That's good," he said. "Because I feel like I've been sleeping under somebody's foot."

"You didn't see Porter before he left, did you?" I asked him, thinking Porter might have wakened him while he was leaving.

"Did he leave?"

"You don't think I drove him away do you?"

"Not really."

"I can't say that I care much."

"I'll have to leave right after lunch, Harry," said Grace.

"You do? Because of him?"

"Sort of."

"Don't go," said Harry. "I do care about you."

"I have to go."

"That guy. The man on the muscle," and Harry shook his head.

"There was a plane crash down the beach," I said. "Max and I are thinking of walking down later and having a look."

"I might go with you," said Harry. "I have never seen a plane wreck."

"You all take it so casually," Grace said.

"I know," said Harry. "But I don't see why we should get depressed, either."

She made a perplexed motion with her head. Then Grace and I went down to the beach and I ran into the surf near Max, who was trying to ride the waves but not doing so well at it. I tried to show Max how to ride the breakers but he could not catch on. The breakers always hit him before he could ride them.

Harry came down after a while and swam while we rested. Coming out of the water he put on his big white beach robe. It was much too big for him. It made him look funny and slightly pathetic. We laughed, and he did, too. Again his confession came back to me. I saw him walking naked among many other naked young men being examined and his holding that letter from the doctor saying something was wrong with him, and the examiners looking at him and at the letter. I heard him talking to the Army psychiatrist and telling him all the things of his sickness and fear of that time. Then I put it all out of my mind. I did not want to think about it any more.

"Coney was never like this," said Max.

"We should have brought some Pepsi and hot dogs so you would not feel lonely."

"That would help," he said.

"Why didn't you invite the local girl down?" Harry asked him.

"I did. But she was too shy."

"That lousy status business again. Nobody can forget it, even for a minute."

"How is your status, Blake?" Max asked.

"I don't know whether I have any."

"Maybe we can fix you up in the underground. There might be an opening."

"Thanks."

We went into the water once more, and rested, and went up to the house for lunch. We had tuna fish and hard-boiled eggs and a big green salad, and ice cream and coffee. The food tasted unusually good after the swim. Harry called up the railroad station to find out the exact time the trains came through, and then called for a cab for Grace.

I stayed downstairs while Grace packed upstairs. The cab honked its horn on the road behind the house. Grace came down with her bag.

"I'll go to the station with you," I said.

"No. Don't bother, Blake. I want to go alone."

"If that is the way you want it."

"This girl is getting so independent," said Max.

"Thanks for a fine time, Harry," Grace said, taking his hand.

"I'm sorry you're leaving so soon," he said. "Come again next week end."

"So long, Max."

"So long, baby. Stay out of trouble."

I carried her bag to the taxi, and the driver put it in the back of the car. She got in and closed the door. She put her face to the open window and I kissed her.

"Call me tonight," I said.

"I will."

The cab drove off and I walked back to the house. Max was lying on the couch listening to a bail game.

"That was a very sweet scene, Blake," he said, talking as though he knew I had kissed Grace good-by.

"Glad you liked it."

"Good old Max," said Harry. "Always on the make for a situation. He feels frustrated if he doesn't lay at least one situation a day."

"You seem to have become my Boswell," Max said to him.

"I have nothing better to do."

After a couple of drinks we walked down the beach to where the plane had crashed. It was a long and tiring walk. By the time we got there, first seeing from a long way off the crowd, a crew of men was clearing away the wreckage and piling it into a truck. There was not very much wreckage left because the plane had caught fire.

It was a grotesque sight, and it gave me a grotesque feeling. I had never before seen anything like it. It was not at all like an automobile wreck.

"They say the pilot was burned to death," a lady near me whispered to a companion.

"How did it happen?"

"Nobody seems to know."

"I've seen enough," I said to Max and Harry.

"It is a parable of our time," said Max. "It has all the necessary ingredients. Man falls from the heights."

"I'm not in the mood for parables," I said, looking away.

"There you go being personal again," Max said. "Consider this wreck philosophically, Blake."

"It gets you, doesn't it?" Harry said.

We walked away from the wreckage and the silent, staring crowd of people in street clothes and bathing suits, and went toward the town there. It was a well-known literary resort. Harry suggested we look around, as long as we were down there.

It did not take us long to get to the center of the town. There was something about it that smelled chic and literary. You could not mistake it. The cleanness of the ocean air was not here as it was on the beach.

We passed a newsstand and Max asked me to lend him a quarter to buy a magazine. He had left his money at the house. I knew I would never get the quarter back but I loaned it to him anyway. We did not go back to the beach the way we had come, from the wreckage of the plane, Max's parable, but instead, to avoid that wreckage, we walked several blocks along the ocean drive, then cut into the beach, above the wreckage.

It was not as hot now as it had been earlier, and clouds were forming in the sky ahead.

When we got to the house Harry said he would call a girl he knew near by. She might be amusing for a couple of hours. He said she was something of a tease, though.

"You mean she tries to keep too many balls in the air at once?" asked Max.

"That's it."

Harry called her. It turned out that she was having a party Harry said we would be right over. I told them to count me out. I wanted to take it easy this afternoon.

"Don't hang back, Blake," said Max. "Come with us. We need a strong front."

"Too many parties lately," I said.

"Okay. We'll see you later," Harry said. They left for the girl's house and I read for a while. I hit a dull stretch and dozed for I don't know how long. When I woke up I felt a change in the atmosphere. There was not as much light in the room and I sensed a slowed-downness all around me. I looked outside. It looked like rain.

I wanted to take a swim before it did start raining, so I went upstairs and changed into my trunks and got a towel and walked down to the ocean, feeling the slowness and heaviness increasing all around me. The horizon out ahead of me was blurred and gray.

I swam in the surf until I was tired, my breathing coming fast and hard, but it was better this time than it had been before because I had got the breaker-riding down very well. The coloring in the air was now all gray. I came out of the surf, and then it began to rain softly through the grayness. I wiped my face with the towel and walked up the sand through the gray rain to the house.

About an hour later Max and Harry came in. The rain had set in steadily. They were quite wet.

"Make it good," I said.

"I knew it would rain," said Harry.

They went upstairs and changed clothes and came back down.

"The drinks were splendid," Harry said. "Absolutely first-rate. The best gin I have had in a long time. But the people, a lot of uptown intellectualoids. Why do people always have to talk about writing at parties? It ruins them."

"Sounds like something worth having missed," I said.

"And all those good-looking, frigid women," said Max. "Marvelous stuff going to waste."

It was quite overcast now and outside the rain kept coming down through the soft grayness. We listened to the radio and had a couple of drinks, and then fixed something to eat. We decided to take a train that would get into New York around eleven-thirty. I did not want to get in too late. Harry said he would go in with Max and me and attend to a couple of things in town, and come back the next day.

After we had eaten Harry called and arranged for a cab to pick us up twenty minutes before train time. We sat in the front room talking about the places where we were brought up. Max told us some fairly funny stories about his early childhood. Finally the cab honked outside. We turned out the lights in the house and locked up and ran with our bags through the rain to the cab.

We were lucky and got air-conditioned car seats on the train back. During the ride Harry told us about Europe. He had been there twice. When we finally pulled into Grand Central the rain had stopped. We caught an express train downtown. At our downtown stop we walked from one underground level to another to the entrance above ground, outside, where the air was now thin and sweet and fresh from the rain.

We went down Sixth Avenue and turned east at Third Street. At the corner across from the park I turned to look in to see who was there, and I saw Cap Fields. He was standing in the shadows between two park lights. He was talking to two people sitting on a bench in the shadows. I could not tell who they were. I could only make out Cap's identity.

"There's your connection, Max," I said, pointing in Cap's direction.

"Where?"

"Over there, between the lights. He has probably just made a run."

"I see him now. This is a real stroke of luck. Maybe he is holding something. I'll dig you later."

We watched Max walk quickly now into the park shadows to meet Cap who might have some great new charge. And then Harry and I walked to the Sporting Club to have a drink before splitting up.

"This one is on me, Blake," Harry said when we were at the bar.

"No it isn't."

I put a bill on the bar for our drinks. The place was crowded and noisy with a lot of loud-talking new people. And there was the usual quota of literary con men. I did not want to stay around, so I drank up quickly.

"I'm cutting out, Harry. I have to get home."

"Right away?"

"I'm afraid so."

"I'm sorry about telling you all that stuff, Blake."

"I had forgotten about it."

"It wasn't fair of me," Harry said. "Now you are shouldered with the burden of knowing about it."

"It isn't as important as you think."

"Okay, Blake. Thanks. Have a good time. I'll get in touch with you."

"Fine. Thanks for everything, Harry."

"Come again anytime you like, Blake. Come next week with Grace."

"Maybe."

We said good-by and I had to shove my way through the noisy crowd to get outside. I was hoping Grace had not already called me.

CHAPTER XXX

Later on I was shaving in the bathroom when the phone rang. It was Grace. She asked me what I was doing and I said nothing and she said she would come right over, and I said that would be wonderful.

I straightened the place up a little. The downstairs buzzer finally sounded and I pressed the button near the door to let her in. I stood at my open door waiting for her, hearing her walk up the stairs.

"Come on in," I said.

She came in and I closed the door and she turned around smiling and I took her in my arms and kissed her, kissing her long and holding her tight in my arms.

"Oh, Blake."

"I love to kiss you."

"Oh, sweetie."

We kissed again, long, and I let her go. She sat down on the edge of the day bed, and I sat next to her.

"Well, it is all over," she said.

"You told him that?"

"Yes. I couldn't take it any more."

"And how do you feel about it?"

"Fine. Honestly, Blake. Like new."

"I don't know how you stood it this long."

"Neither do I, now that I think about it. I guess it was a kind of sickness with me."

"What did he say?" I asked her.

"Nothing very much. He doesn't really care. He can have absolute mobility now."

We looked at each other, smiling, and I put my arms around her, smelling her sweet perfume, and we kissed for a long time on the day bed and she let me unbutton her blouse, kissing me as I did it.

"Yes," she said. "Yes. Do that, honey. Kiss my breasts. Ah, sweetie, sweetie, kiss me there, please please. Oh lover. Keep kissing me there, don't stop, don't stop, don't ever stop."

An hour or so later on we got up.

"Are you hungry, darling?" Grace asked. "I'm starved."

"You don't feel starved. Where are you starved?"

"You. Let's go out for something to eat and then take a walk. Would you like that?"

"I'd love that."

We dressed and went out. I had never felt so light in my life. Downstairs Grace took my arm and we walked by the Italians who were still standing in front. They stopped talking as we walked by them. One of them whistled softly. I started to turn around but Grace gripped my arm not to, and we walked on. We got off my street and walked north on Sixth Avenue.

"It's so late," Grace said. "Will we be able to find a place?"

"It isn't too late for some places. We'll find one."

"Oh, Blake. I'm so glad it is this way now."

"It should have happened sooner. But it never does, does it?"

The freshness of the after-rain was still in the streets, the streets now empty, cans driving very fast along the avenue, a quietness in the air, and we walked arm in arm. At Berkshire Place we saw that the Mexican restaurant was still open.

"Will that do?" I asked.

"Better than that."

We took a corner table in the restaurant. We were the only customers there. We finished eating in a short time.

"Do you know what I would like to do?" Grace said.

"Tell me."

"I'd like to see Jimmy Coster. Would you like to?"

"I've been thinking about it ever since the fight. Why don't we go see him tomorrow night?"

"All right. I'll call him."

"The three of us can have dinner together. I think he would like that, don't you?"

"Oh, he would. I know he would. It would make him feel so good."

The waitress brought our *maté* now.

"It tastes like perfume," said Grace.

"Yes," I said. "But it has more of a kick than China tea."

"Are we drinking it for kicks?"

"No."

"That's fine," she said. "I'm so tired of everything being reduced to a kick."

Then I paid the check and we left. We took a walk up to Sixth Avenue and Fourteenth Street, then came back, arm in arm, and walked to the park. We sat down in the long row of benches facing the archway and the circle. Two people were sitting on the rim of the circle. A policeman was walking across the park swinging his night stick. I remembered that we had sat here, I think on the same bench, when Grace had told me she needed a doctor.

"What are you thinking about, Blake?"

"Us."

"What about us?"

"What we will do. Where we will wind up. When."

"Don't think about it now. Let's just let it happen. I'm superstitious about thinking that way. Think about something else."

"I can't help it."

"Don't. You sound so pessimistic. I don't want to be pessimistic now."

"All right. I'll think about becoming famous. How will that be?"

I put my arm around her and she put her head on my shoulder. The cop came along our row of benches telling the few people sitting there that they had to leave the park now. You were not supposed to be there after a certain hour. We got up before he came to us and walked down West Broadway.

"Why was he doing that?" Grace asked me.

"Bad things happen in parks after midnight," I said. "The cops are just trying to keep down crime and immorality."

"As if they could."

I did not ask Grace if she wanted to go back to my place. I took it for granted that that was the natural place for her to go now. We took our time walking down West Broadway. When we were inside the lobby of my building Grace suddenly put her arms around my neck and kissed me.

"One for the stairs," she said.

"These are long stairs."

"All right. Another one for the long stairs."

Upstairs in my apartment Grace went into the bedroom and set the alarm of the electric clock to wake her for work the next morning. I turned out the light and we undressed and got in bed. As we lay there through the front windows came the steady grinding of the trash truck chewing up the refuse of the day.

"You're so nice in bed, Blake."

"Is that so?"

"It's lovely just being next to you."

"You're pretty easily satisfied."

"No, I'm not. Ah, you darling. Give me another. That was so nice."

In a few minutes, "Do you have any special way of getting to sleep? I mean if you aren't sleepy?"

"Yes," I said. "I get a picture of myself walking down a long empty road with tall houses on both sides."

"And that helps you get to sleep."

"Very often."

"I don't want to go to sleep now," she said. "But I have to."

"Want to try my street?"

"Let's do it together."

I don't know how long we had been asleep when I woke up, rising through layer after layer of unconsciousness to hear the phone ringing. It seemed to have been ringing for a long, long time. I got out of bed and felt my way through the darkness to the telephone stand. After I had finished on the phone I was completely awake, staring into the darkness, not moving from where I was, the shock holding me still.

"What was it, Blake?" Grace asked from the bedroom, and turned on the light."

"It was the police," I moved away from the telephone stand toward the bedroom, the shock making me feel slightly sick. "They found Harry in a gutter of King Street, terribly beaten up. He's in St. Joseph's Hospital. They say he may die."

"Oh, my God."

I was dressing now.

"Oh God what a horrible thing," she said.

"He had my name and address in his wallet, to be notified if anything happened to him and his father could not be reached. It must have been those lousy hoods. Those dirty lousy sons of bitches."

"I'm going with you, Blake," and she was out of bed and dressing.

"You don't have to. It might be better if you stayed here."

"No. I'm going with you."

"What a filthy thing. It must have been seven against one. That is the way they do it. He must have been drunk."

We were both dressed. I had never known Harry had my name and address in his wallet. I left the lights on in the apartment.

"What can be done about it, Blake?" Grace asked me as we left the apartment and started down the stairs.

The shock of it still holding me, I said, "I don't know. Probably nothing."

"Oh, God. Let's go away, Blake. Let's get out of this terrible place."

"And go where?"

"Anywhere. Let's just get out. I'm scared."

"So am I."

A NOTE ON THE TYPE

The text is set in 11 point Aldus with a leading of 14 points space. Hermann Zapf designed Aldus for the Stempel foundry in 1954 as a companion to his Palatino typefaces. Originally designed as a display typeface, Palatino gained popularity as a text typeface as well. Believing Palatino to be too bold for settings at small point sizes, Zapf designed the lighter weight Aldus to better suit text settings. The typeface is named for Aldus Manutius, the innovative fifteenth-century Italian printer and publisher.

∽

The display font is Univers. As a student in Zurich, Adrian Frutiger began work on Univers, which would eventually be released in 1957 by the Deberny & Peignot foundry in Paris. The design is a neo-grotesque, similar to its contemporary, Helvetica. The Univers family is comprised of twenty-one typefaces that were designed to work together in a number of ways. Their legibility lends itself to a large variety of applications, from text and headlines to packaging and signage.

Composed by Charles B. Hames
New York, New York

Printed and bound by
Webcom Limited, Toronto